Rozner's Constant

Bonnie

Best Wishes

To a dear friend

Rozner's Constant

Jeffrey L. Waters

As You Like It

Goodfellow Press
As You Like It Imprint
16625 Redmond Way, Suite M20
Redmond, Washington 98052-4499

ISBN: 1-891761-11-0

Library of Congress: 99-97240

Edited by Pamela R. Goodfellow

Cover and Book design by Matthew L. Buchman

This is a work of fiction. The events described are imaginary; the characters are entirely fictitious and are not intended to represent actual living persons.

Author photograph by Vernon Merrill.

White Alligator photography by R. Andrew Odum. Image was graciously provided in return for a donation to the Toledo Zoo Aruba fund.

"Rozner's World" landscape was designed by Matthew L. Buchman using Bryce 3D animation software.

The title and the gator speak are in ArnoldBoecklin.

The page headers are in Lucida Sans.

The text is in 12.5pt Berhhard Modern Roman with 16pt leading.

The manuscript and cover were formatted using QuarkXpress.

For Lady Carol, who believed.

Behold, I show
you a mystery;
We shall not
all sleep,
but we shall
all be changed.

1 Corinthians 15:51

— 1 —

The sky exploded. Water-laden air flashed like sun breaking through clouds, then the white blaze dissipated leaving the familiar, gray, half-light of eternal fog. A heartbeat later, the shock wave slammed him to the path. Lieutenant Aaron Trout plowed, face first, into warm, black muck. He faintly heard the delayed, far-off boom of the explosion before the bright, orange after-image on his retinas winked out. The universe faded to black.

The smell. Mildewed washcloth. No, not quite right. Moldy celery. That's closer. Why couldn't he grasp . . . ?

Aaron opened one eyelid and watched a tiny black beetle with blue-green wings crawl across the soggy ground a few centimeters from his face. A twinge of pain flashed through his left leg.

Swamp muck. That's it. Slowly, he raised his head, then sat up, painfully reaching with his right hand to pluck a chunk of wet sod from the side of his face. He held it at arm's length and stared at it. What . . . ? The ringing in his ears began to ease.

The blast. What the hell had that been? Aaron flung the sod into the black water of the swamp and staggered to his feet. He stared down at his filthy Trail Patrol uniform, then attempted to wipe away the black mud with shaking hands. His left leg buckled and he collapsed on the pathway. He tried to rub sensation back into his thigh through the rough fabric of his uniform but could feel only a faint tingling near the old wound.

Aaron slowly looked around. Branches and shattered pieces of bark lay on the trail and floated in the water near the dike, but the glow of amber lights along each path still stretched away into dense fog. They had been too close to the ground to receive the full brunt of the shock wave.

He sat at a main intersection of the network of causeways on raised dikes that connected the wetlands of Rozner's World. Dark trunks of enormous trees extended from fetid water beside the trail and disappeared into the heavy fog. They always reminded him of ancient columns from ruins of a long-departed civilization. He grabbed a fallen branch and used it as a prop to pull himself to his feet, stared into the saturated air, then glanced at the instrument package on his wrist. He looked up into the leaden sky. The corona of the explosion had burned off, leaving the half-light of late afternoon to be absorbed by the waterlogged atmosphere. It must be nearly nightfall. He glanced at his chronometer as a cold ripple of fear crawled down his spine. The eerie quiet that followed the explosion slowly gave way to the bellow of gators as they recovered from the shock. Aaron shuddered at the sound. If one had discovered him unconscious....

Light rain began to fall. He recognized the pattern. The coming downpour would soon overwhelm the fog and liquefy the stinking black mud, making the trail nearly impassable. Aaron rubbed the back of his neck then turned up his collar trying to remember why he was on the trail network. Something about a shuttle.

Laz. Where was Laz? He had been several paces ahead. Aaron listened for a moment. "Laz?" His chest burned and his voice sounded strained to his own ears. He swallowed to moisten his throat. "Laz?"

"I'm here."

A wave of relief flooded over Aaron. "Activate your locator."

A yellow beacon began to flash in the soup directly in front of Aaron. As he watched, it approached like a huge, drunken firefly. His partner materialized out of the fog at arm's length. Clad in a regulation gray and green uniform, he resembled a mud-spattered toadstool that had sprung up from the earthen dike. The tense muscles in the back of Aaron's neck relaxed.

Laz struggled to pull his rain gear out of his belt pouch. Aaron reached out, grasped his shoulder, and searched his face. Blood oozed from a small cut above his partner's left eye and ran down into the mud on his cheek.

"You alright?"

"Yeah. Knocked me on my ass. What blew?"

"Damned if I know, but it was enormous."

They looked at each other, then Laz loosened his sidearm. "The gators have gone quiet. I'm not sure we're safe here."

Aaron glanced around. "We're not safe anywhere on this planet but I'd sure like to know what exploded."

"The missing shuttle?"

"I don't think so. Too big and too distant. Had to have been in the upper atmosphere."

"Well, it scared the shit out of me. What should we do?"

Aaron leaned against a tree trunk that grew up from the murky water of the swamp and encroached on the trail. He couldn't make his heart stop pounding. He cast the branch aside and rubbed his injured leg.

"I think we better find that shuttle then get back to Salvation."

Laz unclipped the small, black guardian from his belt and pressed the sensor to activate the unit. Instantly the air filled with excited chatter from other search teams. An authoritative voice cut through the noise. "Silence! This is net control. Official traffic only. Monitor this frequency."

Laz stared at the guardian then glanced up at his partner. "You ever heard that before?"

"No. Must be something major. I don't like this, Laz."

"What do you want to do?"

"You heard the man. Let's work our way back toward Salvation. We've already searched the area west of here and we'll be off duty by the time we get in. Maybe we can find somebody who knows what's going on."

"Better put on your rain gear, Aaron. We're about to get some serious water."

Laz turned and headed up the trail as Aaron struggled into his storm gear. He retrieved the branch, used his laser knife to trim off twigs and foliage, then steadied himself with the makeshift crutch as he followed. He could hear the squish of their boots in the mud. He'd fallen into a rhythmic pace punctuated by the rain on his foul-weather gear and nearly ran Laz down when his partner stopped.

"I don't think we're going to find the shuttle, Aaron. It can't have gone down in this quadrant."

"The coordinates have to be wrong. Some spaced-out pilot is always overshooting the pad and dumping one of those things in the swamp. They're probably down in a dead zone."

"Perimeter Control should have pinpointed it."

"Those clowns couldn't point us at an erupting volcano. If that thing nosed in out here, we're not going to find it without a signal."

"There must be something they can do for the crew."

"They may walk out in a day or two if the gators don't get them. It's been done. But I don't see how we can save them. God, I hate this job."

Laz chuckled. "Could be worse. We could still be in that hellhole prison in Djakarta."

Aaron sighed. "Sometimes I'm not sure we traded up."

Lazarus removed his broad-brimmed hat and ran his hand through his wet hair. He jammed the hat back on then studied his wrist display. "You'd think that shuttle would generate a signal from the crash beacon or an infrared signature, but I can't pick up anything. Engines couldn't have cooled already. I think you're right. They have to be down in a dead zone. Let's get back to Salvation. You okay on that leg?"

"I think so, but let's take it easy. It's beginning to hurt like hell."

"You should have the docs look at it again."

Aaron sighed. "They've done all they can."

He leaned heavily on the branch as he limped after his friend, allowing the glow of Laz's yellow beacon to guide him. Rain pelted the ground leaving small craters in the mud. An inbound ore carrier passed overhead. The glow of its running lights washed through the rain clouds and reflected off the dark water of the swamp. Gators bellowed all around them. He'd always wondered why they responded so violently to the huge transports.

Laz keyed his guardian and listened as he walked.

"Anything?"

"Not a sound. This is eerie. This isn't a blackout area."

"You know they ordered silence, Laz. Maybe everybody's just listening."

"I hope so."

Aaron shuddered, lifted his face to the rain and tried to detect any hint of sunlight through the low-lying clouds. He peered intently into the dissipating fog that was slowly revealing the endless swamp. Periodically, the heavy mist was disturbed, as though a large creature had passed, unseen. Water dripped from lichen-encrusted branches into silent, black pools of undetermined depth.

He heard the thud of his partners boots on the rough planking of one of the sturdy wooden bridges and shortly felt the solid timbers under his own feet.

Laz stopped to wait for him. Aaron caught up, leaned his staff against the railing and removed his goggles. He wiped the condensation off the lenses on the only clean spot of his sleeve, once again resolving to spend a portion of his next pay credits on a pair of the new heated glasses. It would deplete his resources, but his chances of buying his way off this cesspool planet were remote. His jaw tightened as the anger resurfaced followed closely by a knot of despair that rested high in his chest. At least Laz was here. Aaron couldn't remember a time without his best friend at his shoulder.

Laz struck out for Salvation. Aaron stumbled and nearly fell into the water as he attempted to follow. A searing pain flashed through his left thigh.

"Hold it, Laz. I've got to rest this leg."

Aaron eased himself into a sitting position on the wet bridge and stretched his aching leg out in front of him. He used both hands to massage his thigh. Laz leaned against the railing and watched. The rain intensified. Water poured from their rain gear.

"You going to make it in?"

Aaron shivered as a chill swept his body. "Yeah, I just need a little time. Tell me again how lucky we are to have these jobs. I keep forgetting."

Laz grinned. "It was your idea. You wanted to get away from your family. Remember? Shun the privileged life and make it on your own. I thought you were nuts, but then I was crazy enough to come with you."

"Oh hell, Laz. You don't know how to stay out of trouble. You've never walked away from a challenge in your life."

"There are a few I wish I had."

A flash of lightning ripped through the clouds followed by the booming tympani of thunder.

Laz squatted down on his heels as the rain intensified. It bounced off the surface of the planks like pebbles and splattered on the railing. "Even with your scintillating company, I don't plan to stay on this mud ball the rest of my life."

Aaron picked at a splinter on one of the vertical supports. "I don't either."

A gator bellowed to the west and loud splashing penetrated the sound of the rain. Laz grimaced. "Dinner's served."

Aaron laboriously pushed himself to his feet. "Speaking of dinner, we'd better get going. It's getting dark."

As they stepped down to the trail from the bridge deck, Pain shot through Aaron's leg and he cried out. Lazarus turned at the sound and steadied his friend. "You can't go on, Aaron. Maybe a few hours rest will help. We better set up camp on the bridge."

Aaron felt his shoulders slump in defeat. "I don't want to spend the night out here surrounded by teeth."

"We don't have any choice."

Laz keyed his guardian. "Net control. Trout and Lazarus requesting clearance to suspend search. We have to abort. Trout injured and unable to proceed until morning. We'll bivouac on the bridge at marker 210. We've seen nothing."

The response came through both guardians. "You are relieved. If you require medical assistance, we could get someone to you but not immediately. With all the activity, everything's tied up. We're always reluctant to leave an injured patrolman out there with the gators, but I don't see what we can do about it. I'm afraid you're on your own for at least four or five hours."

"We'll be all right. We just need to rest. We'll push on as soon as we can."

"Be extremely careful."

Aaron sighed and leaned on Laz's shoulder as they retraced their steps to the middle of the bridge. Laz gently lowered him to the deck and he leaned against the railing. "You stay off that leg. I'll set up camp."

The throbbing in his thigh eased to a dull ache. "I'm not going to argue."

As the light faded, Aaron listened to gators bellow and night birds cry out in the treetops. He watched Laz erect the two-man shelter and tether it to the railings on either side of the bridge. Aaron leaned heavily on Laz as his partner assisted him inside. When he had activated three lightsticks, and placed them in the receptacles designed to receive them, he extracted dinner pouches from their packs and triggered the heating unit in each.

Aaron leaned against the shelter wall, held his packet and waited for the meal to warm. Rain pounded on the shelter making it difficult to hear. "You sure we can't swap these for a sandwich and a case of cold beer?"

Laz chuckled. "I'll call Salvation and ask if they deliver."

"See if they have any fresh coffee. Tell them I prefer the Cirran blend."

A gator bellowed close by. Both men started. Laz reached for his phased-array sidearm. "I better check on our host."

He stepped out of the shelter and returned two minutes later. "He's just passing through. Swam right under the bridge and kept going. Big sucker."

Aaron shifted position, trying to make his leg more comfortable. "We'd better sleep in shifts. I don't think we need to stand guard but one of us should be awake."

"All right. It's eight now. I'll take the first watch and wake you about midnight. You rest."

"Thanks, Laz."

"How's your dinner?"

Aaron opened the pouch. "Smells pretty good."

When they'd finished eating, they sat listening to the night sounds. The rain had stopped. Something bumped the bridge and Aaron flinched. "What the hell was that?"

Laz poked his head out, "I can't see a thing."

He returned to his seat, unholstered his weapon and rested it in his lap. "Do you realize we've been on this mud ball nearly three years?"

"Funny. Seems like only ten."

Laz glanced around the interior of the shelter. "As I recall, our interest in travel might have been stimulated by a global arrest warrant. Good thing the Indonesian police didn't keep up on the latest postings. Even your father couldn't have gotten us out of that one."

"He'd have tried."

"Yeah, he would have."

Laz shook his head. "I still can't believe the Europolice really think we killed that girl."

"Apparently they do. Hell, we didn't even know her name."

"Maybe the warrants have been retracted."

Lightning flashed, bathing the interior of the shelter in a white glow. The thunder arrived almost immediately. Laz flinched. "That was close."

He peeled off his jacket then pointed to Aaron's filthy uniform. "Do you want to get out of those wet clothes?"

"No. I'm too tired to move. The shelter's warm."

When he awakened, the shelter flap was up and gray daylight poured through the opening. Laz stood on the bridge deck outside. No rain fell.

"You were supposed to wake me at midnight, Laz."

"You were out cold. I dozed off and on. How's the leg?"

"Don't know. Haven't moved it yet."

When he did get up, his leg, though stiff, responded reassuringly well. They broke camp and made for Salvation.

Laz took the point. "Watch yourself. I scouted the next section this morning before you woke up. The trail is partially washed away around this bend."

"Yeah, I saw it yesterday on the way out. It's an old break. We can report it when we get in. Other than our bellowing nocturnal friend, any sign of gators this morning?"

"Haven't seen any, but they're out there. I heard one earlier. Why, you missing your friends?"

"One encounter was enough. God, I hate those six-legged bastards!"

Laz chuckled. "Well, be careful."

"Keep your beacon on. I don't want to explain to all of your women that you were lunch for your favorite pets."

Aaron stood for a moment, scanning the swamp. "Any word on the shuttle?"

"Nothing on the guardian. Sounds like they didn't find a thing."

"Poor bastards are gator bait by now. Wonder if the beasts like the change in menu from all those damn ugly fish."

Aaron watched his friend move off, carefully picking his way through the downpour. Tufts of wiregrass threatened to trip Aaron and send his weary body plunging into the swamp. Tangled branches of fast-growing deciduous trees extended over the path. He heard the distinctive zip sound of his partner's laser knife as Laz sheared them off. Aaron watched them tumble into black water.

The weather held through the morning but by noon heavy rain began to fall. Lazarus halted and waited for his partner to catch up. "How close are we, Aaron?"

"Almost to Salvation."

"Sounds like an Earth spiritual."

Aaron simply lowered his head and plodded on through the downpour. Laz overtook him and resumed the lead. In another hour the trail would be impassable.

Laz turned and shouted to make his voice carry through the storm. "If that shuttle crew survived, I hope they made it to one of the bridges. Anyone on the trail is going to have to hunker down, wait for the rain to quit and let the walkway drain."

Aaron stopped. "I thought they were going to surface the causeways."

Laz shook his head. "They keep promising."

As they approached Rest and Recreation Facility Number Four, Aaron watched the shimmering lights materialize through the rain. His entire body sagged with relief. Weary crews had quickly tagged the huge dome "Salvation" because it provided the only respite from mud and rain-soaked boredom. As they passed through the airlock, computerized sentries read the retinal patterns of their eyes and verified their identity: "Trout, Aaron- Lieutenant. Lazarus, Winton - Lieutenant. Stand for water removal."

Aaron stripped off his rain gear, dropped it into the receiving slot, placed his hands against the wall of the chamber and waited. It felt good to be off the trail. Moments later, strong blasts of warm air pounded him from all sides. Pressure built up in his ears. Water, forced from his clothing, drained out through the floor. The process took several minutes.

Laz dozed, leaning his forehead against the wall waiting for his uniform to dry.

"Your suits are now at fifteen percent humidity."

Aaron glanced down at his gray and green uniform. The material was filthy but dry. He ran his fingers through his wild hair as the inner door opened. Laz roused himself and tucked in his shirttail. As Aaron entered the cavernous space beneath the vast dome, he instantly noted the subdued buzz of conversation that replaced the usual cacophony of pounding music and raucous laughter. He stood for a moment feeling the warm air on his face and smelling the spicy food, uncertain of his next move.

"Something's definitely wrong, Laz."

"You figure that out all by yourself? This place is a tomb."

Aaron spotted a group of fellow patrol officers, quietly drinking themselves into oblivion. Empty glasses littered their table. He plucked at Laz's sleeve and headed for the others.

Jergan Angst glanced up from his beer. "You two okay? What did you do, Aaron, plant your face in the mud."

"We're all right. Why so glum, Jergan?"

"What planet have you been on, Trout? Weren't you out there, yesterday, when she blew? I'm surprised you're alive. Didn't you hear the blast?"

"Yeah, we heard it. What was it?"

"Only the *Majestic Vagabond* going nova."

The air rushed out of Aaron's lungs. He couldn't breathe. They were all dead. The huge intergalactic starship carried a complement of twenty-three hundred men and women, many of these people were his friends. Everybody on Rozner's World knew some member of the *Majestic Vagabond* crew. He could feel the terror in the crew's nanosecond of recognition. They wouldn't even have had time to cry out.

He opened his eyes to find Laz staring silently at the table. He forced his attention back into the room and refocused on Jergan Angst. "How? She's been in parking orbit."

"She was scheduled to depart this morning."

"What happened?"

Jergan set down his glass. "She plunged into the upper atmosphere. No one knows why." He leaned forward. "The admiral thinks they fucked with the Constant."

Aaron reached out and grasped the edge of the table. "Jesus Christ and all his disciples!"

Several people at the next table glanced up at the outburst but said nothing, then returned to their drinks. Laz dropped heavily into a chair. Aaron sat, then with both hands, lifted his injured leg and rested his foot on one of the benches along the wall. Damned thing ached like an abscessed tooth. He reached to the center of the table for a glass and poured beer from the community pitcher.

Aaron scowled. "What happened?"

Jergan turned on him. "Are you even vaguely connected to the universe, Trout? Haven't you been following the discussion on the vid?"

Aaron felt the heat rise in his face. "We've been on duty, Jergan. We just got in. Some of us were actually out searching for the downed shuttle."

Jergan ignored the jab and focused on Lazarus. "You should request a new partner preferably one who's conscious."

"He's okay. Why don't you give us the condensed version?"

"Think either of you can fit it into your busy schedule?"

Aaron felt heat rise in his cheeks. "Try me, and quit being so belligerent."

Laz waved a dismissive hand. "Jergan's just being a prick. It passes for a personality."

Jergan glared at him but said nothing.

Aaron noted that the mechanics from shuttle repair had commandeered a table near the food and were holding a quiet conversation of their own. He caught Laz intently searching the mechanic's table and smiled at the flicker of disappointment in his partner's eyes. Shelly LaCoste wasn't with them.

As head of the shop, she had no doubt been called back on duty. Her people probably knew as much as anyone about starship operations. He made a mental note to speak with her later. If anyone understood all of this, she would.

The weather lock cycled and several others entered; some in Trail Patrol uniforms and a few in lab coats. Laz glanced over his shoulder and nodded to a slender redhead who smiled as she removed her rain hat. Aaron grinned. She was another member of Laz's collection.

As he reached for his beer, the massive holographic vid screen on the west wall flashed to life. A hush fell on the assembled patrons as an obviously shaken anchorwoman dressed in the tunic and pants of the network appeared on the screen. Her image solidified into a three-dimensional figure which stepped into the room and stood suspended above the patrons. She cleared her throat twice before she could speak.

"AP Intergalactic: Earth Date 2406.31. On the heels of the *Vagabond* disaster all of civilization mourns the passing of Dr. H. Maximillian Rozner this date on RA-9, Serial 4, better known as Rozner's World. He was eighty-four and is believed to have died by his own hand."

Aaron froze with his glass halfway to his mouth. The vast interior of Salvation lay totally silent. Only the hiss of the cycling weatherlock broke the stillness.

She continued. "Dr. Rozner was the principal architect of Rozner's Constant, the ion starship drive that makes interstellar travel practical. He first came to Rozner's World, then an obscure satellite of RA-9, fifty years ago, after an unmanned probe returned to Earth bearing a soil sample. He built his first starship using the nodules found in the soil sample. Employing a huge engine of his own design, he emigrated to Rozner's World to establish production facilities close to his source of fuel. The story of this amazing quest and the subsequent development of the Rozner Constant drive is detailed in Lawrence Shakleford's biography, *Starman - The Life of H. Maximillian Rozner*.

"He is survived by his granddaughter, Dr. Jillian Rozner, a marine biologist at the Pacific Institute in La Jolla California, USA, Earth. Transmission ends."

The image of the newscaster retreated to the screen and vanished. Aaron stared at the blank panel. He took a long drag on his beer, letting the cold liquid run down his throat. He studied the surface of the table noticing how the rings from wet glasses formed an interlocking pattern.

Jergan Angst still stared at the vid as if trying to extract additional details from the inert device. "Now ain't that a bitch? I wonder why he killed himself."

An officer Aaron wasn't familiar with waved his hand in dismissal. "He's been ill for years. Everybody knew it."

Jergan glared at him. " I didn't."

"You have to keep up, Jergan."

At the far end of the table Laz slowly rose to his feet. He glanced around the room then refocused on his friends as if seeking guidance.

"I never met the old man and I can't say I'm enjoying this job, but you've got to admit, he made one hell of an impact.

I didn't know he was ill, but I hope he's found peace." He slowly lifted his drink. "To Dr. Rozner."

As the initial shock wore off, others at the table raised their glasses. "Dr. Rozner."

Similar toasts were being offered throughout Salvation. At the mechanics table, two of the women wept softly.

Aaron glanced up as four patrol members passed through the water removal lock and entered the room. He recognized three of the four. They headed straight for the bar and joined the group gathered there. He saw the shock on their faces as they learned of Rozner's death. Some of these people looked on Rozner as a surrogate father, others simply as an employer. A few even hated him but no one doubted his greatness.

Jergan slowly shook his head. "We're screwed."

Aaron was pulled back to the table by his lowered voice. "How so?"

"Who's going to figure out what happened to the *Majestic Vagabond*? Rozner was probably the only one who might actually have had a clue."

On the big screen, a canned biography of H. Maximillian Rozner commenced. Aaron had seen it before. He slid his stein around on the table leaving a wet trail. "What do you think happened?"

"I think the crew of the Vagabond pushed the Constant or missed their LaGrange point."

Aaron glanced up. "How can you miss a LaGrange point? It's elementary physics."

Jergan shook his head. "It's dicey stuff. Locating the point of neutral gravity between any two masses isn't that easy."

A mechanic whom Aaron had noticed eavesdropping on their conversation, pushed back his chair and sauntered over to their table carrying his empty glass. "Maybe I can help. Do you mind?"

Jergan glowered at him but said nothing. Aaron shoved back a chair and pushed a pitcher of Bull Gator toward him.

"Have a seat and enlighten us. We lowly patrol officers aren't often exposed to the wonders of the universe."

The newcomer filled his glass. "It's not that easy but Dr. Rozner insists that a starship, using conventional engines, has to maneuver to a LaGrange point. It's brought to a relative standstill between two planets or a planet and one of its moons. Then the ship is nudged toward a gravitational well. As she begins to accelerate toward the gravitational source, you cut in the Rozner's and veer off into space."

Aaron refilled his own glass. "Why can't you go directly to velocity?"

Jergan's partner, Rasher snorted. "You really don't know much about space drives, do you, Trout?"

Aaron ignored him. The mechanic continued. "If you try to force acceleration, you explode. Each of the Rozner Constant Drives has a fail-safe mechanism that prevents engagement if the ship is moving outside of set tolerances."

Laz waved away the explanation. "What did you mean they could have pushed it?"

"Tried to go directly to acceleration."

"And you think the Majestic Vagabond's crew attempted to override the fail-safe and go directly to velocity?"

"That's Admiral Benington's contention, but we won't know until the investigation is completed."

"Wait a minute. If starship crews know all of this, why would they attempt to circumvent the system?"

Glasses clinked behind the bar as the biography ran its course. The screen went blank. Jergan leaned forward and lowered his voice. "Maybe the Admiral's wrong. Maybe they didn't."

"What other possibility is there?"

"Sabotage."

Aaron felt a chill at the base of his spine. "Sabotage! Who would intentionally destroy a starship and kill thousands of people?"

"Keep your voice down, Trout. It's only a possibility."

"But why?"

Rasher responded. "You have to understand the economics involved. There are powerful interests battling for control of Rozner's empire. It's still a private corporation, you know."

A patrolman that Aaron didn't recognize emptied his stein and reached for a full pitcher. "We ought to drag the bastards into the swamp and leave them for the gators."

Rasher glanced at him. "Which bastards?"

The would-be executioner muttered something and returned his attention to his glass.

Aaron noted that several groups at nearby tables drained their glasses and headed for the weather lock. Association with theories of conspiracy could be unhealthy for one's career. He nearly followed them but his curiosity was aroused. He left his beer on the table and leaned back.

"Where do you get your information."

Rasher glanced at Jergan Angst. "I keep up with these things. You never know when a little knowledge will come in handy."

Aaron felt the hair rise on the back of his neck. Something about Rasher and Jergan together made him nervous.

Lazarus jumped in. "I thought the Galactic Commission controlled the Constant."

"They license it. Rozner not only owned the lion's share of the stock, no one else knows how the Constant actually functions. The core data is genetically coded to the old man's DNA. No employee is allowed to work on more than one stage of the assembly, and the drive units are sealed when they leave the factory. It's probably the best-kept industrial secret in the history of the universe."

Aaron shook his head. "I can't believe that nobody else knew how to build the damn things, or at least how they worked. That just doesn't seem possible. I don't buy it."

Rasher leaned forward and folded his arms on the table. "It's like Winslow Pharmaceutical's T-cell transfer that virtually eliminated cancer. At most, two people actually know how that works."

Aaron shook his head. "I don't believe that either. You can't hide these things, Jergan."

"In any event, as long as Rozner was alive, the lid stayed on the Constant."

A server appeared unbidden and placed two pitchers of Bull Gator on the table. Rasher passed his hand over the sensor in the table, accepting the charge to his personal account. Aaron nodded his thanks.

"What happens now that he's dead?"

"That's what'll keep the Commissioners awake nights."

Laz was clearly puzzled. "Why couldn't someone reverse engineer it?"

"They might if they could open it. They're all tamper proof."

"Tamper proof?"

Rasher folded his hands behind his head. "About three years ago, a group of engineers on Talgo II tried to open a unit. They're still finding pieces of it scattered around the desert. Didn't leave enough of the men to bother shipping home."

"He has to have recorded it, somewhere, or told someone." Aaron stood up. "He's not going to let his life's work vaporize at his death, Rasher."

"There are rumors."

"What rumors?"

"Just rumors."

Lazarus had been leaning back in his chair. He let the front legs drop to the floor. "You gentlemen speculate. I'm going for a nap."

"You nap, Laz. I'm going to find a terminal and see if I have enough credits for some sun time in Heaven."

"You were just up there last week, Aaron."

"I know, but I'm really saturated, and that damned fungus is back. I'm also feeling the onset of a migraine. If I deal with it now, I may be able to head it off."

Rasher lifted an eyebrow in mild surprise. "I thought migraine sufferers sought darkness. It's pretty bright up there."

Aaron studied him for a moment trying to decide how much to tell a stranger, especially a friend of Jergan's. Something in Rasher's eyes encouraged him to continue.

"Once it fully develops, bright light is excruciating, but if I apply a med patch and relax in the sun, sometimes I can bake it away before I'm laid out."

Rasher stared into his beer. "My mother used to get them." He glanced up. "How debilitating are yours, Aaron?"

"At first you're afraid you'll die, then you're terrified you won't."

Rasher nodded. "You'd better get going."

Aaron waved as he turned away. "Right."

He picked his way through the tables and groups of people speculating about the fate of the starship and Rozner's death. The room was slowly returning to normal. Activity at the bar was picking up as everyone sought solace in the familiar. He felt as if he'd been on a bad drunk and he really needed to get out of his filthy uniform. Pressure continued to build in his skull. How much was migraine and how much was the shock of the *Majestic Vagabond* news coupled with Rozner's death, he couldn't decide. He limped over to a terminal set in a small, isolated alcove and carefully positioned himself directly in front of the screen, allowing the computer to scan his retinas for identification.

"Lieutenant Aaron Trout. How may I serve you?"

"I need to check my balance to see if I have sufficient credit for sun time in Heaven."

"Of course."

The screen immediately displayed an amount that caused him to flinch. It was sufficient but would leave him disturbingly low.

"Charge me."

"Your account has been debited." The screen went blank.

He resolutely set his course for the other side of the dome and the lift station on the other side that would take him to Heaven. He suspected that the heavy tariff charged for sun time was designed to limit access as much as to raise revenue. If Heaven became crowded, it would no longer be Heaven.

He and Laz had speculated endlessly about the possibility of Rozner Corp using some of its vaunted technology to bring sunlight to the surface of the planet or at least burn off some of the cloud cover for brief periods of time. Rozner's people insisted that it might be possible elsewhere, but not here. The same energy emissions from the swamp that caused failure of many high technology tools over large sections of the planet's surface prevented them from doing it. They didn't go into detail.

The attendant at the gate smiled sweetly and held the lift door for him. "Enjoy, Lieutenant." In this mechanized society, the personal touch made the experience all that much more alluring.

Alone in the glass-walled cylinder, he gazed alternately at the passing wall of fog and the indicator beside the door. As the lift passed a hundred meters the vapor and low clouds thinned and it broke into brilliant sunlight. Aaron immediately closed his eyes and groped in his vest pocket for his polarized lenses. When these were in place, he stared out at the vast panorama of treetops protruding through the top of the cloud layer. The warmth of the sun on his face brought a broad smile. He closed his eyes.

"It's worth it."

The upper terminus of the lift opened into a small reception area staffed by a young woman. She wore a soft, white tunic that ended mid-thigh, revealing a considerable length of long, shapely leg. Her feet were bare. Long, dark locks framed her delicately featured face and curled gracefully past her shoulders. Her eyes matched the color of the sky above the dome. A small golden charm suspended from a thin chain rested between the exposed upper portion of her tanned breasts. She smelled faintly of citrus. Everything about her said clean. After the muck of the swamp, the simple freshness of her beauty caused an unfamiliar catch in his throat. Before he could speak, she greeted him.

"Good afternoon, Lieutenant. I verified your credentials while you were ascending. You will find everything you need through that portal."

Aaron made no move toward the door, but stood his ground, studying her. He had no legitimate reason to hesitate. He simply didn't want to leave.

He tried for casual. "I haven't seen you here before."

"I've only recently been assigned to this desk."

"How do you like it?"

"I enjoy the sunlight."

He knew he was staring, but he couldn't take his eyes off her. "Are you here every day?"

She smiled. "I have every fifth day off."

Aaron was acutely aware of the banality of the conversation, but still unwilling to separate himself from her presence. While he was attempting to formulate a new line of inquiry, she directed him toward the dressing area, where quiet strains of classical music drifted through the air. He abandoned flirtation. The door whispered open and closed behind him, leaving him in a small, private room. Immediately, a soft feminine voice, undoubtedly computer generated, broke the silence.

"Welcome, Aaron. Please remove your soiled uniform and lay it on the shelf to your right."

As he peeled off the muck-encrusted garment, he winced at the sharp pain in his left thigh where the tight suit pulled against the long, jagged scar. After nearly a year, the gator bite was still tender. That little encounter had almost cost him a leg. If he closed his eyes, he could still see the enormous reptile leaping out of the swamp and feel the powerful jaws clamping down on his flesh. He could hear his own screams and see Lazarus dropping to one knee and leveling the ion rifle. The blast had nearly deafened him. All of the gator from the neck back had vaporized leaving the huge jaws attached to his leg. Laz had dragged him back onto the dike and pried the maw apart, releasing Aaron. He'd awakened in the infirmary, heavily bandaged. He still wondered how he could ever repay his friend.

He bunched the suit on the extended shelf and watched as a panel slid aside and his garment disappeared into the wall.

"Your uniform will be cleaned and returned to you when you are ready to depart. Please extend your arms and close your eyes."

Moments later, a high-pressure spray of warm water and herbal-scented cleansing agent pounded against his body.

"Turn around, slowly, please."

Aaron rotated to assure that the solution covered his entire body then repeated the process for the rinse cycle.

"Air or towel?"

"Air, please."

"Grasp the hand holds now extending from the side walls."

He complied as the blower came on, nearly lifting him off his feet. When it subsided, the computer continued.

"This Sunroom is intended for the relaxation and pleasure of all. To insure a pleasant experience for everyone, we insist that you speak quietly, as others are resting. Food and beverages are to be consumed only in designated areas."

Aaron rolled his eyes. "I know the routine."

"Patrons may elect to sunbathe in various stages of nudity. You are requested to respect their privacy. Overt sexual advances will not be tolerated. Each visitor must feel completely safe to relax without fear of disturbance. While you may wish to arrange a liaison for a later time, no sexual activity of any kind is appropriate on these premises."

"Or rarely anywhere else in my experience."

"We would like to caution you that sunburn is a very real possibility for those not often exposed to ultra-violet light. Use the sunscreens provided. You are strongly urged to comply with warnings from the attendants. They are here for your protection."

Aaron grinned. "What have you sunburned lately?"

"Violation of any of these contract provisions will be grounds for immediate expulsion without refund of admission credits. Place your right palm flat against the screen to record your acceptance of the terms of the contract.

Aaron completed the required gesture.

"Enjoy!"

The inner door slid open and he stepped into a tiled dressing area, where he found a locker with his name flashing on the tiny panel near the top and opened the door. A plush, white robe of rare natural fiber hung inside, and the small shelf offered oils, sandals and two books in the old-fashioned paper form. Heaven was the right name for this place.

At the Pacific Institute in La Jolla, Dr. Jillian Rozner leaned back in her leather chair and studied the holographic image that slowly rotated in the middle of the lab. The tiny seahorse, now magnified to more than two hundred times its actual size, gave no hint of pathology. All four of Jillian's post-doctoral students gazed at the image from their positions around the perimeter of the lab. Jillian nodded to the tall redheaded man in the corner.

"What do you see, Larry?"

He pursed his lips. "A perfectly healthy seahorse, though somewhat larger than normal. Look at the vertical scale projected beside him."

"Good. Anybody else?"

Ruth Barnum stepped forward to study the image. "Looks okay to me."

Merton walked all the way around the hologram. "The color's a little off."

Bennett finally set down his mug and entered the conversation. She'd been waiting for him to speak, knowing that when he broke his silence, he'd add something worthwhile.

He pointed to the seahorse. "This is the largest one we've seen. I'm remembering an article on the net. Johnson from Wood's Hole refers to the size of this year's males but doesn't take it any farther. I think there's a pattern. It appears to be a cycle. The largest adult on record was recorded almost exactly eleven years ago. Other adults maturing the same year were also oversized. Five years later, they were all much smaller."

Jillian ran her fingers through her hair, smiling broadly. She knew he'd see it.

"Very good, Bennett. I received a formal request last night to look into the cyclical nature of growth patterns in our small friends. It may be an indicator species."

She looked at each of them in turn. "Here's what I want you to do. Bennett, you stay with the literature search. Larry, concentrate on solar cycles. See if there's any correlation. Ruth, I want you to examine water quality for changes in salinity. Merton, concentrate on food supplies."

"My grandfather says that great science is methodical plodding interrupted by white-hot flashes of inspiration. I want you to plod through the data and wait for the impending flash."

Ruth frowned. "When it comes, I hope we're not blinded by it."

Jillian chuckled. "In any event, we're finished for today. I'll see you all back here in the morning."

She glanced at Ruth. "How's that paper on antigens coming?"

Ruth flinched noticeably. "I will have it completed by Monday, Dr. Rozner."

🐊 🐊 🐊

After her students had gone, Jillian closed up the lab and strolled through the campus, stopping briefly at the dolphin tank to watch Jim Archer work with Squeak and Bullet. The two Pacific Bottlenoses were paying rapt attention to their trainer who spoke softly to them in strangely accented English. They apparently finished their conversation and the dolphins dashed away to the other end of the pool.

Jim glanced up and waved. "Through for the day, Jillian?"

"Pretty much. I thought I'd stop by the Rusty Harpoon for a tot. Care to join me?"

He picked up a blue plastic ring from the deck and tossed it into the corner. "I'd love to, but Marge is holding dinner. It's Grant's eighth birthday and I've been instructed to be on time. He's feeling very adult and wants a formal dinner."

Jillian felt a twinge of disappointment. Jim was good company. "See you tomorrow."

She strolled out the front entrance of the institute and crossed the street to the local watering hole. Loud music blasted through the door as she pulled it open and stepped into the crowd. She was startled by the chaos in this normally quiet establishment.

"Jillian. Over here." A group of three faculty members had commandeered a corner table. She eased her way through the mass of humanity and slid into the only empty chair. "Thanks. This place is a mad house."

Peter Nugent pointed to the opposite corner. "Landholm's been appointed head of invertebrate physiology. He's buying drinks for the house."

Jillian waved to Dr. Landholm, delighted that the board had acted on her recommendation then turned back to her friends. "Good thing the promotion comes with a hefty raise. He's going to need it with this bunch."

Ted Arms chuckled and signaled a passing waitress. "What are you drinking, Jillian?"

"Chardonnay, please."

On her right, Beth Altman drained her glass. "When this breaks up, we're all going over to Teddy's for a clambake. You really should come. His father-in-law sent down fresh salmon from Alaska. The clams are appetizers."

Her wine arrived and she tasted it. Not great but passable. Ted leaned over the table. You will come to my clambake, won't you, Jillian? I promise you better wine than that. I have a cabernet that will bring tears to your eyes."

"How can I refuse?"

The door swung open and several more faculty members squeezed into the room followed by a cadre of grad students. They all grabbed glasses and toasted Landholm. He swayed and held onto a table.

Ted chuckled. "I was going to invite the man of the hour, but I'm not certain we could find a plank to carry him on."

Jillian chuckled. "Best leave him in the care of his minions."

Three students jumped up onto the bar, threw their arms around each other's shoulders and sang a bawdy version of lyrics they'd composed to "Hail to The Chief."

Peter raised his glass. "Party's picking up."

Beth glanced around the room. "If it picks up any more, it'll be a full blown riot."

While the proprietor tried to shoo the singers off the bar, a loud disagreement erupted in the far corner. Something about shuttle races on Cirrus IV. Jillian couldn't make it out. She saw a pitcher of water raised over the belligerent's head and upended. The shouting promptly ceased.

Ted stood up and scanned the room. "It's tough to tell through all the bodies, but I don't see Landholm. I'm not sure he's still vertical."

Beth tugged on his sleeve until he dropped into his chair. "Well, if the guest of honor's down, it's probably okay to leave. I vote for clams and salmon. Anybody hungry?"

They abandoned their table and pushed their way to the door. Once outside, they strolled down the street in a group. Jillian looked out over the ocean and a wave of contentment swept over her.

On the beach, in front of Ted's lovely home, he soon had a huge pot of clams steaming in seawater and salmon broiling on racks over a fire. He'd delivered on his promise of a better wine and Jillian was basking in the glow of sunset and friendship. Ted's wife arrived with another contingent.

But as the evening wore on and Jillian listened to stories of the couples' adventures, she felt isolated. Most of her friends were happily paired off. Normally she felt perfectly comfortable as a single, treasuring her solitude. She thanked her hosts and strolled down the beach wondering why she always neglected this part of her life. Grandfather kept telling her she needed to pay some attention to men. For the hundredth time, she resolved to do something about it. Maybe she should discuss it with Alice.

Tiny wavelets lapped at Jillian's bare, brown feet and tugged the sand from beneath her heels. A minuscule crab climbed her large toe, halted half way across and reversed course. He didn't know what he was doing either. She was still feeling the confusion that began at last night's party.

Jillian stared out to sea. The gray haze on the horizon promised a storm. She loved the great Pacific blows that brought the enormous breakers crashing onto the beach, tossing their cargo of flotsam ashore. Often, she would walk the surf line at the height of a squall and revel in the raw power of nature's tantrum. Afterward, she loved to comb the shoreline, taking note of the changes in the topography of the dunes.

La Jolla lay too far south for the terrifying North Pacific monsters that periodically crushed the Aleutians and ripped into Vancouver Island, but the winter gales that circled out of the Gulf of Alaska could produce excitement, even this far south. The massive waves that thundered ashore sent ripples of excitement through her whole body.

She had spent the day analyzing what she believed to be fossilized remains of a new sub-species of sea urchin she had found in the Mesozoic sandstone of one of the larger tide pools. Now it was time for a glass of wine and dinner. The choice of the entree was not particularly important, but the wine selection was critical. It was her one vice. She considered the Oak Creek Private Reserve, but decided to save it for a special occasion.

Jillian dug her toe into the sand. "What special occasion, Doctor? Dinner with a cultured, passionate lover? Good Luck!"

She chuckled as she skirted the tide pool and stood with her back to the setting sun, casting a shadow across the surface of the water. The cool evening air sent an inexplicable shiver up her spine. A common sculpin, very much alive, rested in the shallow pool.

"Where's your lover, big boy? You all alone, too? Care for a glass of California's finest?"

The sculpin didn't respond.

Jillian sighed, then glanced at the setting sun. As she strolled toward the rolling sea-grass covered dunes where she'd parked Alice, the fiery ball settled below the rim of the Pacific.

At the base of a towering sand dune, the ancient, red aircar sat patiently waiting. Other than good wine, Alice was Jillian's only extravagance. For years she'd poured far too much of her income into restoring the Harley-Davidson Floater, but Alice gave her an exhilarating sense of freedom that nothing else could match. She smiled as she covered the last few feet to the vehicle.

"Door please, Alice."

The aircar's computer, keyed to Jillian's voice, released the lock and the bubble dome that comprised the entire front of the vehicle swung upward. Jillian settled into the pilot's reclined seat and sat for a moment, absorbing the heat of the sun-warmed leather. She glanced at the control panel.

"Close please."

The bubble canopy settled into place.

Jillian started to say, "Home, Alice," and let the on-board computer take her there, but tonight she needed to feel the controls.

"Manual mode, please."

She reached out and rapidly flipped switches activating electrical circuits and guidance systems, then eased the controls back.

Alice rose gracefully above the dunes, turned inland and sped homeward, passing over the twinkling lights of the city.

"Alice?"

"Yes, Jillian."

"Why am I alone?"

"You have many good friends."

"Why don't I make room for a man in my life? I'm always going to be alone unless I do something about it."

"There was that young doctoral candidate, last fall. You made time for him."

Jillian felt the heat rise in her cheeks. "All he wanted was my endorsement of his thesis. Men are all alike. They only want one thing from a girl – her mind. Why can't I find one who wants my body?"

"You have had men."

She smiled at her own rare touch of melancholy. "Not recently. It's not a totally unattractive body, is it?"

"Your proportions are classical for a woman your age. Your legs and torso are somewhat longer than the norm, but this extension is almost perfectly offset by your larger breasts and wider hips. The Asian slant to your eyes lends mystery and belies your European heritage."

"What do you mean 'for a woman my age?'"

"You are thirty-eight, Jillian."

"I know." Jillian lapsed into silence as she approached her dwelling on the seventy-ninth floor of the Sea Breeze Plaza.

"Garage, please, Alice."

A panel on the side of the building slid open and Alice nestled into her home.

After bedding Alice down for the night, Jillian spoke her own name and the door to her apartment irised open. As she entered, the walls began to glow with pale light that perfectly matched the spectrum of early evening on the Pacific coast. She made straight for the refrigerated wine cabinet and poured a glass of the Stormy Peak Merlot. She knew that her more cultured friends scoffed at her taste for chilled red wines, but she loved to indulge her senses in the awakening bloom of the great reds as they warmed.

Carrying the glass in one hand, and a piece of cheese in the other, she headed for the bath, anticipating a long, leisurely soak. She was halfway across the room, when the flashing message light on the vid panel caught her eye.

"Message, Please." She finished the cheese.

Instantly, the screen brightened and filled with the image of her grandfather. While he often left her endearing greetings, he had never before communicated from behind his massive desk in the headquarters of the Rozner Corporation on Rozner's World. Her breath caught in a quick gasp and tears sprang to her eyes. He looked terrible and she couldn't even greet him. In all of his transmissions over all of these years, she had never seen him so haggard.

"Greetings, Minnow. I don't have a great deal of time, but I wanted to tell you a bedtime story. No one else has ever heard this tale."

Jillian began decoding as the term 'bed time story' triggered a response born of years of secret correspondence. She listened intently as Dr. H. Maximillian Rozner spoke in their private childhood language, comprised of storybook characters, number sequences, and color substitutions for words. His first instruction was to take no notes. He'd never done that before.

Over the years, their personal form of communication had become extremely complex as each added encryptions from their respective professions. Her love for her grandfather was rooted in this special dialogue. Since her parents died in the shuttle crash on Beta II when she was nine, Grandfather was the only relative she had known.

"In the land of Ra, Prince Random set a large platter of blue squared positive ions before the king. Quantum units of circling yellow butterflies delivered thrust driving descending linear Boy Blue to near madness."

"The prince approached the throne. 'Lavender pressure now equals zero, Sire, but we will require twelve platinum coaches for Sister Mary Magdalene to attend court. I, Prince Random, can access level four.'"

"The king raised his glass. 'Let swallowtail rush to negative flux, and fetch my steed.' "

As she translated, her hand began to shake. She set the wineglass on the end table. Jillian then settled onto the couch, mesmerized by the old man's discourse. This was no ordinary bedtime story. Buried in the flow of kings and dragons, castles and maidens, and elaborately numbered butterflies ran a brilliantly condensed and extremely precise scientific treatise.

His tired voice droned on for nearly an hour. By the time he signed off with special endearments, Jillian was shaking so hard that she couldn't rise from the settee. Her frightened gaze darted around the room, seeking help from any quarter. Then the grief hit her in a massive wave. She buried her face in her hands and wept, knowing with absolute certainty that her beloved grandfather was dead. In his final hour, he had burdened her with the universe's most terrible secret. Dr. Jillian Rozner was now in sole possession of Rozner's Constant.

She slowly shook her head. "You bastard. How could you? You devious, scheming, selfish, old bastard. All these years. All our wonderful, secret messages, they were training. All my life, you were preparing me to receive this transmission."

Jillian leaped off the couch and rushed forward, shaking her fist at the blank screen. "I loved you."

She let her hand drop to her side and sank onto the couch. "Oh, Grandfather, how could you? What am I supposed to do with it? Who do I tell? How do I remember it all?"

Slowly, she raised her head as the full brilliance of the old man's method sank in. "I don't have to remember it. It's all in my vid memory. I can replay it any time I want to."

Jillian began to laugh. "I could play it in an auditorium full of Nobel laureate physicists, and it wouldn't mean a thing. I'm the only one who can decode it. To anyone else, it's a non-sensical fairy tale, told by a senile, old man."

She sat staring at the blank screen. "No, that isn't true. Some whiz with enough crunching power could eventually crack it. I have to put it somewhere safe. Somewhere no one would look."

A sudden current of energy swept through her body. She retrieved the recorded cube from the unit and was halfway to the garage before she realized where she was going. "Wake up, Alice. Door, please."

The bubble canopy swung upward, and Jillian settled into the pilot's couch. She stabbed the amber button, opting for automatic mode.

"To the beach, Alice."

Alice complied by opening the garage door and sliding silently into the night. "Any coordinates in particular, Jillian?"

"It doesn't matter. Just put me on the shore. Where we were this afternoon, is fine."

They soared over the tiny lights of the sleeping city, headed for the ocean. After a brief silence, Alice spoke. "Why are we going to the beach, Jillian? This is your sleep period."

"I need to think."

"Oh."

As Alice settled onto the sand without a detectable bump, the bubble canopy swung upward. "You do want to get out, don't you Jillian?"

"Yes, Alice. But first, I want you to take the information from this cube and store it deep in your memory banks. Then wipe the cube. You must never reveal you have this recording or its contents to anyone but me. Do you understand?"

"Yes, Jillian."

She slipped the cube into the receptacle. It disappeared. Tiny lights flickered across Alice's panels as she absorbed the data. "This doesn't make any sense, Jillian."

"I know. Don't worry about it. Just keep it safe for me."

"Do you want out, now?"

"Yes. I won't be long." Jillian rose from the pilot's seat and stepped onto the sand. She walked for more than an hour, stopping to stare into moonlit tidepools. Occasionally, tears rolled down her cheeks and were whipped away by the wind. Finally, she sat on an old beach log and gazed out at the breaking waves, their white crests shimmering in the moonlight. "Oh, Grandfather, what have you done to me? What am I supposed to do? I don't want to leave Earth. My work is here. My life is here. I don't know anything about space travel or corporations."

She turned and looked back down the beach at the distant aircar. She could just make out the tiny silhouette surrounding the faint glow of the interior. Alice was using her interior lighting as a beacon.

Jillian slowly shook her head. "Why couldn't you select someone else, Grandfather? Someone who knows about these things. Someone older and wiser. Is it really that important? Does it really matter who controls the Constant?"

Jillian closed her eyes and heard again the droning voice of the old man delivering his life's work into her hands. She took a ragged breath and let it out slowly. "It mattered to you and you placed your trust in me."

She ran her hand along the worn surface of the sea-polished wood. At the core of her soul, butterflies of excitement fluttered above a chasm of despair. Slowly, her gaze shifted upward and focused on the twinkling stars.

"I have no choice. I must go to Rozner's World."

With the decision made, a sense of peace settled over her. She rose and walked further down the beach watching the moonlight on the waves. Finally she returned to the log, sat on the sand leaning against it, and dozed.

Alice lifted smoothly off the beach and headed inland. "Jillian, I sense a release of tension in your voice. You have made a decision. Should I know what it is?"

"I'm going to Rozner's World."

Alice remained silent for a moment, obviously accessing her data banks. "Rozner's World is a highly inhospitable planet comprised primarily of swamps. The principal life forms are birds, large reptiles, and colonists in the employ of the Rozner Corporation. Why would you want to go there?"

"My grandfather has summoned me."

"Your grandfather is dead. I monitored the Galactic Network News while you were on the beach."

Jillian felt a small wave of fear pass through her body. "I know. I must assume control of his corporation."

"This is not a rational decision. Are you abandoning your position at the Pacific Institution to accept this assignment?"

"Yes, at least temporarily."

"I cannot endorse this course of action."

"No one asked you to."

They banked over the sleeping city. Jillian watched the twinkling lights of the ground traffic, below.

"Jillian."

"Yes."

"Did you not charge me with protecting you?"

"Yes, Alice."

"I cannot protect you if you act irrationally."

Jillian heard the irritation in her own voice. "I know."

The first, golden rays of the rising sun tinted the eastern sky as Alice slid into her garage. Jillian stumbled into her apartment and headed for the bath. This time she didn't even glance at the vid.

"Draw bath."

The household computer added a capful of the Jasmine salts she loved, and regulated the temperature to precisely the setting she preferred. As she stripped off her clothes, she couldn't help checking her figure in the mirror.

"You're right, Alice. It's not a bad body."

The water burned her feet as she stepped into the pool, but soon her skin adjusted to the delicious heat. Jillian settled into the bath and rested her head on the padded support so that only her face broke the surface. She closed her eyes and tried to clear her mind, but the questions kept coming.

"Do I give up directorship of the institute? I suppose I'll have to. How do I get to Rozner's World? It must cost a fortune. I can't just stroll into the executive suite and announce that I have the secret. No one will believe me. Grandfather can't really expect me to run the place. I don't know anything about corporations. Maybe I'm not supposed to go at all. Maybe he's simply using me as a repository. I probably should have asked him what succession plans he had made. I really didn't think it was any of my business. I just assumed he had people who would take over for him."

🦖　🦖　🦖

Jillian awoke with water lapping at her chin. She sputtered, sat up and sneezed. How long had she been asleep? The water hadn't cooled, but then the computer would have maintained temperature.

"Time, please."

"Nine-twenty-six, AM, Sunday, June seventh."

She'd slept for three hours. Jillian lifted her hands from the water and stared at her wrinkled fingers. "Good job, Doctor. You're a prune."

Too exhausted to think, she crawled out of the pool and dried herself with an enormous, fluffy towel. The spa began to drain as it detected her absence. She shuffled into the bedroom, fell onto the bed using the last of her strength to pull up the sheet, and fell instantly asleep.

🦖　🦖　🦖

She awakened just after four, ravenously hungry. She climbed out of bed, reached for her blue, silk dressing gown and set sail for the kitchen, where she held a glass under the juice dispenser.

"Orange." She watched the glass fill.

"Coffee." She was rewarded with the sound of the brewer delivering hot, black Colombian to her favorite mug.

"Cereal with sliced peaches, whole-wheat toast, and crunchy peanut butter."

"This meal is out of sequence."

"Override."

The individual appliances complied without further harassment from the computer. She carried the tray into the living room, and set it on the coffee table. Only then, did she notice the blinking light on the vid.

Jillian sucked in a full breath and picked up her coffee mug. She held the familiar vessel in both hands, letting the heat seep into her skin.

"Play."

The three dimensional image of her grandfather filled the screen, speaking in their code. Shaking, Jillian translated.

"Greetings, Minnow. While this vid is being cut at the same time as the first, I am setting it to transmit several hours later. I can only hope that you have had sufficient time to vent your understandable anger."

Jillian took a deep breath.

He grinned. "Oh, yes, I knew you'd explode when you received the first transmission. I know you so well, my little Minnow, and I love you more than you could ever understand."

Jillian sighed. "I love you, too, Grandfather, but what have you done to me?"

Dr. Rozner continued. "By now, you will have guessed that I am dead. I shall take the appropriate medication when I finish this recording. Do not grieve for me, Minnow. I have had a full and rewarding life, but I am gravely ill, and I choose not to continue. You need some answers. I can only hope that you are ready to receive them."

Jillian stared at the screen. She had no idea he had been sick. He'd hidden it well.

Her grandfather continued. "First, I must tell you that you are the light of my soul. I could not be more proud of you. You may wonder why I didn't do more for you while you were in school and beginning your career. I had to let you struggle. It was necessary to build the strong character you need, and you are going to need it."

"Your financial struggles are over. My will settles upon you my entire holdings in the Rozner Corporation, an amount equal to sixty-eight percent of the outstanding, common stock. The balance is scattered among suppliers and colleagues. My lawyers assure me that my will is unassailable, although there will certainly be attempts to break it."

"Dear Little Minnow, you are wealthy to a point where it has no meaning."

Jillian set down her coffee mug, her eyes glued to the screen. Rozner turned serious. "To the inevitable question, 'Why me?' the answer is deceptively simple. You are the most honorable person I know. I have watched you grow into a fine, young woman of impeccable integrity. You have a first class mind and a superb wit. You're going to need both."

Jillian's jaw dropped and she stared at the screen. A warm glow rose in her cheeks. Her grandfather had never before paid her such compliments. She felt proud but disquieted.

He continued. "Using that mind, you will by now have rightly concluded that you must come here to take over. I know you have a thousand questions. My attorneys will be in touch with you to answer them and to make arrangements for your travel. You will discover you have allies. Some will greatly surprise you."

"Oh, I have not forgotten Alice. She is to come too, and upon arrival, receive a complete rehab. I know how much she means to you."

Jillian smiled. How like grandfather not to forget Alice.

"Finally, dear Minnow, I am acutely aware of the unfairness of all of this. What else could I do? Millions of lives ride on the continued success of the Constant. I have left it in the best possible hands. I can only hope that you will understand, and in time, forgive me. Know always, that I love you. Goodbye and may God be with you."

Dr. Jillian Rozner finally understood that she was heir to the greatest fortune in the known universe and holder of nearly limitless power, yet grief overwhelmed any joy she might have felt. She stared at the blank screen, her emotions in chaos.

– 3 –

In his greenhouse on Rozner's World, Adak Pierce gingerly extracted the nearly microscopic embryo from its agar sprouting medium with a glass pipette, and deposited it in a sterile test tube. He held the glass vessel up to the light and examined his latest hybrid. He felt the corners of his mouth turn up in a faint smile. This cross between two rare cymbidia orchid strains should tolerate the low light conditions of Rozner's World. He deposited the vial among its nearly three hundred peers on the intensely illuminated growing racks. Later they would be transferred to low light stations for acclimation to swamp conditions.

After glancing around the lab to make certain that all was in order, he passed his hand over the control panel dimming the wall lights and left through the side door. As he climbed the stairs to the main house, he sighed.

Adak passed through his study. "Vid, please, Replay recording from last night. Wait five."

Four minutes later he'd returned from the bar with a cold beer and a well-packed gator sandwich. Adak dropped his two-meter frame into his favorite recliner and took a long pull on his beer before the requested selection began. After a brief commercial message concerning a new anti-fungal cream, the replay of last night's investigative news program commenced. A blonde reporter he didn't recognize appeared on the screen.

"Good evening. I'm Laurie Watson, and this is Newsbeat. As you can see, I'm standing on one of the many small bridges spanning gaps in the dikes where seasonal flood waters rush out of the marshes, carrying tangles of floating vegetation and the occasional animal carcass to sea. These dikes form the network of trails in the swamp here on Rozner's World. We are fortunate to catch one of the rare occasions when the fog has thinned out enough to allow us a glimpse of the surrounding landscape."

"Botanists are perplexed by the apparently spontaneous development of rare cattleya and phalaenopsis strains of orchids that have been sighted along all of the major networks. They are apparently thriving but no one can account for their origin. You can see some of the orchids growing out of the forks of the trees behind me. The mysterious appearance of these marvelous flowers was first reported on this program, last year. With me, is Dr. Robert Bowman, professor of botany and a landscape architect for the Rozner Corporation."

The camera focused on a tall, distinguished man who kept brushing his wet, gray hair back from his forehead. Laurie held the microphone close to her face. "Thank you for joining us, Doctor. What do you make of all this?"

Doctor Bowman peered directly into the camera. "These orchids are not indigenous to this planet. It's possible that they are a form of botanical contamination."

Pierce froze with his sandwich half way to his mouth. A small vein began to pulse in the side of his neck. "Contamination, hell."

On the screen, the reporter raised a well-groomed eyebrow. "I'm not certain I understand."

"Well, Laurie, history is replete with examples of plants being inadvertently transplanted to new ecosystems. In the twentieth century, Eurasian Milfoil was accidentally transported on the propellers and rudders of ships to the North American continent. This noxious weed nearly choked the life out of most fresh water estuaries before they got it under control."

"Are you saying that these orchids are intergalactic weeds?"

Bowman gazed into the surrounding swamp. "In a sense, Laurie, that's exactly what they are, but these didn't arrive by accident. These have been hybridized by someone who appreciates their beauty and has the considerable technical expertise required. Given the low light conditions, they should not grow here at all. Yet they are thriving. I can only conclude that they have been genetically altered to survive in conditions of lower light and wider temperature fluctuations."

Laurie tilted the microphone to her mouth. "Don't most orchids grow in tropical jungles under similar conditions?"

"Not this extreme."

Adak waved at the screen. "Years of work, my friends."

The reporter continued. "How do your colleagues at Rozner Labs view this development?"

"We are, of course, enthralled by their beauty but we have grave reservations about upsetting the ecological balance of the swamp. You never know what introducing a new species into an ecosystem will do."

Pierce leaned back in his chair and laughed. "You bozos wouldn't know an ecosystem from a sewer system."

On the screen, Dr. Bowman continued. "We have given some consideration to removing them, but frankly, there are too many and they are rapidly reproducing."

Pierce shook his fist at the screen. "Touch one of my orchids and I'll remove your reproductive system, you old fool."

The tape ended and Pierce settled back into his chair. Why couldn't they understand simple hunger for beauty on this monochromatic planet? All he wanted was just a touch of color among the drab greens and browns. The orchids light up the swamp and delight the soul. What's wrong with that?

The vid defaulted to the preset news channel and the same blonde read the latest AP Intergalactic copy.

"In other news, condolences on the passing of Dr. H. Maximillian Rozner continue to pour into Rozner corporate headquarters. The sudden death of this scientific genius has left the fate of the Rozner empire in question. Rumors continue to circulate that his granddaughter and sole heir, Dr. Jillian Rozner of the Pacific Institute, Earth, is on her way to assume control of the galaxy's most powerful private corporation."

Pierce vaulted out of his chair. "What! The old bastard's dead? Nobody told me. Oh, they can't be serious. They're not really going to put his whelp at the helm? Outrageous."

He turned and slammed the beer bottle down on the chairside table. Foam overflowed the bottle and spread across the hardwood surface. "I won't have it."

The reporter continued. "Rozner first postulated the theory of constant acceleration through the use of mercury suffused nodules nearly half a century ago at age forty. Together, with his student and partner, Dr. Adak Pierce, then twenty, he struggled for nearly ten more years before producing an operative system. But before the triumphant introduction of the Rozner Constant drive, Pierce departed the firm to pursue a competing technology, which ultimately failed. He remains in seclusion on Rozner's World."

Pierce flinched and threw up his hands. "It didn't fail, you ignorant fool! I simply ran out of capital before I could complete my prototype. By the time I got reorganized, Rozner had demonstrated his drive. There was no way I could catch up. I poured my life into that work, you stupid woman."

The reporter wrapped up. "On the Universal Exchange, Rozner Corporation common stock plunged following the announcement of his death, but has recovered considerable ground on speculation of Dr. Jillian Rozner's assumption of the chair. Dr. Rozner is a highly respected scientist, and many believe she has been groomed for the position for years."

"No way. No way is some twit with clamshells for brains going to take over my company. I don't care how long they've groomed her. I'm still a major stockholder. You owe me, Rozner."

He collapsed into his chair. A Newsbeat file photo of Dr. Jillian Rozner filled the screen. Pierce glared at the portrait. "Don't get in my way, bitch."

Captain Suzanne Eaton Wyman stood at her command post on the bridge of the *Windflower Vagabond* watching the star-cluttered, black depths of space. She never tired of the awesome spectacle. The great Rozner-powered starship, now cruising at nearly the speed of light, was outbound from Earth for Cygnus IV. At over six kilometers in length and nearly half that in width, the *Windflower Vagabond* was the newest and largest addition to the Vagabond fleet. Only the *Majestic Vagabond* that recently exploded in orbit around Rozner's World had approached her in mass.

That wasn't going to happen to her ship. As she looked around the bridge, Suzanne felt pride well up in her chest at the memory of being chosen as the inaugural commander of this magnificent vessel. She had been fortunate.

After a decade of jockeying tramp freighters from one seedy spaceport to another, she'd been plucked from the bridge of one of the seediest and brought before Admiral Benington. She could still recall every nuance of that meeting. The admiral had attempted to put her at ease and offered her tea, then launched into his presentation.

"Suzanne, you've been with us for nearly ten years and your record is exemplary. We think you're ready for a new challenge. Do you know that we are launching a new starship, the *Windflower Vagabond*?"

Suzanne nodded. Oh yes, she knew. It had been the sole topic of conversation among Vagabond fleet pilots for months. Everyone was vying for a slot on the crew roster. Suzanne had harbored dreams of being appointed second or third in command. She would take cargo officer if it would get her aboard. She fought to keep her expression calm.

"Yes, Sir."

The admiral set down his teacup and looked directly at her. "We want you to command the *Windflower Vagabond.*"

Suzanne stopped breathing and felt the muscles in her face go slack. She heard the muted ticking of the admiral's antique wall clock in the otherwise totally silent room, and turned to look into his eyes.

"Are you serious, Sir?" She managed a gasp.

He laughed. "I told the board you wouldn't believe me. They asked me to show you this."

He retrieved an engraved plaque from his desk and handed it to her. She stared at it.

"Know all men by these presents, Captain Suzanne Eaton Wyman is hereby appointed inaugural commander of the *Windflower Vagabond.* Earth date 2405.12. Seek the stars."

The admiral lifted it gently from her hands. "This will be mounted on the bridge."

Suzanne was trembling. "I... I'm not qualified. I've never piloted anything that big."

He laughed. "No one has, Suzanne. There's never been anything this big."

She leaned back in her chair and studied her superior officer. "Why, me? You have other qualified pilots, many with more experience."

He set down the plaque and read from the screen in his desk. "Suzanne Eaton Wyman, graduated first in her class at the academy, served as navigation officer aboard three different freighters, served as second officer aboard one and later assumed command. Promoted to captain.

"Awarded the Certificate of Merit for the successful delivery of medical supplies into a plague area and the Legion of Honor for the rescue, under extremely hazardous conditions, of the crew of another supply ship."

He glanced up and smiled. "I think you're qualified, Captain. The job is yours."

She took a deep breath. "I won't let you down, Sir."

Standing on the bridge, she glanced back over her shoulder. The plaque was mounted on the rear bulkhead. She smiled as she reached up and brushed her long, blond hair back from her face. She knew it was impractical in space but didn't care. Suzanne felt it complemented her tall, slender figure. She was determined to be both feminine and captain. So far, it appeared to be working.

Major Jac Sabot spun around in his chair and addressed her from the communications station. "Captain, I'm receiving an 'eyes only' transmission for you from fleet."

She nodded. "I'll take it in my quarters, Jac."

"Yes, Sir."

When she had retrieved a cup of tea from her stateroom wall unit she settled into her lounge chair.

"Captain Suzanne Eaton Wyman, *Windflower Vagabond*, Commanding. Clearance Alpha 1, Slash 2-0-2-2. Decode.

"Captain Wyman, you are hereby ordered to abort mission to Cygnus IV and proceed on with all deliberate speed to RA-9, Rozner's World."

"Imperative you maintain secure identity of cloistered passenger who is aware that scheduled events on Cygnus IV are a blind. Deliver passenger earliest possible to Rozner's World. Extensive briefing for cloistered passenger to be transmitted separately. Further instructions follow. End transmission."

Suzanne leaned back in her chair and let out the pent up breath she didn't realize she'd been holding.

"Understood. *Windflower Vagabond*, out."

She sat digesting the message and trying to understand. What did they mean, "... scheduled events on Cygnus IV are a blind?"

She clenched her fists. They should have told her. What was she supposed to do with the cargo?

Heading for the bridge, she wondered how her secret passenger could have so much clout.

Adak Pierce opened his eyes and stared at the ceiling. His body responded of its own accord to the rhythm of the tall brunette sitting astride his hips. He lowered his gaze to watch the head nurse from the Rozner infirmary.

Tanya towered over him, though most of her two-meter stature resided in her spectacular legs. As she rocked, her large breasts swayed and he listened to her ragged breathing. Her long, brown hair brushed her shoulders. Raising both hands, he gently cupped her breasts and allowed them to bump against his palms, marveling at the soft resilience of her flesh. She moaned and quickened her pace. She always did.

Adak felt the pressure build in his groin and gritted his teeth trying to hold back. He fought to stay focused. The sudden eruption of his body surprised him as he released inside her. Tanya thrust twice more, then tipped her head back and cried out as her own climax overwhelmed her.

As her breathing slowed, she straightened her legs and stretched out on top of him. She lay quietly as he slowly retreated. When he had disengaged, she rolled off and lay beside him.

"Where are you, tonight, Lover?"

Adak turned his face toward her. "Is it that obvious?"

"Uh huh."

"I'm sorry. It's this Rozner thing. Now that the old man is dead, I finally have a chance to take control. I just can't figure out how."

"What are you going to do?"

He pounded the bed with his fist. "I don't know, but I'm sure as hell not going to stand around while that granddaughter of his takes over."

When he spoke again, the storm of anger had partially dissipated. "Rozner was my mentor and the closest friend I ever had. In many ways, he was the only father I ever knew. We worked together for years on the Constant. We finally disagreed on a fundamental point of theory. We used to get falling down drunk and argue about it all night. So we decided that he would pursue his course and I would form a new entity to explore mine.

"We never intended to become rivals, at least I certainly didn't. I naively had always assumed that we would share whatever success we had. Then, without even warning me, he demonstrated his drive. I was stunned. My name wasn't even mentioned.

"Any backing I might have garnered to support my own research collapsed. I spent every last credit I had to follow him here to try to reason with him. He wouldn't even see me. I had a large block of stock but that did me absolutely no good. I didn't have enough to mount a takeover and it paid no dividend. Periodically I sold off a few shares to support my interests but I didn't want to sell much. It was the only toehold I had.

"I've stayed here all these years as a lab assistant waiting for a chance to get even. Now this granddaughter of his is taking over. It's too much."

When he'd wound down, they lay on their backs listening to the night sounds of the swamp; the occasional bellow of a gator covering all others. Tanya began to slowly stroke him, her hand gently tugging on his member.

She turned her head toward him. "You do still hold a sizable block of stock?"

"Yes, but she has control. The old man saw to that."

"Can't you have her declared incompetent or something?"

"On what grounds? She's a highly respected scientist."

"But isn't her field marine biology? What can she possibly know about propulsion?"

Adak sighed. "She doesn't need to know anything. Rozner gave her control and now the company's brain trust is ready to support her."

"Can she manage it?"

"I suppose she can. That's what's so galling about it."

A gator bellowed close to the house. From deep in the swamp, another responded. In the awkward silence that followed, Adak could hear his own breathing.

Tanya turned her head toward him. "You've been treated badly, dear Adak, but let it go for tonight."

He lay quietly for several minutes before turning his head and smiling at her. "All right, but if you keep touching me, you're going to have some added responsibilities."

"I can handle it."

"I'm sure you can."

Captain Suzanne Wyman stood in stunned silence on the bridge of the *Windflower Vagabond* as the admiral's image faded from the overhead screen. A cold chill started at the top of her head and passed down her entire body. Rozner dead? Not possible. She shuddered and let out the deep breath she'd been holding. Unthinkable.

Instinctively, she glanced at each of her officers. They all sat frozen by the enormity of the event. She watched as they shook off the impact and returned to their duties talking quietly among themselves.

Her first reaction was that the Admiral should have notified her privately but by then it would be all over the news. He'd broadcast on the most open channel available. The entire crew would have heard.

This would be an excellent time to tour the ship. Her people needed to see their captain. She would stay calm and reassuring, only wishing she felt that way. How Rozner's death would affect the fleet remained to be seen.

Suzanne strode the long main corridor of the *Windflower Vagabond* that the crew had dubbed the gun barrel on her routine tour of inspection. It ran straight down the spine of the ship on the main level. Decks above and below had passageways but no others that cut an uninterrupted swath through various work areas for the full three-mile length of the *Vagabond.* She could easily have taken one of the deck gliders but decided to walk. She needed the exercise and the stroll would allow her to review the condition of many areas of the ship. As she passed through on the way to the stern where she wanted to personally check on the Rozner drives, she would have time to sort out her own feelings.

The instructions to abort her mission to Cygnus IV and proceed to Rozner's World now made sense. They must have known Rozner was terminal. No wonder they were concerned.

She hadn't had time in recent days to tour the ship. Years in space had taught her that direct visual inspection by the commanding officer could head off problems before they became serious.

In the vast, humid space of hydroponics she found the staff busily sowing seeds for the next crop of vegetables. They seemed subdued but snapped to attention as she entered.

"Carry on. I'm just passing through."

A young woman she didn't recognize approached from her left.

"Is it true, Captain? Is Dr. Rozner really dead?"

Suzanne glanced at the crewmember's security badge. "Apparently, Neely. You heard the same announcement I did."

"How will that affect us, Sir?"

Suzanne took a deep breath. "I'm not certain I can answer that, but I can't see how it would change our duties."

Neely nodded, accepting the reassurance at face value. "Begging the Captain's pardon, Sir, but I thought you might like to see our latest little triumph."

Suzanne smiled at the youthful enthusiasm on the woman's face. "Of course. What have you done?"

Neely pointed upward. Suzanne let her gaze travel up into a web of netting several meters above her head. Green vines with dark, irregular leaves sprawled across the entire construction covering several acres of surface.

She glanced at Neely. "What are they?"

The beaming young crewmember's eyes sparkled with excitement. "Watermelon, Sir. We always wanted to grow them but they require too much bench space. Even the bush varieties take up more room than their productive ratio allows. We negotiated with the boys in cargo for a fine netting, didn't want any melons dropping down, and utilized the overhead."

Suzanne's grin broadened. "Well done. Let me know when they ripen."

"You'll have the first slice, Captain."

"Thank you. I'll look forward to it."

As she exited through the other end of the section, she glanced back at the verdant tables that stretched for nearly as far as the eye could see. Hydroponics always brought a sense of well being to her soul. The lush, green of growing plants with their output of oxygen rekindled memories of Earth. She loved her job but she missed her home. Reluctantly, she passed through the lock into engineering.

Instantly, her ears were assaulted by the clamor of heavy machinery. No one even looked up as she entered. She recognized the tall figure of chief engineer Lanny Greenleaf huddled over an ion-plasma cutting torch. She didn't want to startle him. Carefully, she eased around into his field of vision. He glanced up, flicked off the torch and lifted his face shield.

"Sorry, Captain. I didn't see you come in."

"No problem, Chief. How did they press a torch into your hands? I expected to find you in your office."

"We need all the hands we can get for the rush on the new baffles you requested for the sick bay air ducting. You checking up on us?"

"No. I'm on walkabout."

He smiled at her reference to his native Australia. "We'll have these finished in the next forty-eight hours. I hope that's soon enough."

"I'd like them earlier, Chief but if that's the best we can do, the Meds will have to live with it."

He scratched his head with a dirty hand. "We'll do what we can, Captain. What do you make of the old boy popping off?"

"I haven't had time to sort it out. I suppose we'll all find out how it will affect us in the next few days. Carry on, Chief."

He nodded and relit his torch.

She picked her way through the machinery and detritus of the shop and passed into stores. This double area was nearly a quarter mile long. Vast racks of lockers towered over her as she walked through the entire warehouse area without encountering a soul. She made a mental note to check security in this sector. The next section was divided, infirmary to starboard, crew mess to port. She opted for the eating area knowing that nothing improved the quality of staff cuisine like an occasional drop-in visit from a boss who didn't hesitate to sample the fare.

She strode through the seating area, smiling at the pleasing effect of tables scattered into groupings broken by plantings and marine aquariums. This was a far cry from the regimented rows of tables on the smaller freighters.

In the kitchen, she found the staff busily preparing for the first dinner sitting. The senior chef, following protocol, greeted her and offered a cup of Cirran coffee. She took in his perfectly pressed white uniform and towering toque and nodded approval.

"Thank you, Maurice. I could use it."

She sipped the hot, rich blend and raised the cup in salute. "Good stuff."

Maurice smiled. "Would the Captain care to sample tonight's dessert?"

"I thought you'd never ask."

Maurice disappeared among the huge kitchen appliances and reappeared a moment later with a white ceramic dish of crème caramel. He handed Suzanne the concoction and a spoon and stood back to await her reaction. The custard literally melted in her mouth. She rolled her eyes heavenward.

"Maurice, I think the crew is in excellent hands. My compliments to the chef. And if a few of these happened to make their way to the bridge this evening, your captain would be most grateful."

He chuckled. "I think that can be arranged."

He watched while she finished the dessert. "Sorry about Dr. Rozner. It'll be a long time before we produce another mind like that."

"Yes it will, Maurice, but I'll bet he couldn't make a custard like this."

He smiled as he accepted the dish.

"My highest regards to your cooks."

She glanced at her wrist display as she eased through the next portal into the crew's quarters. She'd been walking for sixty-three minutes. Cries of "Officer on deck" rang through the open space and everyone came to attention. This always startled her although she knew she should have anticipated such a reaction. She'd just never gotten used to it.

"At ease, everyone. I'm just passing through."

She made her way to the rear exit, pausing to return salutes and shake hands with all who offered and answering questions about Rozner's death. Near the portal, a young ensign sat tossing tiny spools through loops of fine white thread in an intricate pattern of lace that expanded between her hands. Suzanne was mesmerized. The girl looked up and started to rise.

"At ease, Ensign. I'm fascinated by what you're doing. It's very beautiful."

The girl blushed. "Thank you captain. It's a19th century Earth craft called tatting. Most lace was produced in this manner. My grandmother taught me the art."

"Please continue. I'd just like to watch for a moment."

The girl settled back to her project. As Suzanne looked on, spools flew through the air and dropped through carefully calculated holes in the pattern causing the entire project to grow like a gossamer spider web. When she finally slipped away Suzanne was shaking her head at the girl's skill.

In the doorway, she paused and looked back over the crews quarters with pride. A warm glow spread over her as she surveyed the worthy assembly of men and women.

The next section was her final destination. After placing her palm flat against the identity panel and receiving clearance, she passed through the double lock and entered the highly restricted, cavernous engine room of the *Windflower Vagabond*. The two huge Rozner drives lay in parallel synergy along each side of the compartment. A faint blue halo of light enshrouded each of the thirty-five-meter long power units. They were totally silent. Suzanne wondered for the hundredth time how something so massively powerful could be so quiet. The starboard unit's aura was dimmer and didn't penetrate quite as far into the room.

Three crewmen huddled around an open port on the weaker drive. One held a small recorder while the other two had both hands buried in the beast. She recognized the observer.

"Good afternoon, Lieutenant Sloan. How is the patient?"

He glanced up. "Suffering from a slight case of indigestion, Sir, but we're nursing her back to health."

"Good. Carry on."

She walked between the drives for the full length of the room, then retraced her steps. As she approached the door, the repair team closed the hatch and began packing their tools.

She looked back at the drives and reached for the link on her belt. "Bridge. Captain. How's the balance on the Rozners, now?"

Her second-in-command responded. "The starboard drive is still five percent under spec. Stand by for rebalance."

As she watched, the aura expanded until it matched the port engine's.

"That did it, Martin. Keep an eye on the starboard unit."

"Aye, Captain."

She stepped onto one of the deck gliders that rode a reverse polarity magnetic field a few centimeters above the floor and took a circuitous route back to the bow of the ship. As she passed through officer country directly behind the bridge, Suzanne veered into a side passage and stopped before the entrance to the Admiral's cabin. After glancing around to be certain that she was unobserved, she placed her right hand on the identity plate beside the door. Immediately, a small screen directly above the panel glowed with text.

"Occupant in state of suspended animation. All vital signs within normal parameters."

She nodded and continued to the bridge where she stood looking at the plaque. She couldn't help thinking about young Dr. Rozner being thrust suddenly into a position of great authority. Suzanne knew exactly how she felt.

She shook her head. I wouldn't want to be Jillian Rozner.

− 4 −

Aaron opened his eyes and stared at the gleaming surface of the pool. Sunlight bounced from the aquamarine water and reflected off the dome, casting bright diamonds of light onto the tiled floor. He glanced up at the wall display. He'd slept for forty minutes. Thank God for payday. He hadn't been up here in Heaven for over a week.

His back felt hot and his legs were beginning to sting. At least the migraine had relented. He raised his eyes to see the tanned attendant striding toward him.

"Better cool down, Lieutenant. You're starting to burn."

"Thank you. I'll take a swim then move into the shade."

Aaron didn't bother to rise. He simply slid across the tile on his belly like a seal and slipped into the pool. The cool water took his breath away. He surfaced in the center and floated on his back, watching fluffy, white clouds drift across the sky beyond the clear dome that enclosed Heaven. It reminded him of the pool at his parents' home only this one was smaller.

Everything Father did had to be on a grand scale. Only the best for Leon Trout and that included his son. The old boy did know how to live. He just didn't know how to relate to a son who idolized him but had his own ambitions. He couldn't understand that Aaron had no interest in the family business. Cartage meant simply moving objects from one place to another. How could you care about that?

Aaron wanted to have an impact, to count. For a while he considered being a doctor, but mucking around with other people's bodies didn't appeal to him in the least. Trail Patrol came close. It was dirty, frustrating, often backbreaking work, but he'd saved lives.

A small, white cloud drifted across the dome. Aaron watched it slowly dissipate as it floated from east to west.

Father had given him values he considered important. For all the old man's bluster, he had absolute integrity. Aaron could not recall a time when his father failed to do what he thought was right, no matter the cost. Once, it had nearly lost him his corporation. Aaron had never forgotten that.

He glanced around and realized that he had the pool to himself. Everyone else lay basking on the deck or reclining in folding lounges, talking softly or reading. Everyone, that is, except the ash-blond sitting in a full lotus position, completely nude, at the east end of the pool.

Her eyes were closed and her lips turned up in a faint smile. Her perfectly formed breasts rose and fell with her slow breathing. With a start, Aaron realized that she was the attendant who had recorded his credit deduction and admitted him to the elevator on the lower level of Salvation. Obviously her shift had ended and she was availing herself of the fringe benefits of her job.

No overt sexual advances would be tolerated. Aaron snorted. He was good at covert sexual advances. He could be very subtle if necessary.

He stood up in the middle of the pool where the water came up to his chin and wondered what it would take to be transferred up here. Beats the hell out of mud. The view was certainly better. Maybe he could apply for Heaven's security detail. They must have one.

As he watched, she suddenly opened her eyes, looked directly at him, and smiled. Aaron's heart stopped. Slowly closing her eyes, she continued her meditation, totally oblivious of the devastating effect she had on him. She was completely at ease with her nudity, and probably came up here every day. Her entire body was lightly tanned.

Aaron reluctantly looked away. He loved watching her but felt slightly embarrassed by her lack of modesty. He was also nude but she was so comfortable with it. He found himself staring again.

Think of her as a work of art, Trout. Appreciate the beauty without calling up your baser instincts. Sure.

It had been a long time since those baser instincts had been indulged. There had been the brief encounter with Jana from supply, but that had been nearly two years ago. She had wanted too much of his soul.

The nude woman shifted positions and settled back into her meditation. God, she's lovely. I'd better leave before I make a complete ass of myself.

As he started to climb out of the pool, he suddenly realized that his body had betrayed his thoughts. He could have hung his towel on his protruding member.

Maybe I'll just sit in the water and think about something else for a while.

He eased himself back into the pool. He could think about his job or exploding starships. He could concentrate on his finances. That would deflate him. But he couldn't keep his eyes from drifting toward the east end of the pool. She hadn't moved. She sat, still as a statue, soaking up the sunlight and breathing slowly.

Ah, to Hell with it.

Aaron vaulted out of the water, throwing his towel over his shoulder, not caring who noticed his condition and strode into the locker room. The computerized voice greeted him.

"Massage or shower, Lieutenant Trout?"

"Massage, please, then a long cold shower."

"Excellent choice, Lieutenant. The massage chamber can relieve your discomfort."

He started to say, "What discomfort?" then glanced down. "Right." He'd never thought of the aching need as discomfort, but it was probably as good a term as any.

A panel in the locker room wall slid aside and the chamber glided silently into the room. With a faint hiss the top raised to reveal a full-length massage table. Aaron climbed aboard and the door whispered closed. Soft music filled the dark space, then the rollers and mechanical fingers went to work.

Forty minutes later, the interior walls of the chamber slowly brightened and the door raised to reveal the locker room, now suffused with soft, blue light. Aaron leisurely sat up then stepped onto the heated, tile floor. Indeed, his discomfort had been relieved. His release had been deep and satisfying.

"Your shower is ready, Lieutenant Trout."

He stepped into the enclosure and immediately a needle spray of cold water pounded against his body from all sides. Aaron gasped then tried to breathe evenly. It wasn't easy.

After air-drying his body, he dressed in the clean uniform from his locker and strolled into the reception room.

The same stunning brunette occupied the reception desk. She flashed a brilliant smile as he crossed the lobby to the elevator. Aaron turned to speak to her. "Have a nice day."

When the doors had closed, he leaned his forehead against the bright metal. "My God, Trout, you could have thought of something more original."

The elevator descended.

🐾 🐾 🐾

Sherman W. Ellis, managing general partner of Williamson & Ellis, Attorneys at Law, strode into the 212 story Pacific Building in downtown Seattle. He crossed the lobby and entered the private negative gravity lift that levitated him to his firm's suite on floor 210.

As he ascended, he replayed last night's conversation with Adak Pierce. Even with the delay caused by the enormous distance, he could feel the determination of his firm's most difficult client. He reached up and rubbed the back of his neck, attempting to ease the tension. This was not a course of action he could endorse. Every fiber of his body cried out against it. In twenty minutes, he would convene the board meeting. It had better go the right way. Pierce was not a man you chose to alienate.

Arlene waited in his office. She stood before the wall screen that displayed the prepared documents. He nodded to his assistant.

"Did all the affidavits arrive?"

"Yes, sir. The last one just came in. We have signed proxies from all the board members who cannot be here, including Adak Pierce. Jones, Swenson, Anderson and McCall are in the boardroom."

"Good. Good. This has to come off without a hitch. You're certain that the proxies all name me."

"Yes, Sir. I checked each document. You have full voting authority for everyone who is absent."

"Well, that's a relief."

Ellis took a deep breath and pulled open the massive oak doors that led to the boardroom.

The men and women in the room were all congregated at the far end of the table. He greeted each, then waved them to their seats and took his place at the head.

"This ad hoc meeting of the board of directors of the Rozner Corporation is called to order. Computer, let the minutes show that a quorum is present. We have only one item of business. With the sad passing of Dr. H. Maximillian Rozner, we must elect a new Chairman, who will act as CEO."

Helen Anderson leaned forward. This was the moment Ellis had been dreading. "I thought it was understood that his granddaughter, Jillian Rozner inherited his controlling interest and would assume the title. Shouldn't she be represented? She's the majority stockholder."

The other three nodded. None of them knew her, but the logic was irrefutable. Ellis held up his hand urging patience, then palmed the sensor on the table. A document materialized on the screen buried in the tabletop before each participant. Ellis waited until they had finished reading and looked up.

Jones reread one of the texts. "This is an insurance funded buy-sell agreement. It names Adak Pierce and Dr. H. Maximillan Rozner as mutual beneficiaries with rights to buy any or all shares of the first deceased."

Ellis nodded gratefully. "It would have worked in reverse if Pierce had predeceased. It supercedes the will."

Swenson was beginning to track. "But this leaves his granddaughter with nothing."

Ellis shook his head. "Hardly, Larry. As heir to his estate, she receives the proceeds of the insurance policy. Jillian is a very wealthy woman. She will also have a substantial position with the firm if she desires it."

Bruce McCall had not said a word through the entire proceedings. Now he stared at Ellis and his eyes narrowed. "How do we know this document is authentic?"

"View the next frame. That is a superior court certification."

The room filled with crosstalk as they absorbed the news. Ellis let it continue until the conversation began to die out. He knew they needed a few minutes to absorb the concept if they were going to go for it.

He took a deep breath. "In view of these developments, I will entertain a motion of unanimous consent to elect Adak Pierce chairman and CEO of the Rozner Corporation. I have proxies for the absent board members."

After a brief hesitation, Anderson looked up. "So moved."

Jones nodded. "Second."

Ellis took a deep breath. "All in favor?"

A chorus of 'Ayes' rang out.

"Opposed?"

Silence.

Ellis leaned forward and rested his elbows on the table. "Hearing no objection, I declare the motion passed. Adak Pierce is chairman and CEO. Since there is no other old or new business, I declare this meeting adjourned. Thank you for your time."

While the others milled around the room discussing these extraordinary events, Ellis excused himself and strode through the reception area to his private office. He closed the door and leaned against it. He had just violated every moral code he knew, but he had no choice. Oh, God. If it had gone the other way.... If anyone ever found out....

When he could stop shaking, he poured a double scotch and downed it in one gulp.

Helen Anderson passed through the doors of the Pacific Building and stood on the plaza that surrounded the towering structure. Fragments of the meeting raced through her mind. How could this be? They had just turned Rozner Corp. over to Adak Pierce. Maybe she should have objected but it all happened so quickly.

She had never met the granddaughter but surely she should have been represented at the meeting. She shook her head. "I wonder if the young Dr. Rozner even knows about this?"

As president of her own corporation, Helen knew enough corporate law to detect the ring of authenticity in the legal work. Still....

She strolled over to the massive fountain that dominated the plaza. Two small boys stood gaping at the geyser that rose nearly as high as the tenth floor before falling back to splash into the pool. She sat on the raised rim and stared up at the building. The tension in the back of her neck ratcheted up another notch. She had to do something.

She could contact Jillian Rozner, but as a member of the board she wasn't certain that was ethical. She cared about the other board members. They could be stuffy and often obtuse but she felt their intentions were honorable.

A shift in the breeze brought a fine spray of mist from the fountain to cool the back of her neck. She turned and watched the water. The boys were gone. She smiled. One maxim of her father's had never failed her. When in doubt, seek the council of an old and trusted friend.

She stood and strode back into the building and located a private communication booth. Placing her hand flat against the sensory panel she waited for the computer to identify her and activate the vid screen. Helen took a deep breath.

"Connect me with the office of John Marshall, Chief Justice of the World Court."

After a slight delay, a young woman appeared on screen. "May I help you?"

"This is Helen Anderson in Seattle. I urgently need to speak to Justice Marshall."

"The Chef Justice is not available. My name is Shannon O'Neil. Perhaps I can help."

Helen took a deep breath. She had anticipated a gauntlet of protective bureaucrats. "May I speak to his administrative assistant, please."

The young woman smiled. "I doubt that we need to disturb Ms. Henderson. I'm certain I can answer any question you may have."

Helen clenched her fists, fighting for control. "I have no questions, young lady. Just put me through to Margaret Henderson. This is very urgent. She will recognize my name."

"One moment please."

The screen flickered and a new face appeared. "Helen. How nice of you to call. I'm afraid the Chief is off planet. Is there anything I can do for you?"

Helen hesitated. "I need his council, as a friend."

Margaret chuckled. "There is no better. If it's really important, I can reach him."

Helen leaned back against the wall of the booth. She couldn't decide how much to reveal. Finally, she realized she had no choice.

"Tell him the board of directors of the Rozner Corporation has just named Adak Pierce Chairman and CEO. For my own peace of mind, I need to know if we've done the right thing. There's something disturbing about all of this."

Margaret took a moment to absorb the statement. "What about the granddaughter? The one that's been in the news?"

"That's what's bothering me."

Margaret nodded. "I'll let him know. Will you be home later if he wants to speak with you?"

"Yes. Thanks, Margaret."

"You're welcome. Goodbye, Helen."

🐾 🐾 🐾

"Jillian."

She heard her name but couldn't locate the source of the voice. She swam up through the drug-induced fog and opened her eyes. The softly glowing panels of an unfamiliar ceiling hung centimeters over her head.

"Jillian."

"Hmmm."

"Jillian. It's time to wake up."

She reached up and rubbed her eyes. "Who....I don't understand. Where am I?"

The voice seemed to emanate from the walls. "You're aboard the *Summerset Vagabond*, outbound from Earth to Rozner's World. The shuttle will depart for the surface in nineteen minutes. All life support and cryogenic monitoring systems have been removed from your transit couch. You are free to move around your cabin."

She turned over on her side and stared at the room. The floor was several meters down.

"I feel a little light-headed."

"That's the effect of the stimulants. You will feel normal, shortly. Take your time."

Glancing around the room, she attempted to locate the attendant but saw no one. Vague traces of memory began to reassert themselves. She recalled the exhilaration of the shuttle ride up from Earth and her shock at the vastness of the ship. A young medical assistant had helped her onto the couch. He had administered a nose vapor sedative and she'd passed out. Nothing after that.

She swung her legs over the edge and the platform descended smoothly until her feet touched the deck. A panel at the head of the bed slid open revealing her sandals. She retrieved them and slipped them on her feet. Only then did she notice that she was fully clothed. Someone must have dressed her and fixed her hair. That was disconcerting. A faint taste of mint lay on her tongue.

There was a slight dizziness as she stood up. Somehow, she had expected to have more reaction to cryogenic stasis. Her joints were not stiff and her muscle tone appeared to be normal. They must have been bringing her around slowly for some time. It was the quickest two years of her life.

Steadying herself with one hand on the bed, she carefully launched her body for the door. The portal slid open as she approached. The long, dimly lit hallway led off in both directions. A glowing pale green arrow in the opposite wall pointed to her left. She followed the instruction and arrived at the departure lounge.

A male attendant in full uniform awaited her. "Good Afternoon, Dr. Rozner. Your shuttle is waiting. All of your personal effects have been transported to the surface. We wanted to give you as much time as possible to recover."

"Do I need to check out?"

He laughed. "No. Everything has been taken care of. Just make yourself comfortable and we'll leave in a moment. There is one other passenger."

In a few moments, a harried looking man with tousled gray hair bustled into the lounge and made directly for the shuttle. Barely nodding to the attendant, he settled into the seat across from Jillian and began strapping himself in. Jillian took the cue and pulled the braces across her chest clipping them into their brackets.

Her stomach rolled as they dropped away from the ship, then the engines fired and she was gently thrust back into the thick padding. She could see the orange glow from the nose of the craft as it entered the atmosphere.

She closed her eyes. "I hope you're right, Grandfather."

The shuttle settled onto the pad with only the slightest bump. The man across from Jillian glanced up. "Cheated death, again." He wasn't smiling.

When the door slid aside, she stared out at the huge, white building that filled her vision. Through the fog she could make out the sign across the top of the wall: Rozner Laboratories. She felt dwarfed by the imposing structure.

Jillian rose and walked to the doorway. As she approached, a stairway slid out of the belly of the craft reaching to the ground.

"Well, don't just stand there. I've got work to do."

She turned and glared at her fellow passenger. "Give me a minute. This is all new to me."

"Contemplate it later. Either exit or get out of the way."

She strolled down the stairs as casually as possible, taking a perverse pleasure in making him wait.

Once on the ground, she looked around. Stout trunks of trees filled her vision in every direction, their branches decapitated by the heavy gray fog that hung just a few meters overhead.

A damp grassy smell so unlike the fresh sea breeze of home rode on the air. Already, she longed for the brilliant sunshine and clear blue skies of La Jolla.

As she started for the building, a deafening bellow filled the air. Jillian nearly leaped back into the shuttle.

"Oh for God's sake, haven't you heard a gator before?"

She steadied her breathing and stepped aside to let him pass. "No, as a matter of fact, I haven't."

He shook his head, brushed past her and strode off toward the entrance of the building.

The door slid aside and a tall man in a white lab coat walked purposefully toward her. He extended his hand as he approached. "Welcome to Rozner's World, Doctor. I'm Marcel Covington. When they haven't got me hunkered down in the lab, I act as Chief of Protocol."

Jillian smiled. "Thank you for meeting me. I'm afraid the other gentleman wasn't impressed."

Marcel glanced around as if searching for someone then laughed. "Oh, you mean Dr. Wiggins. Don't mind him. He's irascible, but absolutely brilliant. He's our metallurgist and runs the test lab."

Jillian smiled then nodded toward the building. "Is this where the real work gets done?"

He grinned. "We like to think so, but the people in Assembly would give you an argument. Would you like to see the facility or would you prefer to go to your quarters?"

Jillian was tempted but decided she'd have plenty of time later to tour the plant. Right now, she wanted a decent glass of wine and a hot bath. She also needed to check on Alice. "I'd like to get settled in."

Marcel touched a small plate on his wrist. A well-used runabout slid out of a compartment in the side of the building and glided to a stop beside them. He spoke to it as one would to a co-worker.

"Take Dr. Rozner to her quarters."

"Sir." The voice came from the craft.

Jillian extended her hand. "Thank you for your courtesy, Marcel."

"My pleasure, Dr. Rozner."

She slid onto the seat and the small craft accelerated away from the landing pad. They swept through a spacious corporate campus, past several large buildings and over carefully tended lawns bordered with tall ferns and low-growing mosses. The neatly maintained landscape provided a stark contrast to the surrounding swamp.

The pressure of the old anxiety rose in her chest. This was insanity. These people were never going to accept her. She was too young, too inexperienced. She could not replace Grandfather.

She felt small, insignificant, like a child sent on an adult's errand.

A light rain began to fall as they drifted to a stop in the covered portico of the tallest building. "Your quarters, Dr. Rozner."

Jillian stepped out of the ground car and it accelerated away. As she approached, the clear doors slid open and a slender man in a dove-gray suit approached from the interior.

"Welcome, Dr. Rozner. I'm Lewis, your Concierge. If you need anything at all, call on me day or night."

Jillian slowly extended her hand. "Thank you, Lewis. I'm a little surprised. Isn't the building automated?"

"Of course, ma'am. We have all of the latest conveniences, but your grandfather liked to provide the personal touch. I'll show you to your apartment."

They ascended to the penthouse and Jillian stepped through the portal into a beautifully decorated home. All of the surfaces were done in muted cream-colored panels and the furniture was appointed in pastels.

She turned to speak to Lewis and discovered that he had slipped out. Jillian was alone on Rozner's World. She walked over to the clear wall and watched the rain pour down on the saturated campus. "Okay, Grandfather. I'm here. Now what in this world am I supposed to be doing?"

Rain pounding on the transparent wall of her bedroom woke her at dawn. For her first night on Rozner's World, she had ignored propriety and left it clear. A simple command to the household computer would have rendered it opaque, but in this dreary climate, she needed all the light she could get.

Jillian chuckled as she remembered her initial encounter with the household computer that identified itself as "Wilson." Whoever programmed the unit had a lousy sense of humor. When she insisted that the wall remain open, Wilson had informed her that according to his sources, "Nice girls don't do such things."

She lay listening to the rain then heaved a small sigh. At least her stay here should not be long. She'd tie up the loose ends, then go home. An impish grin spread over her face.

"Wilson"

"Yes, Jillian."

"I'm tired of the rain. You can turn it off now."

To her complete astonishment, the entire wall turned translucent then displayed an animated panorama of the beach at La Jolla, complete with breaking surf and wheeling gulls. The reflected colors lit up the room.

She sat bolt upright and stared. "It's wonderful, Wilson. Where did you get that?"

"Your grandfather thought you might like it. Would you like sound?"

"Please."

The room filled with the roar of surf punctuated by cries of sea birds and wind-rustled dune grass. Jillian nearly wept for joy.

She requested Wilson to reduce the sound to background level. She considered damping it completely but couldn't bear to come home to a silent ocean panorama. After a few tries she had it dialed in perfectly, a shade above a whisper.

For now, she had a mission. Jillian had decided that she would spend her first morning, alone, in her grandfather's office. She needed to feel connected to the great man who had taught her to love knowledge and adventure. Certainly, he had personified that code.

She rubbed her eyes and let her hands drag down over her face. Then, pushing herself upright, she headed for the shower, pulling her gown over her head as she walked. The needle spray commenced as she entered the enclosure. For a few moments, she stood and let the hot water pound on the back of her neck, then lathered her hands and began washing her hair.

As she exited the shower stall, the water stopped. "Air or towel, Dr. Rozner?"

"Towel."

A panel in the wall slid aside and a large, white cloth extended into the room. Jillian accepted it, scrubbed her short, dark hair, then began drying her legs. A tingle of excitement sparkled over her body. Despite the gloom of the planet, this was going to be some adventure.

Jillian finished drying and stepped over to the basin. Her toothbrush, fully loaded, extended from its holder. She retrieved it and guided it toward her teeth, stopping with it halfway to her mouth.

"Wilson?"

"Yes, Dr. Rozner?"

"Connect to my grandfather's office, audio only." She began brushing her teeth.

"Your grandfather's office does not respond."

She froze with her hand in midstroke. "What do you mean?"

"Code sequences have been altered."

"That's absurd. Retry."

"Impenetrable."

"Who ordered the change?"

"The president of the Rozner Corporation."

Jillian lowered the brush and let her hand fall to her side. "I'm the president of the Rozner Corporation."

"There has been a change."

Jillian felt a cold chill pass up her spine. "Identify."

"No information available."

"Connect me with Grandfather's secretary."

After a short pause, an unfamiliar voice responded. "Rozner Corporation."

"Lucy Warren, please."

"Ms. Warren has been transferred."

Jillian could feel tension gripping the back of her neck. "Where's my grandfather's secretary? Who are you?"

"Janice Smally. Is this Dr. Rozner?"

She slammed the brush down on the counter. "Yes. What the hell's going on?"

The voice on the other end was soft and glacially calm. "I have been instructed to order you to report to the office of the president."

"Order? What do you mean order? I am the president."

"There's been a change, Dr. Rozner. Please report as soon as possible."

She retrieved the toothbrush and passed it under the stream of water. "Report? To whom?"

"To the president."

"Who is this president?"

"He prefers to introduce himself when you arrive." The connection terminated.

Standing over the sink holding her dripping toothbrush, she felt the cold chill envelope her entire body as she recalled her grandfather's words. "My will is unassailable, but there will certainly be attempts."

She gazed into the mirror. "So, now it begins."

She swept into her dressing room, grabbing up the clothes she'd laid out the night before. She could hear the kitchen appliances preparing her breakfast and smelled the aromatic coffee. She glanced around the apartment, so far from her beloved La Jolla on Earth, and heaved a sigh.

"I've always wanted adventure. This is just more than I ever contemplated."

She straightened her shoulders. "I can do this." She ordered the computer to switch off the appliances and headed for the door.

After donning her foul weather gear, she greeted Lewis on the way out and strode purposefully across the compound to the administration building he had pointed out to her.

After displaying the identification card she'd found in a welcoming packet in her apartment to a nervous guard, she was escorted to her grandfather's office suite.

Approaching the office complex, she read the luminous plaque on the door. "Adak Pierce, President."

As she opened the door, a tall woman in navy blue business attire looked up at her from behind the reception desk. "How may I help you?"

Jillian approached her. "I'm here to see Adak Pierce. I'm Dr Jillian Rozner. Who are you?"

"I'm Janice Smally, executive assistant to Mr. Pierce. He's expecting you."

Jillian felt the heat rise in her cheeks. "I'll bet he is."

"One moment, Please. I'll announce you."

"Don't bother. I'll announce myself."

Jillian took a deep breath, squared her shoulders and stormed past Janice Smally to the inner office entrance. She plunged through the irising doorway without knocking.

Stepping into the room, Jillian was confronted by the biggest man she had ever seen. Even seated, he had to be two meters tall and weigh a hundred-and-fifty kilograms. A mane of dark hair, streaked with silver, crowned his enormous head, and his chin sported a full, black beard tinged with gray.

He stood and extended his right hand. "Good morning, Dr. Rozner, so kind of you to come on short notice."

Jillian approached him as she would a Kodiak bear from Earth. He looked the part, but his grip was normal enough.

"Kindness has nothing to do with it. What are you doing in my chair?"

Pierce walked around and sat on the corner of the desk. "Calm yourself, Doctor. I understand your confusion. I'm sure you have questions and in time, they will all be answered. First you need to know that I am the lawful successor to the presidency of the Rozner Corporation."

"By what conceivable authority?"

Pierce stood and gestured to the guest chair. "Please take a seat, Doctor Rozner, and I'll explain."

She ignored his offer for the moment. "Who are you?"

"Did they not tell you? I'm Adak Pierce. For many years, I was your grandfather's partner in the development of what later became known as the Rozner Constant. Actually, it should have been patented as the Pierce-Rozner Constant, but that's a long story."

Jillian settled into the chair. "My grandfather said nothing about a partner, though your name is vaguely familiar. His will specifically left control of the corporation to me."

"I'm afraid it was not his to bequeath."

Jillian felt the chill on the back of her neck begin to grow. "What do you mean?"

Pierce slid off the desk and casually walked around to the other side. When he had seated himself in the executive chair, he rested his elbows on the desk and steepled his fingers. "How familiar are you with intergalactic corporate law, or for that matter, corporate law of Earth?"

"Not very, but my lawyers are."

"Are you familiar with the ramifications of insurance funded buy-sell agreements?"

"No."

Pierce opened the center desk drawer and retrieved a document. "This has all been reduced to computer records, but this is a copy of the document drawn up by your grandfather and me thirty-five years ago. The original is stored in a safe place. In the event of the death of either of us, the survivor may use the proceeds of a corporately-funded, single-premium life insurance policy to buy out the interest of the deceased. It's common practice in ventures with two or more initial principals and takes precedence over an individual's will."

Jillian felt a dull pain forming at the base of her skull. "Why didn't his lawyers know of this?"

"It was a long time ago, Dr. Rozner. He had different legal counsel. Perhaps the new firm was never advised. Your grandfather probably forgot all about it."

She glared at him. "Why should I believe you?"

"You don't need to. Check the records of the King County courthouse in Seattle, on Earth. They will allay your suspicions. It may seem that I have acted precipitously, but we could not leave the corporation headless."

Jillian stiffened. "It was not headless. My grandfather's will left me in command the minute he died."

Pierce rose from his chair and walked to the window. He stood with his back to her and stared into the rain. "We've already covered that ground, Jillian. The board has sanctioned my appointment."

He turned to her. "But we have by no means excluded you. You have been named Vice President of Public Affairs. It's a vital position and requires the authority of a highly respected scientist as well as the skills of an articulate spokesperson. We need to shore up our image after your grandfather's untimely passing. It's crucial that we maintain the confidence of our larger clients.

"I've arranged full security clearance and we've established a beautiful office for you in the executive suite. I'm sure you'll be very happy there. Give it some time."

He returned to his desk and stood behind it. "Now, if you'll forgive me, I have a great deal of work to do. Miss Smally will show you to your office when you're ready. We'll talk again, later."

Jillian took a deep breath. "This is not over."

She stood abruptly and strode with great dignity out of the office, her mind awhirl. The news made her dizzy. She needed time to sort it all out and she knew exactly where to do it but first, she wanted to see what Pierce had in mind.

She stopped on the way out to get directions to her new office from Janice Smally who pointed down the hall to another suite. As she entered an attractive gray-haired woman in a beautiful teal suit greeted her at the door.

"Welcome, Dr. Rozner. I'm Lucy Warren. We have spoken once or twice. I was your grandfather's executive secretary and I've been assigned to your suite to assist you. I hope that meets with your approval."

Jillian gave a start. Pierce had given her grandfather's assistant. He wasn't afraid of her at all. The arrogance, the sheer audacity of the man caused her to shake her head.

Lucy didn't appear to notice.

Jillian liked her. She radiated quiet confidence.

"Yes, I remember. So nice to finally meet you in person." Jillian nodded toward the door. "I've come to see the office."

"Of course. Right this way."

She led Jillian across a large receiving room tastefully appointed in muted colors and displaying large light panels of the Vagabond fleet on the walls. At the wave of her hand, a panel slid aside revealing her new office. Jillian stepped in and Lucy closed the door leaving her in solitude.

She stood drinking in the surroundings. The dominant feature was the massive desk, so like her grandfather's, that straddled the northeast corner of the room. The surface was completely bare. She crossed slowly to the executive chair and sat facing into the room.

"I'm here, Grandfather. I won't fail you. It may take time but I promise you, this will not last. I can learn and when I'm ready, I will strike."

She glanced up at the models of spacecraft suspended from the ceiling. All employed the Rozner Constant drive. There were so many.

The seating area in the opposite corner offered large comfortable-looking chairs surrounding a low table. Jillian immediately decided that was where she would work. Even though it reminded her of her grandfather, the desk was too intimidating.

"Computer."

"Yes, Dr. Rozner."

"Did my grandfather leave a message for me?"

"None that you have not already acknowledged."

She rose and walked around the desk, trailing her fingers lightly across the surface then crossed back to the seating are. Settling into one of the large chairs, she stared out at the rain.

– 5 –

A lice soared above the landscape and banked into a sweeping turn that would take them above the compound then out over the swamp. From her comfortable seat, Jillian looked down on her new home through thin fog. The huge rectangular edifice that housed Rozner Labs took up the entire east end of the campus. Maintenance and storage facilities were attached to the north side of the building like limpets on a rock.

"Jillian."

"Yes, Alice."

"You've been going to your new working place for six days. Is it like your old working place in La Jolla?"

Jillian heaved a huge sigh. "No, Alice. It's nothing like La Jolla."

"I sense tension in your actions when we arrive there."

"I know."

Two-man shelters that served as crew quarters for both the miners and the Trail Patrolmen squatted like boulders along the southern edge of the dry land that supported the development. Staff housing lay along the northern perimeter. In the center stood the residential tower for corporate officers. Jillian had the entire top floor.

The dominating feature was the vast dome of "Salvation," the rest and recreation facility. It provided a desperately needed semblance of normalcy in a hostile environment. The smaller elevated dome of "Heaven," on its five hundred-foot tower, passed by the starboard side of Alice at eye level. Through the clear enclosure, Jillian could see patrons lounging around the inviting pool.

"Jillian."

"Yes, Alice."

"Why are none of those people wearing clothes? Don't you remove yours only to bathe?"

"They're sunbathing."

Alice cogitated for a moment, obviously checking her references. "Sunbathing - to lie in a sunlit place wearing little or no covering for the purpose of absorbing ultra-violet rays." The lights on Alice's dash blinked. "UV will kill you, Jillian. Their actions are irrational."

Jillian smiled. "They wear sunblock, Alice. It filters out most of the UV."

Alice was quiet until they had passed the trailhead and were out over the swamp. "Is this another of those things that I will never understand, Jillian?"

"I'm afraid so, but don't worry about it. You'll just have to trust me on this one."

Alice remained silent for a moment. "Trust? Is that like when we launch out of my garage and you have to believe that I can fly?"

"That's it, exactly."

"I like trust, Jillian."

"It can be a very good thing, but it can be abused."

"Like military power?"

"In a way."

They swept over a large building on a point of land south of the compound. "What's that, Alice?"

"My map identifies it as the private residence of one Adak Pierce. There is no other information."

A red wave of anger welled up in her chest. "Aha. So that's his lair. We have to learn a great deal more about him,

Alice. He's taken over Grandfather's office. Hell, he's stolen the company. Let's get a closer look."

The rapidly blinking pattern of lights on Alice's console indicated mild confusion. "Didn't your grandfather leave you in command?"

Jillian took a deep breath. "It's very complicated."

Alice reduced her power and glided down toward the compound. They slowly circled the buildings but could detect nothing remarkable with the exception of the large translucent surface covering the east wing.

"What is it, Alice?"

"I have no definitive data. It may be a growing place for plants." Alice added thrust and gained elevation.

For the next two hours, they cruised low above the eerie landscape as Jillian tried to sort out her predicament. She watched water drip from moss-covered branches into dark pools that concealed the bases of ancient, cypress-like conifers. The huge trees soared into the low clouds. Great roots broke the surface of the swamp in long loops like giant, discarded garden hose cast into the fetid water by long-departed landscapers. Decaying vegetation perfumed the air with pungent odors that assaulted her nose. Shrill cries of unseen birds drifted through the portal Jillian had slid partly open in Alice's cabin wall and provided counterpoint to the hoarse bellow of enormous, gator-like reptiles, below.

"Jillian?"

"Yes, Alice."

"We have an ore carrier coming in on our port bow. He's quite large and probably not very maneuverable. I'm going to alter course to give him plenty of room."

"Very well, Alice."

They turned toward the northeast and climbed fifty meters. As they leveled off, Jillian detected sluggishness in the aircar's response.

"Jillian?"

"Yes."

"I'm losing power to my radial converter."

"What's happening?"

"I have no other data."

"Is this serious?"

"Yes."

Jillian glanced quickly at the map display. "Can you stay in the air long enough to get us back to the compound?"

"Not according to my calculations."

Jillian's throat tightened as she slowly turned her head to survey the swamp. Tall cypress-like trees and black water stretched away in all directions.

"I don't see any place to land, Alice."

"I know. I'm not sensing any dry ground in range."

"How long can you float?"

"I don't know. I've never tried."

A tiny knot of fear formed beneath her breastbone and expanded to fill her whole chest. "How much time do we have?"

"Not more than a few minutes. I'm losing internal power."

Jillian checked the instruments, then focused on the navigational computer. The upper half of the screen was very dim. "Let's head back toward the base. We can at least shorten their search. Begin transmitting distress signal."

"Yes, Jillian. I am already broadcasting."

They skimmed the dark water, rising now and again to clear stumps and floating logs. Once, Jillian glimpsed one of the strange, six-legged gators gliding through the shadows. She shuddered and pulled her cape around her shoulders, trying not to think about all those teeth.

"Jillian?"

"Yes, Alice."

"I'm picking up a solid mass one thousand meters ahead."

"It's probably one of the raised pathways"

"That would fit the data."

"Can we land on it?"

"Possibly, I need to survey."

As they swept over the dike, Alice banked, then turned back over the causeway.

"It will be close, but we can land."

Jillian took a deep breath. "Put us on the ground, Alice."

"It will not be smooth like a baby's bottom. Is that the correct phrase, Jillian?"

"Uh, yes. That covers it."

"Glue your buns to the seat and grab structure."

"Alice, where are you getting this language?"

"I'm monitoring the net. I like the way the pilots talk."

Jillian reached back and retrieved the free ends of the emergency restraining harness. With shaking hands, she wrapped the webbing tightly around her body, clipping the loose ends into their sockets. She reached up and grasped the built-in grab bars on either side of the pilot's couch as the aircar settled into a long glide above the dike then abruptly dropped the last few meters.

Alice bumped once on the muddy surface, then settled into a long, sickening slide that ended abruptly as the antique aircar pitched up against a huge log. Despite the harness, Jillian slammed forward, striking her head on the instrument panel.

"Jillian? Jillian, are you awake? This is not your sleep time."

Slowly Jillian opened her eyes and glanced around the familiar cabin. She raised her head, then carefully sat up. A sharp pain flashed down her leg.

"We're down, Jillian."

"I can see that, Alice. I don't understand. I can't remember."

"You have been in sleep mode for twenty-two minutes. We had to make an emergency landing. We're on one of the raised trails about fifty-kilometers northwest of corporate headquarters. Are you intact?"

"I believe all vital parts are still attached."

Jillian attempted to shift position. She cried out as a sharp pain shot through her left leg. Somehow she got settled again in a reasonably comfortable posture. Her voice was a hoarse whisper.

"What do we require to make repairs, Alice?"

"A new radial converter would be an excellent beginning."

"I'm afraid that'll have to wait until we get back to the base. Are you hailing on all emergency frequencies?"

"Yes, but there is no response. Our signal must not be getting through."

Jillian gazed around the landing site. Fog rolled in on the western horizon. Only a few hours of daylight remained. A gator bellowed. A cold chill crept up her spine. The thought of spending the night in the swamp terrified her.

"I don't understand, Alice."

Alice was silent for a long time. Jillian wasn't certain that she'd heard. Lights blinked furiously on Alice's control panel.

"What is it, Alice?"

"I'm detecting massive interference on virtually all systems. I have no reference for this."

Jillian shivered, not certain how much was cold and how much was fear. "Keep trying. Can you give me a little heat?"

"No. The heat cells draw heavily and I'm on emergency power. I need all I can generate to transmit."

Jillian shuddered, then reached into the door pouch and retrieved the emergency kit. She removed flares, dehydrated food packets and medical supplies. Finally locating the heat reflecting blanket, she wrapped it around her shoulders, and tucked in all the corners, then settled down to wait.

Just before she fell asleep, she remembered the flares. She sat up, located the hand-held launcher, and loaded one of the two red cartridges into the breach. Leaning as far forward as possible, she slid the starboard window wide open, stretched her arm into the damp air and pulled the trigger. The bright fire of the flare drifted through the fog infusing the swamp with an eerie red glow. Jillian waited five minutes then repeated the process with the other cartridge.

Thoroughly exhausted, she fell back in the seat, wrapped the blanket around her body and fell into a deep, dreamless sleep.

Alice's com link crackled. "This is Trail Patrol. Who's beaming on this emergency channel?"

Jillian leaned forward and waved her hand over the transmit icon on the panel. "Trail Patrol. This is Dr. Jillian Rozner. I'm stranded on one of the dikes."

"Say again. You're breaking up."

"I've crashed on one of the dikes."

"If you're still transmitting, we can't hear you."

"What's wrong, Alice?"

"I'm detecting heightened resistance in my antenna circuit. We may have snapped it off when we impacted. I'll keep putting out the low power signal on the ground wave. Maybe they can lock on to us. This is very peculiar."

"Is there anything I can do?"

"No. Rest. I'll keep hailing."

Jillian tried to sit up but was instantly overcome by a wave of nausea. She attempted to lay back on the pilot's seat, but her right leg refused to move. Reaching down with both hands, she tried to lift her knee and was instantly rewarded with searing pain. She cried out.

"Are you alright, Jillian?"

"I think my leg's broken."

"Can we get a replacement when we pick up my radial converter?"

"No, Alice. They'll have to repair this one."

"Are you in pain?"

"Yes. I'll use the analgesic mist from the emergency kit"
She pawed through the remaining contents of the pack,

locating the small cylinder in the lower left pocket. Holding the nosepiece in place with her free hand she shot a quick puff of painkiller into her nostrils. Within seconds, the agony diminished to a tolerable throb. Another wave of nausea swept through her body and she nearly vomited. Despite the painkiller, her head ached as though her brain was suddenly too large for her skull.

"Alice, what are the medical indications of concussion?"

"Nausea, severe head pain, and drowsiness."

"Maybe that's why I'm so tired."

"Rest, Jillian. My medical entry on concussion insists that I wake you each hour. I don't know why."

"It's okay, Alice. I do."

"I'll keep hailing, but I have nearly depleted my emergency power."

Jillian leaned her head against the cabin wall and drifted gratefully into unconsciousness.

🐾 🐾 🐾

"Is the pilot dead, Aaron?"

"No. She's breathing, but badly beaten up. I think her right leg's broken and she probably has a concussion. There's a nasty bruise over her right eye."

"It's a woman?"

"Yes."

"What's she doing out of the transit corridors in this old relic?"

Aaron pulled his head out of the cockpit. "I have no idea, Laz, but we better get her to Salvation soon, or it isn't going to matter. Jump on the com and tell them we're sending in an accident victim. Better use full power, we're in a dead zone. Tell medical to stand by and we need transport for one."

Aaron lifted the unconscious pilot out the front of the aircar, being careful not to bump her injured leg. She opened her eyes, smiled weakly at him, and passed out again.

Lazarus had already spread the heated body pad from the emergency kit in his backpack in the center of the path and laid out an assortment of medical devices. Aaron gently lowered the injured woman onto the prepared surface. Laz guided her broken leg, then started back toward the aircar. At least the bone didn't pierce the skin, Aaron wrapped a splint around it. The woman groaned once and opened her eyes.

"Alice?"

Aaron leaned over to hear her. "Who's Alice?"

"Alice .... Okay?"

Aaron straightened up. "Hey, Laz. She's asking about someone named Alice. Is there a passenger in there?"

Lazarus poked his head into the vehicle. "There's nobody in here."

"The woman tried to raise her head. "Must know about Alice .... damaged?"

Aaron lowered her to the ground. "Lady, who's Alice?"

"Aircar. Is Alice severely damaged?"

"Alice is the aircar? That pile of junk we hauled you out of? Look lady, you're lucky to be alive. We'll get you to the medical center, then haul that derelict to the recycle yard. Maybe they can salvage parts."

She tried to sit up and failed. "No! You can't. Take her to Rozner Corporate Headquarters."

"You're nuts, lady. They're not going to let me in there with that wreck."

"They know Alice. Tell them Ji...." She passed out again.

Aaron leapt to his feet and yelled at his partner. "Laz, tell them we need that sled, now!"

🦅 🦅 🦅

Jillian opened her eyes and stared at the pale glow of the white ceiling as its internal light gained intensity. She glanced around the room at the array of medical equipment, then tried to sit up. Her right leg wouldn't move. She watched a nurse enter the room, check her chart, and then glance up.

"How do you feel, Dr. Rozner?"

"Tired."

"That's partially the effect of the medication. Try to get some rest. And your leg will be fine."

"Oh." Jillian gave into the wave of exhaustion. She lay back and drifted into twilight sleep.

When she opened her eyes, a tall, young man in a clean Trail Patrol uniform stood at the foot of her bed. Something about him was familiar. She moistened her lips.

"Do I know you?"

He grinned. "My partner and I hauled you out of that wreck on the dike yesterday. My name is Aaron Trout."

"Oh, I remember. You carried me out of Alice. Well, thank you, Aaron. I must have been in worse shape than I realized."

Jillian raised up and was instantly hit by severe pain in her head. She collapsed back on the bed, breathing raggedly.

Aaron stepped forward. "Shall I call someone for you?"

"No. I'm okay."

"The med team said you had a concussion, assorted abrasions, and a broken right leg. They just told me that the concussion would require rest, but that molecular knitting has restored the leg. You'll be able to walk on it in a day or two. I just stopped by to see how you were."

"Thank you." A deep furrow creased Jillian's brow. "How's Alice?"

"Ah, yes, Alice. Frankly, I'm not certain. We went back out to get your aircar this morning. Laz towed her to the Rozner Compound, while I stopped here to check on you. When we were at the crash site, the Rozner people were all over the com. It was all I could do to keep them from sending out a crew of engineers. What is it with that pile of junk?"

Jillian felt the heat rise in her cheeks. "Alice happens to be a very rare 2018 Harley Davidson Floater. I restored her myself, and she can fly rings around most of the newer models. Her radial converter failed. It could happen to anyone."

"Lady, they haven't used radial converters in eons. All the new stuff is linear."

Jillian bristled. "There's nothing wrong with radial."

Aaron shook his head. "Why don't you trade her in on a decent machine. Maybe one of the new Fiat Challengers. The Two Thousand will accelerate in a full vertical climb."

"I don't want a new machine. Alice and I get along very nicely, thank you." She looked away at the white ceiling.

"Right. That's why you crashed in the swamp. It's your neck, lady. Only, next time, I may not be there to rescue you."

Jillian looked back at him sharply. "We'll just have to survive without you."

"Fine, but if you're going to tear around the swamp in that derelict, don't ignore the charts."

Jillian felt the heat in her face. "I'll take Alice anywhere I please. She has perfectly good maps of this planet. You just do your job."

She saw his eyes widen. He looked directly at her. "You're not using some externally published map?"

Jillian felt the first twinges of uncertainty tingle at the base of her skull. "Alice has a full library of planetary configurations."

He shook his head. "The charts the corporation gave you in your arrival packet show all the safe transit corridors though the dead zones. You just program them into your aircar."

Jillian tried to sit up in bed but couldn't. She was too weak. "All the what?"

She saw the incredulous look that filled his eyes. "You do know about the dead zones and the safe corridors? I can't believe you didn't view the arrival vid and reprogram your aircar. Did you even open the gator safety kit?"

Jillian felt weaker by the moment. She heaved a huge sigh and lay back against the pillow. "I have no idea what you're talking about. I received no arrival package and I don't even know what a gator safety kit is. Now, please leave and let me rest."

Aaron took several deep breaths, then walked to the side of the bed. "Look, Lady. I'm sorry. I didn't come here to antagonize you."

"Well, you have. Just leave."

He started to say something, thought better of it, then turned and stormed out of the room. He didn't exactly slam the door, but the distinction was academic. It bounced off the frame and remained ajar. Through the doorway, Jillian saw a shorter man in Patrol uniform approach Trout.

"How is she, Aaron?"

"Why don't you ask her, Laz? She has all the answers."

The one addressed as Laz stepped back and studied his friend. "You didn't upset her, did you?"

"Who cares?"

Jillian saw the panic on Laz's face before he spoke. "You may, my friend. That is Dr. Jillian Rozner."

🐾 🐾 🐾

Lucy Warren charged past a stunned Janice Smally into Adak's office. Pierce set down his tea, rose from his chair and glared down at her. "How dare you enter without permission?"

Lucy ignored his indignation and stormed up to his desk. "Did you really send that child into the swamp without a chart of the blackout zones? You knew full well she didn't have a chance of staying in the transit corridors without it."

Adak stood perfectly still then his shoulders slumped. "I didn't send her anywhere. I knew she had an aircar but I never dreamed she'd go without an escort."

Lucy stared at him. "Oh, you're good, Adak. You're really good. If I didn't know you, I'd almost believe it. Did you even tell her about the dead zones? Did you tell her that there are entire areas of this planet where no communications are possible; where very little of our technology even works?"

He drew a deep breath and thrust out his chin. "What I did or didn't do is no concern of yours. I strongly suggest that you return to your office."

She stared at him and slowly shook her head. "I'll be watching you, Adak." She turned and stalked out of the room.

Jillian leaned against the hospital bed supporting herself with one hand. Despite the medication, the pain in her leg was unrelenting. "I don't care what the doctor ordered, I'm not going home until I check on Alice."

The nurse's demeanor was quickly passing through irritated on its way to indignant. "I have orders to see that you go directly home and rest. You can call Shuttle Repair from there."

Jillian glared at her. "Just order a sled and I'll take responsibility. I appreciate your concern but I have to see for myself."

The nurse threw up her hands and left the room. The vid chimed. "Dr. Rozner. You're transportation is ready."

"Thank you."

Jillian pushed off from the bed and headed for the exit. The sled stood patiently waiting at the front of the building. Her name flashed in the small display above the entrance. She slid onto the seat and made herself as comfortable as possible.

She spoke to the empty vehicle. "Shuttle Repair."

"Yes ma'am."

They glided smoothly away and banked briefly to adjust course. Sooner than she expected, the great hanger facility was before her. She stepped from the sled through a narrow doorway and into the cavernous space.

Several craft of varying designs littered the floor with technicians huddled over most of them. A small, blonde woman in a white mechanic's uniform crossed the room and extended her hand.

"Welcome, Dr. Rozner. I'm Shelly LaCoste, Director of Mechanical Services."

"Good afternoon. I've come to see about Alice."

Shelly smiled. "Alice is fine. I worked on her myself. We salvaged a radial converter from the bone pile and refurbished it. They're not easy to find, but it's functioning properly."

A wave of relief flooded through Jillian. "Thank you. That's wonderful."

"She's right over here. As long as we had her, we checked all of her circuitry and aligned the navigation module. I couldn't detect any local charts, so I added them to her data bank. Alice is in perfect health."

Jillian hesitated but as long as Shelly had mentioned charts, decided to open the subject. "What are dead zones?"

Shelly stared at her. "Didn't they go over all of that when you arrived?"

"Apparently not. Everyone seems to assume that I know."

Shelly shook her head. "We'd better talk."

She glanced around, located two empty parts crates and pulled them close together. "Have a seat."

Jillian eased onto one of the crates being careful not to bump her newly mended leg. Shelly took a moment to collect her thoughts.

"There are large portions of this planet where our vaunted technology simply does not work and other areas where it functions on a limited basis. And I mean everything from communications to propulsion. When Dr. Maximillian Rozner first arrived, he mapped corridors through these dead zones. They roughly parallel the trail system. The ore carriers stay in the corridors."

Jillian's scientific mind grappled with the concept. "What causes the dead zones?"

"Nobody knows. There appears to be a correlation between the strength of them and the concentration of nodules in a given area but no one's actually proved it."

Jillian glanced at Alice across the room. "I take it that the module you installed in Alice will keep us in the corridors."

"Shelly shook her head. It will only tell you when you stray out of them. It's not designed to limit your mobility but I strongly urge you to abide by its counsel."

Jillian followed Shelly to the other side of the hanger and found Alice resting with only her parking circuits activated.

Shelly laid a gentle hand on the rear deck. "Wake up Alice. You have a visitor."

Lights blinked on and panels glowed. Jillian walked all the way around the aircar searching for damage from the accident. Nothing was evident. "You look fine, Alice."

"Thank you Jillian. Shelly says I'm good as new and she gave me all up-to-date charts of the planet."

Jillian returned to the front of the aircar. A faint wave of nausea passed through her. "That's wonderful, Alice. Open, please. I need to get off this leg."

The canopy raised silently providing easy access to the pilot's chair. Jillian eased herself into the seat and Shelly stood leaning against the doorframe.

"Did they give you a new leg, Jillian?"

Shelly and Jillian laughed together. "No, Alice. They rebuilt the old one."

Jillian looked around the shop. "Looks like you're pretty busy, Shelly. Everything under control?"

Shelly sighed. "We're overworked and understaffed but it's the only way we're content. An idle mechanic is an unhappy one."

"When can I pick up Alice?"

Shelly raised an eyebrow. "She's ready now. Would you like to take her with you?"

"What do you think, Alice? Shall we go home?"

"That would be very nice, Jillian. Thank you, Shelly."

Shelly smiled warmly. "You're most welcome. Come back anytime."

The canopy closed and Alice rose three meters to clear the other vehicles between their position and the entrance then gently accelerated through the opening doors into the afternoon rain.

As Shelly watched Alice disappear into the wet, Elsa Minnox, her fuel expert, came up beside her. "What do you make of Rozner's granddaughter?"

Shelly grinned. "My first read is that it would be a serious mistake to take her lightly. You don't get to be the director of a major oceanographic institute without some smarts."

Elsa inclined her head toward the rear of the hanger. "The guys think she's just temporary window dressing. Pierce is the real power. He's the one in the president's office."

"Perhaps. But Alice holds her in high esteem and I'm not sure old Alice would be that easy to fool."

Elsa's laughter was a sharp bark. "Well, you'd expect that, wouldn't you? Alice is her aircar for Christ's sake. I hear Aaron Trout took her on in her hospital room but he probably caught her in a weakened condition."

Shelly stared into the rain. "All the same, I think there's real strength there. I wonder what Aaron and Laz think of her?"

After three days of recovery in the hospital and two at home, the confinement of her apartment began to depress Jillian. Small irritations she would normally wave off loomed large. She upbraided the household computer for the temperature of her bath and the firmness of her bed. She brooded over her morning tea and wandered about her home searching for pillows to straighten.

On the morning of the fourth day, she flicked off the vid screen and headed for the garage.

"Arise, Alice. We're leaving."

"Where are we going, Jillian?"

"Anywhere but here."

Alice considered the instructions while Jillian settled into the pilot's couch. "I don't have coordinates for that destination."

Jillian laughed. "Just head out over the compound. I'll think of something."

As they passed above the vast complex of buildings that housed Rozner corporate headquarters, Jillian suddenly knew exactly what she wanted to do. "Land on the receiving pad behind the lab. I need to see someone there."

Alice settled with no detectable bump. "This is not the entrance you normally employ, Jillian."

"I know."

Alice's blinking dash signaled confusion. "Are you not going to your office, Jillian?"

"Not right away."

As she exited the aircar, one of the guards at the portal waved her to a halt.

"May I see your ID, please?"

Jillian handed him the card she had received on arrival. She saw his eyes widen as he read her name. He returned her card and waved his hand to open the large security door for her. "Proceed, Dr. Rozner."

"Thank you." She strode past the guards into the reception area. A stately woman with short, gray hair sat behind a simple black desk just inside the entrance.

She glanced up and smiled. "May I help you?"

"I'm Jillian Rozner."

The woman's expression froze for a moment then softened into a welcoming smile. "I'm Eleanor Swanson."

Jillian nodded. "I would like to speak with Dr. Chester Wiggins, please."

Eleanor thought for a moment. "He's probably in the lab. Would you like me to summon him?"

"Yes, please."

She waited while Eleanor placed the call. "Dr. Wiggins will be right out. Please have a seat. May I get you something?"

"No, thank you. I'm fine."

Jillian had just settled onto a formal settee when the inner door irised open and a short, dark-haired man in a white lab coat stepped through. He nodded to Eleanor then approached Jillian. "I am Dr. Chester Wiggins. I believe you wished to see me."

Jillian rose, taking in the lightly built scientist. There was something familiar about him. She was certain she'd seen him before.

"Thank you for allowing me to interrupt your work. I'm Dr. Jillian Rozner. Is there somewhere we can talk?"

He hesitated, started to say something, and then apparently changed his mind. "Follow me."

He moved like a shore bird as he led her down a long passage that branched off to the right and stopped at the third archway. The entrance irised open. She hadn't known quite what to expect, but a well-ordered workspace was not on the list of possibilities. Somehow she'd expected a lab cluttered with equipment. Her space in La Jolla always managed to gather racks of apparatus that overflowed into her office.

He gestured for her to sit in the guest chair then settled behind his neat desk. The surface was completely empty except for the small model of a Rozner ship on the corner. Images of his family filled the video screens behind him and a row of small crystal trophies lined the narrow shelf on the north wall. Bright red flowers bloomed outside a courtyard against the dark green backdrop of the swamp.

He folded his hands on the desk. "How may I help you?"

Jillian had received warmer greetings from doctoral candidates competing for the same grant when she was a student. She studied his deep blue eyes and the hard creases around his mouth. Her hopes of enlisting him as an ally faded.

"My grandfather mentioned you several times in his messages to me. He said I could trust you. I need your help. He said you, more than anyone else could fill in any holes in my understanding of the Constant."

Dr. Wiggins blinked but said nothing.

Despite the chill, Jillian continued. "He told me all about the processes inherent in producing the Constant. I have the science but I don't have any feel for how it's applied. Oh, I understand that it allows huge starships to move through space but I don't really have a grasp of the principals involved. Am I making any sense at all?"

The lines around his mouth deepened. "Not really. Shouldn't you be talking to Dr. Pierce?"

Jillian considered how much to tell him. "I've already spoken with Pierce." She allowed some of the bitterness she felt to enter her tone.

Dr. Wiggins sat perfectly still, then finally he leaned back in his chair. His shoulders slumped and he shook his head. "Your grandfather and I were very close. We were both theorists but he was a visionary. I was more practical."

He gazed out the window for a moment then returned his attention to Jillian. "But for all our camaraderie, the old buzzard never would reveal the internal structure of the drives. That was all neatly compartmentalized within the manufacturing process. No one has access to more than one phase. I'm probably the only one remaining, other than Pierce, who does understand much of it. As Chief of Production, I had a need to know but not even I could duplicate the design."

He leaned forward and rested his arms on his desk. "You have obviously been enlightened. May I ask what you intend?"

Jillian sat back, startled by the question. "I plan to re-take control of the corporation as my grandfather wanted."

He froze, then sat measuring her for a long time. The bluntness of the statement obviously shocked him. "Won't Pierce have something to say about that?"

"Probably."

Dr. Wiggins slowly shook his head. "You're taking quite a risk telling me."

"You were Grandfather's friend. I think I can trust you." She decided to try a bluff. "I seem to recall Grandfather saying you had no great love for Pierce, either."

He leaned back in his chair for another of his long pauses. "May I offer you tea or something stronger?"

The tense muscles in Jillian's neck relaxed a little. "Tea would be very nice."

She watched his bird-like movements as he retrieved steaming cups from the wall server. His hands were almost delicate. He sat in one of the guest chairs and handed her a cup. The tea gave off a rich aroma.

"One thing bothers me. Pierce has to be concerned about you. Why would he give you the run of the place?"

Jillian nodded. "He thinks he's bought me off. He does not appear to have much respect for my intelligence."

Dr. Wiggins didn't pursue it. Jillian leaned forward. "Tell me about the Constant."

He nodded. "Your grandfather was a genius of the very first rank. I doubt that any other man alive could have designed the Constant engine. His great contribution was marrying the principal of constant acceleration with the fuel source found only on this planet. He then produced a drive that employs both."

He took a sip of his tea. "If you're going to understand the principals involved, I'll have to give you the math. But first I must tell you about the nodules."

Jillian smiled. This was familiar ground. "Grandfather mentioned those. They're mined in the swamp."

A clap of thunder echoed through the building. Dr. Wiggins didn't appear to notice.

"That's right. The nodules are composed of some of densest materials known to man. Each of those six-centimeter, black spheres weighs seven or more kilos. Several of those nodules are sealed in a chamber suffused with mercury vapor, then the interior of the chamber is super-heated. The resulting reaction releases an ion stream that produces an energy source of unbelievable power. When that stream is directed through a series of baffled chambers at the rear of a starship, we get the space drive known as the Rozner Constant."

Jillian nodded. "You're clarifying some of the information he gave me."

Dr. Wiggins leaned back against the cushions. Rain began to pound on the window and Jillian briefly thought of Alice but decided she'd be fine.

He brought Jillian back into the room with a question. "Do you understand the math involved?"

"Most of it but not how it's applied."

"Okay, let's see if we can fill in the rest. Rozner's Constant not only refers to the interstellar drive, but to the mathematical principal that underlies its function."

Jillian nodded.

"Shortly before your grandfather's death, we had a great tragedy costing thousands of lives."

Jillian shuddered remembering vids of the incident that she'd watched on Earth. "The *Majestic Vagabond.*"

"Yes. We think they violated the mathematical principals inherent in the Constant. It works this way. A starship the size of the *Majestic Vagabond* has unbelievable mass. It takes incredible force to get it moving, and conversely, incredible force to stop it. Rozner reasoned that if you steadily exerted a large force over an extended period of time, you could move anything in the vacuum of space. No friction, of course."

Jillian nodded. "So what's the problem?"

"There are two. First you need a virtually unlimited energy source."

"And the second?"

"You need incredible patience. It's the early stages that are nearly unbearable. If you hadn't been in cryogenic stasis, you would have noticed that on the trip out from Earth."

"Expand, please, Professor."

Dr. Wiggins smiled. His gray eyes flashed with humor then resumed their serious state. "Dr. Rozner was very specific. Acceleration can be no greater than a doubling of velocity per S.T.U. or Standard Time Unit; roughly the equivalent of a 1900's week. Think of it this way. From nearly a dead stop, you accelerate so that at the end of S.T.U. one, you're traveling the equivalent of one kilometer per hour."

Jillian was stunned. "That's all?"

"It gets worse. At the end of the second S.T.U., you're doing two kilometers per hour."

Jillian set down her tea. "We're really cooking now!"

"After three S.T.U.'s, you're going four per hour. After four, eight. After five, sixteen, and so on."

"At this rate, I could walk to the next system."

He chuckled. "You pass through the speed of sound between the tenth and eleventh S.T.U.'s."

"Let me get this straight. I've been on a starship for nearly three months, and I'm just now breaking the old sound barrier?"

"That's right, Dr. Rozner."

She leaned back in her chair and shook her head. "No wonder you said the crews grow impatient! I thought starships traveled beyond the speed of light. At this rate how do they ever get beyond the Earth's moon's orbit?"

Dr. Wiggins nodded. "It's not just the compounding of numbers but the nature of the acceleration that counts. Maybe I can illustrate it."

He turned to face the flat panel in the wall behind his desk, and used a laser scribe to etch his diagram. The tool left a faint trail of smoke as it burned a hair-thin line across the surface without incinerating it. He quickly sketched a mathematical table:

STU	Velocity
11	1,024
12	2,048
13	4,096
14	8,192
15	16,384
16	32,768
17	65,536
18	131,072

Jillian stared at the table. "All right, now we are getting somewhere."

"True, but we've been at this nearly six months. Watch what happens when I extend the table."

STU	Velocity
19	262,144
20	524,288
21	1,048,576
22	2,097,152
23	4,194,304
24	8,388,608

"When do we reach the speed of light?"

"In slightly less than one Earth year. Of course, that's when we used to encounter insurmountable problems with mass. Now, most of the distance is traveled in the next few S.T.U's and then we begin to decelerate, an equally slow process. That is something nobody living understands about Rozner's Constant; how it lets us cross that threshold." He watched her carefully as he spoke.

Jillian put on her best poker face and kept her silence. Let him think Grandfather's secret was lost. At least for now.

He continued. "There are many advantages at lower velocities as well. For one, we have plenty of time to load supplies and passengers by shuttle during the initial stages, but perhaps the greatest value is in the nature of the acceleration, itself. It's extremely gentle. Even in the later phases, there is very little sense of motion. On the commercial runs, the passengers would love it, if they were awake."

Jillian stared at the wall panel. A faint tickle at the back of her mind wouldn't let her relax. Then she had it but the idea left her breathless. "Pierce had plenty of time to set this up while I was in transit. He used it well. I was the one asleep. It's hard to accept that I lost two years of my life."

– 6 –

They had just crossed one of the main dike bridges when Aaron bent down to adjust his right boot. He let a little air out of the ankle bladder and turned up the heat. The blister had reformed on his heel. The damp sock wasn't helping. When he straightened up, Lazarus stood in front of him, motionless.

Aaron studied his friend. "You all right, Laz?"

"Don't move."

A small ripple of fear ran down his spine. Laz would not issue such a command lightly. He watched as Lazarus slowly drew his phased array weapon, aimed it over Aaron's shoulder, and held it steady. Laz spoke, almost without moving his lips.

"There's a huge gator nosed up against the dike, directly behind you."

"What's he doing?"

"Nothing. He's just watching us. Turn around, very slowly."

Aaron remained crouched and pivoted on his left foot. The monster lay in the brackish water with just his head resting on the swamp grass at the base of the dike. A deep scar, like a badge of honor, ran across the bridge of his snout. Aaron could smell the rank breath from the creature's nostrils that ruffled the foliage. He could see the huge, jagged teeth that protruded from both jaws.

The fear that filled his belly was strangely muted by the posture of the creature. It lay motionless with most of its body submerged. The gator's enormous, blue eyes slowly shifted between the men as if trying to decide some vital question.

Aaron tried to rise but his legs wouldn't answer his brain. He placed one shaking hand on the ground and pushed himself upright. The gator raised his head to follow his movement. Laz leveled his weapon. Aaron tried to lick his lips, but he had no saliva. Attempting to avoid any sudden movements, he walked carefully toward Lazarus.

Laz kept the weapon pointed at the gator. "He's so still. His tail isn't even moving. Maybe he's injured. Is he dying?"

"I don't think so. I can't see any trauma, at least on the part that's visible. Don't shoot him unless you have to. I don't know why, but somehow I don't think he's aggressive."

"Well, let's not put that to a test. You ever meet one of these bastards that wasn't? I'll keep him covered, but I'm telling you, Aaron, if he makes the slightest threatening move, I'll fire."

The gator slipped back into the water and drifted along the dike toward them. When he drew opposite their position, he eased his nose onto the grass and resumed his vigil.

Laz lowered his weapon. "Why shouldn't I just blow him away? This isn't rational."

"I know. It's just a very strong feeling."

"Well, that feeling could get you killed."

"Don't shoot this gator, Laz."

Laz shrugged and holstered his weapon. "Aren't you forgetting your last little dance with one of these slimy bastards?"

Aaron instinctively reached for his left thigh. He rubbed the jagged scar. "This is different."

Laz stared at him for a long time. "I hope you know what you're doing."

They worked along the causeway, searching for breaks in the structure. Each time they stopped to repair a bridge or replace a lamp, the gator glided up to the dike and watched them work. Aaron eyed him warily. Several times Laz drew his weapon, studied the gator for a moment, and then holstered it.

Aaron crouched near one of the trail lights. Every rational process told him he should be terrified but he wasn't. "If he hasn't attacked by now, he probably won't, but keep an eye on him. Maybe he's just curious."

"How did you arrive at that brilliant conclusion?"

Aaron shook his head.

Lazarus shrugged out of his pack and stepped over to the edge. Their companion lay below. "Why do I feel like an hors d'oeuvre? I still think I should blast him. That hide would make a great wall hanging for our hut. I wanted to shoot him when he first appeared."

Aaron joined him at the edge. "You hit him with that thing and there won't be enough left for a wall hanging."

They studied their silent companion. Aaron tilted his head. "I don't think he's hostile. He doesn't act hungry. It's more like he wants something."

"What?"

"I have no idea."

They turned and resumed work on the broken power cable well aware that death lay a few meters away. As Laz made the final connection, a gator bellowed deep in the swamp. Their companion answered with a deafening roar that caused Aaron to drop his toolkit.

"Mother of Venus! He scared the piss out of me."

As they watched, the sentinel slowly turned and glided away into the fog.

🐾 🐾 🐾

"This is the last section, Aaron. I can't believe we've been at it for thirteen days."

Aaron stood up and stretched his back. "I can. Light repair's a bitch. Damned power surges." He rubbed his legs. "My knees are gone. I need a shower and a hot meal."

Heavy gray clouds hung like soggy pillows over their heads, but the driving rain that had pounded the swamp for three straight days had finally ceased. They had spent the entire morning patrolling the dikes and making small repairs to the trail lighting system that provided illumination when the fog rolled in. Without the amber lights, the trails through the safety zone would become extremely hazardous. It wasn't his favorite part of the job, but it certainly wasn't the worst.

That had to be dike reconstruction. It involved hours of backbreaking toil stuffing heavy bags between the massive stone blocks, then inflating the bladders. Once the bags were in place, there was still filling the gaps with riprap. That took a heavy toll on the body as well as the spirit. Finally, the unmanned jitney carts would arrive with loads of dirt and sod to overlay the entire structure. In most places, the repaired surface rose a mere two meters above the fetid water. Aaron often wondered why more of this process couldn't be automated. Each time he asked, the engineers muttered something about "persistent emanations from subterranean occlusions". And that explained it, at least to their satisfaction.

The huge gator who had become their constant companion for the past two weeks lay with his nose against the dike. He shifted position as they moved, always keeping them in sight. They had gotten used to his presence.

Laz glanced at the gator. "Old Scar Face is still hanging around."

Aaron lifted the lens cover off the lighting matrix and examined the seared interior. "I keep hoping he'll get as bored as we are and leave."

"Well, your flash charge certainly didn't deter him."

Aaron poked at the circuitry. "This one's shorted out, too. Must have been some power surge. Have you got an extra R-19 connector, Laz?"

Lazarus knelt beside the junction box, ten meters up the dike. His feet were covered with piles of power cable strands he had stripped from the circuits. He didn't raise his head to answer.

"If I do, it's in the lower pocket of my pack. Dig around in there and see what you find."

Aaron watched him work for a moment, then strolled over and rummaged in his partner's pack. He retrieved the connector and returned to his own task. As he worked, a slowly increasing pressure filled his head like the onset of a migraine. He reached for his medical kit.

Behold.

"What'd you say, Laz?"

"I didn't say anything."

"Yes, you did. You said something like 'Behold.'"

"You into the pain killers, again, Aaron?"

"Skip it."

Aaron slapped a tiny adhesive medicinal dot onto his neck to try to head off the migraine then tightened the clamps around the base of the light array. There were eight more to check in this quadrant. They should be able to finish before nightfall. The pressure in his head decreased. He'd inject stronger medication when he returned to his quarters.

Behold. You are chosen.

"Chosen for what, Laz?"

Lazarus climbed slowly to his feet, letting the gossamer strands tumble to the ground, and strolled toward his friend. "You all right?"

Aaron studied Lazarus closely. "Tell me you didn't just say I was chosen for something."

"I didn't say a thing."

"Well, somebody just said, 'Behold. You are chosen.'"

Lazarus laid his hand on his shoulder. "Listen. There's nobody out here but you, me and that demented gator that keeps following us around."

Aaron glanced at the reptile. The gator stared back with fierce intensity; its huge blue eyes riveted on Aaron's face. His mouth went dry with a strange combination of terror and exhilaration. He shuffled to the edge of the dike, drawn by the creature's piercing eyes. Aaron slumped to the ground; an agonizing pressure pulsed at his temples. No migraine had ever been this severe. He was afraid his head would burst.

Behold. I show you a mystery.

He pressed his palms over his ears, knowing with absolute certainty that he hadn't heard the gator, but felt it. Slowly, he raised his gaze to stare into the bottomless pool of the creature's eyes. His head filled with images of huge star ships against a field of velvet black broken by tiny pinpoints of light. Again the deep voice sounded in his brain.

We shall not all sleep but we shall all be changed. In time, all shall be revealed.

The pressure increased, then suddenly abated completely. Aaron slumped to the ground. He couldn't get his breath, and his heart pounded in his chest. Lazarus knelt beside him.

"You all right, Aaron?"

"I don't know. You didn't hear it, did you?"

"Hear what?"

"It was the gator. He was speaking in my mind."

Laz stared at him. "You mean like telepathy?"

Aaron struggled to his feet. "I guess so."

"You've been out here too long, Dr. Dolittle. There's no such thing. Do any of the other creatures speak to you? Had a good talk with a tree lately?"

Aaron sucked in a deep, ragged breath. "I know it sounds nuts, Laz, but that gator spoke to me as clearly as you do."

Laz offered a hand, trying to steady his friend. "What did he say?"

"He said that in time, all would be revealed."

"That's one hell of a message. You sure it was the gator?"

"Absolutely."

Laz stepped over to the edge and peered into the water. "He's gone, Aaron."

"I know."

"Jesus. Do you understand what you're implying?"

"Yes. They're intelligent, or at least this one is."

Aaron lay awake listening to the night sounds of the swamp. The occasional bellow of a gator penetrated the rhythmic symphony of frogs, crickets and night birds. His eyes burned from lack of sleep. When he drifted off, strange dreams of the huge scarred beast destroyed his slumber. He lay trembling and sweating profusely. Lazarus snored quietly on the other side of the room.

Aaron raised his arm and glanced at his luminous wrist display. Two AM. He decided that the incident had never occurred. It had all been a fantastic dream. That was it. By four, he harbored serious doubts about his sanity. He couldn't stop trembling. At five, he had to act. There could be no peace until he knew.

The first hint of color suffused the horizon as he sat up and brushed his wet hair out of his eyes. Moving with the stealth of a burglar to avoid waking Laz, he abandoned his cot and pulled on his tunic and pants then carried his boots outside the small structure he shared with his partner.

Across the compound, Sanctuary glowed with brightly colored hues. The all night party crowd, principally those who were not on duty the following day, was just now staggering off to bed.

He reopened the door, reached inside and scribbled a brief note on the electronic pad by the entry table. "Gone for a walk. Back for breakfast."

Crossing the compound, he reached down and checked his weapon. It rested securely in its holster. The knot of fear in his chest tightened as he passed the outer marker. He knew that entering the trail network without backup was not only unwise but also in direct violation of regulations. No one but a fool would venture out here without his partner. But he had to know and he had to go alone. He couldn't drag Laz any farther into his insanity.

A light fog shrouded the swamp, and the pungent odor of decaying vegetation drifted on the night air. Aaron switched on his belt light and picked his way along the convoluted path to the first bridge. Glancing around to verify that he was out of sight of the compound, he turned off the light, leaned against the railing and tried to clear his mind. As he listened, the night sounds became more distinct. The wind on his face caused his eyes to water and blurred the pre-dawn landscape. An involuntary shudder shook his body. He gasped once, took a deep breath and let it out slowly. Employing a technique he used to suppress his headaches, he focused all of his consciousness on a spot one centimeter behind the bridge of his nose.

When he felt as centered as possible, Aaron closed his eyes and tried to visualize the huge gator with the scarred nose. Feeling more than a little self conscious, he let the question form in his mind then concentrated all his energy on it. This was what the telepaths did in the vids.

"Are you there?"

Silence. As he listened, he became aware of the frogs and the cry of night birds, but nothing else.

"Are you there?"

Nothing. Aaron's shoulders slumped. He let out a long ragged breath. After several minutes, he heaved a deep sigh and turned to walk back to the compound. At least he'd put the nightmare to rest.

The awful pressure built in his temples, but not as painfully.

Behold. I come.

He turned and leaned against the railing straining to see any movement in the water on either side of the bridge, but could detect nothing. The horizon gradually lightened with the coming of dawn and finally revealed a shallow wake coming directly out of the rising sun.

Aaron unsnapped the safety strap on his weapon and loosened the piece in its holster. He tried to see what created the bow wave, but couldn't. Finally, as it approached, he could make out a large dark object, low in the black water, leading the disturbance. It stopped several yards from the bridge but the bow wave washed on toward him.

J am here.

Aaron was shaking so hard he couldn't have used his weapon if he'd wanted to. He stood, transfixed, staring at the gator.

Be at peace, Aaron Trout. Harm shall not befall you.

A strange calm settled over Aaron and his curiosity resurfaced. He brushed aside the wisps of fear that raced through his mind and concentrated on forming a single, silent question. "What did you mean, I'd been chosen?"

You shall be our messenger to this generation. You shall make the crooked straight and the rough places plain. We have been silent far too long.

Aaron had difficulty breathing. "Messenger about what?"

It shall be revealed.

"What shall be revealed?"

In time, Aaron Trout. In a moment. In the twinkling of an eye.

Aaron's frustration erupted. "Why me?"

It is known that you are good.

"Good at what?"

Honorable.

Aaron could think of no response. He stared at the gator.

Go in peace, Aaron Trout. My yolk is easy and my burden is light but remember, if you do not do as J say, my retribution will be swift.

A cold chill swept over Aaron's entire body. "Wait. Do you have a name?"

The ancients called me Solomon.

The huge gator turned and glided away into the rising sun.

Lazarus leaned against the doorframe, watching his partner cross the compound. Aaron's demeanor signaled distress and exhaustion. He approached their quarters and reached out to brace himself against the building. His hand trembled. Laz extended an arm to steady his best friend. Then he knew.

"You've been to the swamp, haven't you?"

Aaron stared at him without recognition. Laz watched the wildness slowly recede from his eyes. Aaron focused on him.

"Yes."

"Did he show?"

Aaron didn't answer immediately, but slumped against the building, "I'm going crazy, Laz."

Laz reached out to lay his hand on his friend's shoulder then withdrew it. He didn't know how to help. "Maybe. What happened?"

Aaron turned and sat on the step, obviously fighting for control. "I called him, and he came. He told me his name was Solomon."

Laz decided to try and jolly him out of his gloom. "Nice name. What does he want?"

Aaron glanced up. "He wants me to be his messenger to this generation."

Laz stepped back. "What the hell does that mean?"

"I have no idea."

He'd never seen Aaron in this condition. Whatever he had experienced in the swamp had really shaken him. He helped his friend inside and guided him to his cot.

"I think you should report in sick and take the day to rest. I'll get someone to partner me for the day."

He searched Aaron's face attempting to discern the depth of his disturbance. The eyes were wild, and his breathing erratic.

Aaron suddenly reached up and grasped Laz's arm. "I'm going mad, aren't I?"

"I honestly don't know, buddy. I can only tell you that the gators have never spoken to me."

Aaron slumped onto the cot and Laz watched as his partner's breathing slowly returned to normal. When soft snoring filled the room, he slipped out of the building and headed for Salvation and breakfast.

Crossing the compound, he debated requesting an appointment with the psychiatric officer to discuss Aaron's condition, but decided that would be a betrayal of his partner. All he could do was listen to him and try to help him sort it out. A friend in pain was a very heavy burden but Aaron had been there for him on more than one occasion. Like when Laz broke his back sand surfing in Australia, Aaron had cared for him through the long, painful recovery. No one had ever been closer.

He stopped and leaned against the gator warning sign. Perhaps the job was finally getting to Aaron. God knows lesser men had collapsed under the grind of the depressing atmosphere and isolation of this world. Several had been shipped off planet after being found wandering in the swamp muttering to themselves. Thornberg had torn off his clothes and jumped into the water convinced that he had spontaneously combusted. If Aaron thought the gators spoke to him, maybe that was a fairly innocuous safety valve, as long as he didn't tell anyone.

Laz shook his head. Maybe it was time to clear out before the swamp creatures started talking to him too. Laz had joined Aaron on this trip simply for the adventure.

Aaron had always led, even when they were young. No reason, he just had. Maybe Laz should take him home. He shook his head. Aaron would have to make his own decision.

Laz would watch and wait.

He pushed off from the sign and continued toward Salvation.

*   *   *

Jillian had no idea they'd be so big. Oh, she knew all the technical specifications, but actually seeing an RC drive was another thing entirely. She stood on the final assembly floor of the Rozner production facility and stared at the massive engines that surrounded her. Each unit was at least three times the length of Alice. They must weigh tons. She counted 35 drives being readied for delivery.

"Oh, Grandfather. They're magnificent. I wish you could be here with me. I'm learning so much."

This was the final stop on her first tour of the huge facility. She had spent the morning passing through sealed rooms where various components of the drives were being assembled. Only her palm print on the portal readers had admitted her to many of the secure sites. The Rozner name still had clout.

The air crackled with electrical arcs from high voltage tools. She could smell the ozone generated by the equipment. Shouts of instruction rang out as engineers directed their staff in the last minute attachment of parts.

Each gray and silver unit rode a powerful reverse-polarity magnetic field that allowed it to hover a centimeter or two above the floor. Mechanics swarmed over the nearly completed drives attaching final assemblies and testing seals. This batch was scheduled to depart as cargo aboard the *Windflower Vagabond.*

A white-coated worker approached her from the left and glanced at her badge. "Pardon me, Dr. Rozner. Could I ask you to stand over there? We're about to bring the number 23 unit through here to the lab for testing."

Jillian smiled. "Of course. Don't let me get in your way."

She stepped back against the wall as two of the men drew portable negative field generators from their belts and aimed them at the stern of a nearby drive. Gradually, it began to move, floating on its magnetic cushion. Jillian was surprised at how slowly they maneuvered the unit along the floor until she considered its mass. If they ever got it moving more than this agonizingly slow pace, it would continue right through the nearest wall.

She followed the drive through the portal into the testing lab. There men maneuvered it onto the firing stand and secured it. Through a large window she could see Wiggins presiding over the control room.

When the drive was firmly attached to the test stand, the lead technician approached her. "We're all set here, Dr. Rozner. Would you like to join Dr. Wiggins in the control room for the firing?"

Jillian glanced at his name badge. "Thank you, Charles. Yes. I'd like to see this."

He led her around by a narrow hallway and through a door marked 'Restricted'. Once in the control center, she was offered a seat with a clear view of the drive through the chamber window. A klaxon sounded. Wiggins looked up from taking final instrument readings and nodded to Jillian. She felt surprisingly pleased by the attention. Once she'd managed to cut through his protective shell, he'd proven to be friendly and helpful.

He waved his hand over a receptor buried in the console. For a long moment, nothing happened. Then the drive began to give off a blue aura that increased in intensity as she watched. It was totally silent, but Jillian could feel a steadily increasing vibration through the soles of her feet.

Wiggins turned to his assistant. "What have you got, Jim?"

"One thousand at ten percent power. That's right on the money."

"Shut her down."

Wiggins walked over to Jillian's chair. "I'm afraid it isn't terribly exciting, Dr. Rozner. We're simply testing the integrity of the unit. If she'll put out a thousand at ten percent, we can be reasonably certain she'll perform at all ranges, but any deviation will be exaggerated at higher settings. This was the static test. The final evaluation will take place once the drive is mounted in the ship. Each of the units you saw in the final assembly room will undergo this exercise."

Jillian smiled at him. "Thank you, Professor Wiggins. I found this enlightening. Seeing the real thing is quite different from reading the theory."

She was escorted through the shipping department and eventually emerged from the building into dense fog. Only the amber foot lights kept her on the walkway. She considered going straight to her apartment, but turned off at the intersection for Salvation. It had been a full morning. Lunch was definitely in order.

🐾 🐾 🐾

As she entered the portal and passed through the blowers into Salvation, Jillian was struck by the lack of activity. Very few of the tables were occupied.

A small group of technicians in lab coats sat in the corner under the vid eating lunch and watching a piece on gravity wells. Even at meals, they couldn't get away from their job or didn't wish to.

Her shoulders slumped in a sudden wave of depression. She longed for her lab in La Jolla where she'd been productive and needed. Here she had a fancy title and no real duties. Well, that would change.

She took a seat near the door and watched the electronic menu fill the display in the tabletop. After selecting an entrée of local fish and a salad, she signaled the waitress once again, fascinated by the contrast between modern technology and old-fashioned personal food service.

The waitress arrived at the table with a glass of fresh ice water. Jillian was confused. "I didn't ask for this."

"No, Ma'am, we serve it automatically. Most people like it."

Jillian smiled. "How nice. Is the fish fresh?"

The waitress, who's badge proclaimed her to be "Midge" hesitated. "I'm not sure I understand. All of the fish we serve are flown in from the other side of the planet each morning by airtruck. Will that do?"

"That will be fine."

After Midge had taken her order and left, Jillian watched her move about the room seeing to the needs of other diners. There was something charming about personal service. Nothing like this ever happened on Earth. She decided Grandfather had made a wise decision. His insistence on the human touch softened the harshness of this hostile planet. She'd have to remember that herself.

She sat mulling over her last week's conversation with Adak Pierce. He seemed so certain of his position. Grandfather could have executed a contract with his former partner. Pierce might have a legitimate claim but then why would Grandfather have told her that she was his sole heir and in control of the corporation?

Midge returned with a steaming plate of beautifully grilled fish and a bowl of mixed greens. As she turned to leave, Jillian stopped her.

"Is it usually this quiet during the day?"

The waitress glanced around the room. "Pretty much. It'll pick up about sunset when the crews come in. Of course the real action takes place at night. The Free Radicals are playing in the lounge this month. They're a big draw."

Jillian was fascinated. Do you get many entertainers?"

"Oh, yes. They make a circuit of the inhabited worlds. Sometimes we have several here at once."

Jillian tasted the fish, nodded approval and took a sip of water. "What about medical help?"

Midge looked around, checking to see if her duties required her elsewhere, apparently decided they didn't and returned her attention to Jillian. "We have several doctors and nurses here and a small hospital. Usually, one of the starships is in orbit and they have extensive facilities we can call on." She glanced at Jillian's plate. "How's your lunch? Can I get you wine or a Bull Gator beer? That's our most popular."

"I tried one and it's very good, but I think I'll just stick with water. Maybe I'll have some coffee later."

Midge excused herself and headed for the kitchen. Jillian finished her meal in peace and sat watching other patrons dine. The waitress returned with her coffee. Jillian tasted the brew and smiled. "I just realized I haven't seen any children."

"You won't. It's just not safe. There really isn't any place for them to play. Company policy is to deport anyone who's pregnant. Oh, they don't call it that and they're very nice about it, but they insist that you go to Cirrus 4 or back to Earth. It doesn't happen often."

"Do you agree with that?"

Midge thought for a moment then nodded. "Yes, I think I do. What is there here for children to do? Schooling can be handled over the vid, but they can't spend all of their time watching a screen."

"Perhaps we can do something about that. Without families, there really is no community. We could build a playground and bring in coaches for different sports for the older children, once there are any. Do you live in staff housing?"

"Yes, I share an apartment with a mechanic from shuttle repair. He's an expert in guidance. We've been together for nearly three years, ever since I shipped out from Earth. It's better now, but when I arrived, things were quite primitive. I wouldn't have come, but they offered extremely generous wages and promised to transport us home if we ever resigned."

Jillian took a sip of water and watched the ice cubes settle back in the glass. "That's a promise that will be kept."

A flicker of recognition passed over the waitress's face. "Oh my God. I just realized who you are, Dr. Rozner. It's a pleasure to meet you, but I have to get back to work."

Jillian smiled. "Thank you for speaking with me. Perhaps we can talk again later."

Midge beamed. "Anytime."

Jillian left as several patrol officers entered and headed for the bar. Bull Gators all around.

Solomon cruised slowly through the swamp listening to the birds in the canopy awaken to the blossoming sunrise. Golden light penetrated the thin layer of fog and cast an eerie patina over shoreline foliage. The rarity of the warmth lightened his spirits. Pungent odors of decaying vegetation filled his nostrils but nothing disturbing lay on the freshening breeze.

Each morning, he slipped out of his lair, compelled by a deeply embedded impulse, centuries old, and patrolled his region of the wetlands. Solomon was at peace. All was as it should be. All was as the Ancients had decreed; or nearly so.

He had brooded long and hard before approaching the man-creatures. Would the Ancients approve? Had he violated the purpose of his creation? Every fiber of his being resonated with the rightness of his actions. Still, he could not be certain. He could think of no other way to protect the ancient knowledge. He would face the judgement of his creators when they returned.

Solomon veered off into a narrow channel that he knew would deliver him into the shallow bay spanned by the bridge where he'd confronted the one called Aaron Trout. The man-creatures were a threat to the sanctity of the nodules, but he had no choice. He had made his selection partially because he felt an affinity to those who patrolled the network of trails through his swamp. They, too, had their duty to regularly visit each portion of their territory. He now felt he had made a wise choice. While frighteningly naïve, Aaron Trout was honorable and highly intelligent, within the limitations of his species. He could be taught.

Solomon wound his way through the labyrinth of twisting passages. At one point he dived under a fallen tree that lay across his course.

Emerging into the more open water of the estuary, he could see ahead the bridge built by the man-creatures. He drifted closer where he could observe the path leading back to their gathering place. No one approached. It was not yet time. Solomon would wait for his protégé.

– 7 –

Aaron lay on a mat at the edge of the pool. Having blown his last credits to ascend to Heaven, he was not about to waste a minute of the time. The hot sun beat through the immense dome and baked his nude body. Perhaps he could burn out the images that had haunted him for nearly a week.

The memory of the encounter with the gator had begun to fade as the daily regimen of work, eat and sleep took precedence. He turned his head to the other side, heaved a deep sigh and began to doze.

Aaron Trout.

"Hmm."

Aaron Trout. Arise.

"What?"

It is J. Solomon.

Aaron was suddenly, fully awake. He glanced around the pool making certain that no one was watching. Slowly, he sat up and turned to face west toward the trailhead, out at the edge of the compound and 175 meters below. Closing his eyes to center himself, he steadied his breathing and allowed his mind to clear, then conjured up the image of the great gator. He began to tremble, as the pressure built in his head.

"Solomon? Is that you."

I have said so.

"Leave me alone."

Behold. Your hour has come. There is great danger.

Aaron opened his eyes. He crossed his legs into the lotus position and rested the backs of his hands on his knees. He could hear the lapping of the wavelets against the side of the pool and smell the tanning lotion on his body. Closing his eyes, he tried to visualize the huge gator.

"What danger?"

Silence.

"Solomon? What danger?"

Silence

"Solomon? Are you there?"

The pressure built in Aaron's head until he thought he could no longer stand it. He clutched his head in both hands and rocked back and forth.

Arise, Aaron Trout. Come to the bridge. We shall commune.

The pressure dissipated and Aaron knew he was alone. He opened his eyes. The pale blue water sparkled before him. Beyond the dome, fleecy white clouds drifted against the azure sky.

When he was certain he could stand, he unwound his legs and stood up. Retrieving his towel, he hurried to the locker room. The computer tried to anticipate his needs.

"Massage, Lieutenant?"

"No, thank you. Shower, Please."

As he stepped into the shower room, the cool needle spray pounded against his skin. He leaned his forehead against the cold tile and tried to stem the panic in his chest.

"You bastard. You better be real. I'm not going through another night like that last one."

He raised his head and allowed the powerful spray to pound against the back of his neck. "Oh, you're real all right, and you scare the hell out of me." When he had dressed, he made his way to the sky lobby and rang for the elevator, without glancing at the attendant behind the desk. As he descended, the fog closed in around the falling car. When the doors opened into the noisy bedlam of Salvation, he hurried across the bar area and through the double entry, grabbing his swamp gear as he passed the rack.

Turning right as he left the building, he headed directly for the trailhead. Going out alone at night was one thing, but violating rules in broad daylight was something else.

He knew this could cost him his job, but it didn't matter. They were going to bust him on a psychiatric anyway. His body convulsed in a shudder.

Maybe they'll put me somewhere warm and dry. Might be a pleasant change.

No one challenged him as he left the compound and entered the trail network. Aaron had half expected to meet other patrol officers, but none appeared. The lame excuses he'd manufactured dissolved into a sense of relief.

As he stepped onto the bridge, he began to clear his mind. The process became easier with each attempt. When he felt fully settled, he glanced around once more to be certain he was unobserved then closed his eyes and tried to visualize the massive gator.

"Solomon?"

Only the chirping of swamp birds disturbed the silence. Faint whiffs of decaying vegetation drifted on the afternoon air.

"Solomon?"

Pressure began to build in his temples. As soon as he recognized the sensation, he tried to dampen it, willing it to subside and was astonished when it did.

Behold. I come.

Now, he could detect ripples left in the wake of the huge body gliding through water. As the gator approached, Aaron formulated his question and concentrated.

"Why have you called me?"

Your hour has come.

"That's the second time you've told me that. What hour?"

You shall be my messenger.

"Messenger? To whom?"

To the one they call Jillian Rozner.

Aaron felt the air rush out of his lungs. He gripped the railing and stared at the reptile lying in the dark water below.

"Are you out of your mind? She threw me out of her hospital room. I'm just an underpaid swamp patrolman. Why would she listen to me?"

Your soul shines though your eyes like the sun through the branches. She will believe you.

Aaron snorted. "Yeah. Right."

You must succeed, Aaron Trout.

Aaron squatted so he could peer beneath the lowest bridge railing. He studied the gator attempting to judge the gravity of the message.

"What am I to tell her?"

Dr. Jillian Rozner must come to me. I shall grant her enlightenment. You must bring her. You must guide and protect her. She cannot come here alone.

Aaron stood up and rested one foot on the railing. "Let me get this straight. You want me to march into her building, ask to see Dr. Rozner and tell her there's this old gator in the swamp that wants to have a word with her."

I shall be here at sunset. You do not have much time.

"Why don't you simply broadcast to her as you did to me this afternoon in Heaven?"

She would not believe.

Aaron pounded his fist on the railing. "Damned right. Only a common patrol officer is fool enough to carry on telepathic conversations with a gator. Give me one good reason I shouldn't blow you away."

Solomon swished his tail sending geysers of water skyward.

Because you are no fool, Aaron Trout. I would not reveal myself to one of your kind with limited intelligence.

Aaron waved away the compliment. "Why do you want Dr. Rozner to come here?"

She must believe. Much will be demanded of her. She is the sacred vessel into which the truth has been poured. She will need a strong one. You must be he, the protector.

Aaron straightened up. He rather liked the idea of being Jillian's "protector."

Solomon turned and glided away.

Sunset, Aaron Trout. Do not fail me.

Aaron stood on the bridge watching the ancient gator disappear into the swamp. He continued his vigil long after the last ripples of Solomon's wake had dissipated, then dropped his foot from the railing and turned toward home. *How the hell are you supposed to pull this off, Trout?* "Gee, Dr. Rozner, I know your busy but I've got this telepathic gator buddy whose willing to deliver some cataclysmic truth into your keeping. Would you like to take a little stroll in the swamp with me?"

Voices of an approaching patrol jarred him out of his reverie. Jergan Angst and Roth Morgan rounded the bend and stepped onto the bridge. Jergan stopped short.

"What are you doing out here alone, Trout? Where's Laz?"

"Not here."

"You know I'll have to report this."

"Suit yourself."

Jergan studied him. "Are you all right?"

"No."

Morgan leaned against the railing, letting his pack rest on the barrier. "What's going on, Aaron?"

"You wouldn't believe me. I'm crazy."

Aaron brushed past them and broke into a slow trot. He didn't slow his pace until he'd passed the trailhead and entered the compound. A beer, that's what he needed. After clearing security and the airlocks, he entered Sanctuary and looked around for an empty table, finally spotting one in the far corner.

Loud conversation filled the air and the holographic vid screen carried the America's Cup races from Earth. Amazing how little the craft had changed over the last five hundred years. The broadcast was emanating from Perth, Australia, where the ever-faithful wind known as the Freemantle Doctor pushed the graceful ships along at the limit of their hull speed. The Asian Empire appeared to be winning the current match race.

Aaron greeted several friends as he crossed the room, but declined all invitations to join tables. He needed solitude.

"May I help you?"

Aaron glanced up at the waitress, noting the open blouse that revealed a considerable expanse of appealing flesh. "Bull Gator, please."

She smiled politely and left. The Asians were rounding the windward buoy with the North Americans close behind.

After his beer arrived, he sat staring into the foam. A confused sense of frustration and anger welled up in his chest. "Solomon, you bastard. What am I going to do? Oh, I can probably get in to see Dr. Rozner, but I'm the last one she'd believe."

He took a long drag on his brew. "Why should I respond to you like a well-trained dog?"

He set down his glass. "Because if I can do this and she hears you, it means I'm not losing my mind. That's why."

Solomon glided through dark water beneath moss-draped cypress trees, altering course to avoid massive coils of roots.

His sweeping tail propelled him unerringly toward his objective. He listened for the small hiss of his wake lapping against the bank, adjusting his position in the swamp channel by its return echo. He heard birds cry out in the leafy canopy and small animals splash away as he approached. Only his nostrils and eyes broke the surface. As he neared one of the largest evergreens, he dipped his scarred snout and sank below the surface. Three meters down, he leveled off and passed through a convoluted tunnel leading to the entrance of a large, partially flooded cavern. Surfacing inside his lair, Solomon glided to the broad shelf that ran across the rear of the huge cave.

He watched his mate, Sheeba, lift her head and huff, then sidle away from the pile of jet-black nodules. She worked her way down the ledge toward him. She touched her nose to Solomon's jaw. His mind instantly filled with her thoughts. He pushed them aside.

Reach out to me in the new ways.

She projected her thoughts in the language of the infidels.

Why can we not communicate in the old ways? Why must we touch minds in this awkward manner you employ with the others?

We must learn. A time nears when we will require the skill.

She heaved a deep sigh and paused to formulate her query.

It is accomplished?

Yes.

He who must serve, is he willing?

I know not. I could only plead our cause.

Will she appear?

I know not.

Sheeba moved aside, making room for her mate. He climbed onto the ledge. She rested her head on his front leg.

I fear.

I also.

The one to whom we have entrusted the ancient knowledge no longer is, we must anoint another. It cannot be the dark one. He will dishonor the truth, Solomon.

I know.

She lifted her head and peered into his eyes.

Are you certain she has the knowledge? Can we trust that he enlightened her before he ceased to be?

He would not have done otherwise. He was honorable.

So much is at stake.

Solomon did not answer and Sheeba walked over to the pile of nodules, curled around them and lay staring into the dark water.

Aaron paced the floor of his quarters, his mind churning. As he passed the wall-mounted vid unit for the umpteenth time, he stopped and faced the screen. "Communications."

"Yes, Lieutenant Trout."

"Connect me with Rozner Corporate Headquarters."

"One moment."

Aaron sat on the edge of the table, absently swinging his foot.

"Rozner Corporation."

"Dr. Jillian Rozner, please."

"Dr. Rozner is not here. Do you wish to speak with her executive secretary?"

The voice on the other end seemed stilted, as though secrets were being protected. Aaron hesitated. The small hairs on the back of his neck stood up. Perhaps he shouldn't have called her office. Come to think of it, maybe she didn't have an office. He opted for discretion. "No. Is there another way I can reach her? It's really very important."

"You might try her at home."

"Thank you."

The screen reverted to its test pattern of scenes from Earth. A large three-dimensional hillside of orange California poppies waved under a brilliant blue sky.

"Communications."

"Yes, Lieutenant."

"Do you have a residence contact for Dr. Jillian Rozner?"

"Yes."

"Connect. Audio and video."

Aaron shifted his weight on the table and swung the other foot. The screen brightened revealing a pleasant but empty sitting room decorated in pale pastels. A large floral bouquet rested on an end table. On the sofa lay an open book, *Harley Davidson Aircar Maintenance*. Dr. Rozner entered from the left wearing a long ivory-colored garment that clung to her body and she faced the viewer. "Hello."

"I hope you'll speak with me, Dr. Rozner. I'm Lieutenant Aaron Trout of the Trail Patrol. We last spoke in the hospital."

A wry smile played at the corner of her lips. "Ah, yes, the man with the strong opinions on antique aircars. It's been a long, hard day. What can I do for you, Lieutenant?"

He tried to organize his thoughts. His foot had stopped swinging. She certainly looked better than she had in her hospital room. He cleared his throat. "I wouldn't disturb you if it were not absolutely necessary, but I must make a very unusual request."

Her smile broadened.

Aaron ploughed ahead. "I need to have you accompany me into the swamp, before sunset."

Jillian settled onto the sofa and drew one foot up under her. The ivory material shifted revealing a long shapely leg. "Precisely what are we going to do on this evening stroll, and why should I accompany you anywhere?"

Aaron took a deep breath. "I need to have you visit an old gator." There he'd said it.

She was positively beaming. "Well, at least it's an original line. Maybe you could fill in around the edges, a little."

Aaron shook his head. Oh, God, she thought he was asking for a date. This was going to be tougher than he'd feared. He plunged.

"There's this ancient gator named Solomon who has been communicating with me in some telepathic form, and now he's insisting that I bring you to the bridge so that he can impart to you some vital secret. I told him you'd never believe me, but he insisted. He can be very persuasive. I know this sounds insane, but will you come?"

Jillian was silent for a long moment. "Why does this Solomon think I would believe you?"

Aaron took a deep breath and closed his eyes. "He said my soul shines through my eyes like the sun through the branches."

Jillian stared at the screen. "You could not possibly have made that up, Lieutenant. Either you are fully delusional or you are hearing gators. Of course, one does not necessarily preclude the other."

"Will you come with me?"

"Of course."

Aaron gaped at the screen. "What? You will? Really? Just like that?"

Her laughter sparkled. "How can I refuse such an eloquent man, especially one who saved my life? Sounds like a perfect evening. Either I receive a rare cosmic truth, or I get to watch you make a complete fool of yourself. When will you call for me?"

"Uh, in fifteen minutes?"

"I'll be ready, Aaron." The screen went blank.

He stared at the gray panel, shook his head and chuckled. Son of a bitch, it worked. Feisty creature, isn't she? He wanted to hear her laugh again. He had already started a quick shower when it hit him. "She called me Aaron." He felt a broad grin spread across his face.

*   *   *

Jillian waved at the screen breaking the connection. She strolled to the window of her tenth floor apartment and watched the rain pour down on the campus. She felt the lightness drain from her spirit. Nearly every day of the three months she'd been on Rozner's World, had been shrouded in fog. The thick gray clouds that hung over the landscape were different. With no wind, the rain fell straight down, pounding the ground into submission, and bouncing off the paved pathways that spread over the campus like the web of an enormous spider.

She longed for the brilliant sunlight of La Jolla. She could not survive without the surf and the fresh salt breezes. Jillian missed the flowers. She ached for the feel of sand between her toes. She wanted to be standing in a shallow tide pool watching tiny fish dart past motionless sea urchins. She couldn't accept that she might never walk a beach again.

Thinking about corporate politics was no better. She was no longer certain that it even mattered who controlled the Rozner Corporation. She was not interested in propulsion systems. Let Pierce have it. Grandfather's dream was not hers. Let anyone but her have it.

The entry chime signal shattered her reverie yet she stood for a moment still staring out the window, reluctant to share her despair with an intruder. Turning to the monitor, she studied the tall officer in the view screen. He stood leaning against the doorframe in a practiced pose of nonchalance; a difficult feat to accomplish with water cascading off your entire body.

She felt a faint smile at the corners of her lips. "Of course. He knew I'd look before admitting a visitor. I wonder how long he's worked on that stance."

She smiled as she responded, her melancholy forgotten. "Open."

She watched him stroll through the doorway and enter the dryer. His head nearly brushed the frame. The overhead fan blasted rainwater from his storm gear then he stripped off the now-dry foul weather suit and hung it on the rack by the dryer. He strolled across the lobby to the lift station, limping slightly. He was an attractive man. Jillian barely recognized the tiny flutter of excitement that sparkled over her body. It had been a long time.

Startled by her response, she pushed it down mercilessly into the well of repressed feelings she chose not to acknowledge. She had enough to deal with.

She lost sight of him as he entered the lift. Moments later, the computer reported. "There is a visitor at the portal."

"Yes, Wilson, I'm expecting a guest. Open."

Aaron stood in the doorway like a schoolboy summoned to the principal's office; his uniform clean and pressed. "I hope this isn't too inconvenient. It will be a long walk."

Jillian hesitated. "We could take Alice."

A broad grin spread across his face. "I'm not certain that Alice would allow me aboard. I think it's better if we walk, but we'll need to leave right away. There's not much daylight left."

"I don't suppose we could postpone this little adventure until the weather clears?"

"No. This can't wait."

Jillian studied his face and was intrigued by the intensity in his eyes. She started to object, then decided not to push it. This was a very strong-willed man focused on a specific goal.

"Have a seat while I suit up. There's hot coffee in the wall server." While she changed, she could hear him fussing with the brewer. Jillian found something oddly comforting about having Aaron in her apartment. She glanced up at the mirror in her dressing room and smiled. She barely knew the man yet she trusted him. A strange sense of peace swept over her. A good friend would be a very welcome addition.

He finished his coffee as she entered the room.

"After you, Lieutenant."

In the lobby, she watched him suit up, pleased by the economy of his movements.

As they exited the building the full force of the storm descended. Huge raindrops pounding on her rain hat nearly drowned out all other sounds. Jillian had to strain to hear him.

"Ready?"

"Let's do it."

They walked briskly across the manicured grounds of Rozner corporate headquarters toward the trailhead. She hadn't realized how tall he was. Her head barely came up to his shoulder. Even with his limp, his long stride forced her to stretch to keep up. She felt like a young girl attempting to keep pace with an adult. Somehow, it made her feel protected.

She glanced over at him. "You're serious, aren't you Aaron? You really are taking me to meet a gator."

"Yes, I only hope he shows up."

"What is this great secret he intends to convey?"

"I have no idea. Solomon simply instructed me to bring you to him."

"Tell me about him."

Aaron nodded. "He looks ancient. I suspect he may even be immortal. He's enormous and has this huge scar on his snout."

Jillian took a couple of quick steps to keep up. "Is that how you recognize him?"

"It was, initially. Now I just know him."

She halted at the entrance to the trail network and leaned against the barrier, trying to catch her breath without revealing that she was winded. Despite the temperature control of her suit, she sweated profusely beneath its confines. She had to raise her voice to be heard above the driving rain. "Just exactly how does he communicate with you?"

Aaron glanced down and pushed a rock around with the toe of his boot. She watched the ripples it created in the puddle. He raised his eyes and looked directly into hers. "He speaks in my mind. Oh, I should tell you. When he contacts me, there's this pressure that builds in my head. Sometimes it's quite painful."

Jillian grimaced but studied his face. He looked genuinely concerned. "Oh, this does sound like fun."

"I find I can alleviate both the pressure and the pain by consciously repressing them."

Fear tightened the muscles at the back of her neck. "Will it work for me?"

"I don't know."

She shuddered. "And you think he'll speak to me?"

"He asked for you."

Aaron strode out onto the bridge, stopped in the middle and glanced back at her. "Coming?"

"No. This nonsense has gone far enough. I thought you just wanted to go for a romantic walk in the rain, but you're not a well man. You may even be dangerous."

He stood staring at her, water draining off his headgear and cascading down his face. "You are going to meet Solomon. You can walk out here or I'll come back and carry you onto the bridge. Either way, you're coming."

She glanced back at the ground they'd covered.

He took a step forward. "I can outrun you, even with my leg."

She stared at him. She could feel the heat rise in her face. "Don't threaten me, Lt. Trout. I don't like it."

He stood perfectly still for a moment then his shoulders slumped. "I'm sorry. I don't mean to be boorish. I feel it's vitally important that you speak with Solomon. Please."

She shuddered as she pushed off the railing and strode onto the deck.

As she approached, Aaron walked out to the center of the bridge and put one foot on the lower railing. He stood perfectly still staring into the swamp. Jillian eased her way onto the span and stood beside him. His eyes focused on some distant point in the water and his face was set like stone.

The rain pelted the black water leaving tiny craters that quickly disappeared. She gazed out among the tall trees and tried to discern any movement between their thick trunks. Finally, she spotted ripples on the dappled surface as a large object moved silently through the dark water. She tightened her grip on the railing.

As it approached the bridge, she could see the huge body that left the wake. A smaller creature swam behind and to the right. She glanced at Aaron. "Is that Solomon?"

He didn't answer.

Moments later, the gators lay beneath them. Rain pounded on their armored heads. All else lay concealed beneath the water. The larger of the two focused on Aaron. Jillian stared in fascination as both man and beast froze in a tableau of absolute concentration.

The huge reptile turned his head and stared at Jillian. Pressure began to build behind her eyes then a wave of cranial pain drove her to her knees. She pressed her palms to her temples and cried out. She felt Aaron kneel beside her and heard his instructions through the agony. "Repress it. Will the pain to subside. Trust me."

She concentrated on pushing the terrible pressure away and was amazed when it relented. Then she heard a deep bass voice at the core of her brain.

Behold, Dr. Jillian Rozner. It is I, Solomon. You are known to us and you are welcome. This is my disciple, Daniel. He has great intelligence. Wisdom will come with age.

Solomon waved his huge tail and moved closer to the bridge.

I have lived several of your lifetimes, but I am not immortal. Daniel is my chosen successor. He already possesses most of the ancient knowledge. He needs time. I hope I can give it to him. He must hear what I say to you.

Solomon opened his huge jaws in a massive yawn. Jillian jumped back. She couldn't breathe. She could only stare at the gaping maw.

Aaron extended his hand to her. "It's okay. I think he stretches his jaws to balance the pressure in his head."

Slowly, she eased her way to the railing. "I could park Alice in there. What if you're wrong?"

Aaron simply stared at her. Next to Solomon, Daniel lazily swung his tail back and forth in the water. Solomon continued.

Your grandsire, Dr. H. Maximillian Rozner served as a faithful trustee of the ancient knowledge. We shall forever honor him. It was I, Solomon, who chose him, and it was I, Solomon who placed the complex secrets in his brain. His death leaves a tragic void.

The huge Gator yawned again.

What he called the Rozner Constant, we have known for centuries simply as power. We had the knowledge but not the resources to construct the great ships like the ones built by those who brought us here. Your grandsire had such resources.

Jillian's knees felt weak and tightened her grip on the railing until her knuckles hurt. She tried to communicate by staring at Solomon and thinking what she wished to ask. "Are you telling me that my grandfather simply took notes from you?"

No, my child. We would never have entrusted power to anyone unworthy. He had worked out most of it. I simply intervened to prevent the dark one from usurping our secret.

Jillian tried to think. It was all so unbelievable, so incomprehensible. "Who is this Dark One?"

You have met him. He was your grandsire's associate in the early days of the search for power.

Jillian felt the breath rush from her lungs. "Pierce."

Yes, my child. You must not trust the dark one. He must not acquire the knowledge.

Jillian slumped against the railing. "He has control of the corporation, or at least he does until I can get help."

Ah, but he does not have the knowledge. You do. Did not your grandsire pass on the entire secret before he died?

"How do you know that?"

Solomon swished his tail.

It is what he would do. You are worthy.

Jillian turned to Aaron. He was watching her, a puzzled expression on his face. "Are you hearing this, Aaron?"

"No. It must be for you, only."

Without looking, she reached behind her for his hand, found it and held on tightly. She refocused on Solomon. Anger burned in her chest. "I tried to ignore it, but you're right. We must stop Pierce. What do you expect me to do?"

He waved his massive tail in the water causing small ripples to lap against the pillars of the bridge.

For now, it is enough that you keep the trust. We have shared only part of our truth. There is more, much more. We will enlighten when the time is right.

She began to tremble, uncertain her legs would support her. The fear gripping her nearly stopped her breathing. The entire situation was absurd. Solomon was huge. The implications of his message so profoundly disturbing. Nothing in her experience had prepared her for this.

"Why do you call me here if you are not ready to act?"

Would you have believed had I not? It is vital that you do. I have preparations to make. Patience, my child. All is unfolding as it must.

Solomon turned and glided off toward the East. Daniel followed in his wake, a small stately craft behind a massive ocean-going vessel. Jillian stood trembling and heard again her grandfather's promise, "You will find surprising allies." She watched until they disappeared into the rain.

− 8 −

When Solomon could no longer be seen, Jillian turned to Aaron. Rain pounded on his headgear and cascaded onto his foul weather suit. Under the huge brim, his eyes were quiet but concerned as he rested his hand on her shoulder. "What did he tell you?"

She tried to speak, but the words wouldn't come. She leaned toward him. With the gentlest of pressure Aaron pulled her to him and she collapsed against his chest. Great sobs racked her body and her shoulders heaved as her tears mingled with the rain. Anger burned in her brain. Anger at being shackled with terrible secrets; anger at this God-forsaken world with its constant rain and talking gators, but mostly helpless rage for her own weakness that left her cradled in the arms of a man she barely knew. Slowly the storm subsided; she began to breathe more evenly. She spoke into his shoulder as he held her.

"I'm a scientist, Aaron, a trained observer. I believe in a rational universe. Gator's don't communicate with humans, let alone give them complex mathematical models for interstellar travel. I'm losing my mind."

Aaron placed his hands on her shoulders and gently pushed her back to arm's length. She watched the glow of the bridge lights play on his eyes. He studied her face and chuckled.

"That was precisely my reaction when he spoke to me. One of the reasons I brought you out here was to prove I wasn't going nuts."

Jillian felt reassured by the confidence in his eyes. "Maybe we're both crazy."

"Perhaps, but I don't think so. There's nothing more we can do here and it's getting dark. Let's head in."

Reluctantly, Jillian disengaged herself and they started for home. She was silent for a long time remembering how she'd thrown herself into his arms. What must he think of her?

They had just left the bridge when an enormous bellow thundered through the swamp.

Aaron flinched. "Solomon."

"How do you know?"

"I just know."

A moment later, an answering voice erupted from the opposite side of the dike.

Jillian started. "Who was that?"

"I don't know, but I think it's time we got off the trail. I'm not certain what these old boys are discussing, and I'm really not supposed to be out here without another patroller."

The intensity of the rain increased as they left the network and entered the compound. The eerie glow of Salvation barely penetrated the downpour, but the pounding bass of the performer's instruments carried on the heavy air. She flinched as Aaron stopped her by laying his hand on her shoulder. "I'm ravenous. Would you like to go for a drink or something to eat?"

She started to decline, then realized that she was hungry. "Please."

They turned left and approached the weatherlock of the huge recreation center. When they had passed through the outer door, the computer responded. "Stand for water removal."

They extended their arms and legs. The multi-directional fans energized driving water from their suits and sending their hair flying. "Water removal complete. Moisture content is at fifteen percent. You may proceed."

As the inner door irised open, Jillian ran her fingers through her short hair.

"If I'm going to continue coming here, I've got to start carrying a brush."

The din of the vast room, filled with off duty personnel, struck like a physical blow. Pungent odors of numerous cuisines wafted from cooking stations scattered around the perimeter of the dome. They hung their rain gear on the rack and Jillian headed straight for the bar with Aaron in tow. She slid onto one of the tall stools. "A double."

The bartender turned at the sound of her voice. "A double what, Miss?"

"Doesn't matter. High alcohol. White rum."

Aaron ordered a beer.

After Jillian emptied her glass, she glanced up at him. "We did actually communicate with a gator, didn't we? I did not dream that."

Aaron took a sip of his beer. "Solomon, and the smaller one is Daniel. What did Solomon tell you?"

"He's worried about Pierce."

"Who's Pierce? You mean Adak Pierce?"

"My grandfather's original partner in the development of the Rozner Constant. He's taken over the corporation under an old legal agreement that gives the survivor control. I don't remember what it's called and I have no idea if it's valid."

"Why don't you contact an attorney?"

"I tried to reach Grandfather's lawyer, but he's off planet. I left an urgent message for him to contact me as soon as possible. I'm working on other solutions."

"Care to expand on that?"

"No."

He let it pass. Jillian considered ordering another drink but decided that most of the adrenaline had been diluted. "Shall we eat?"

"After you."

She headed for the Old World Italian counter. Aaron followed. She ordered lasagna, a green salad and a half bottle of Chianti. Aaron opted for the ravioli. When they were seated, Jillian opened the wine and poured a full glass. She extended the bottle toward Aaron, but he shook his head. Ignoring her meal, she drank deeply. Aaron nudged her plate toward her. "Better eat something with that."

She searched his face for any sign of disapproval and found none. "Thank you for taking me out there. I have no idea where all of this is leading and I'm not certain that I want to know, but I'm glad you were with me."

She saw his cheeks color as he glanced down at his plate. "Escorting civilians is part of my job."

She began to eat. "Aaron, what do I do now?"

He shrugged "Wait for Solomon to contact you again. You probably won't have to go back to the swamp. He may speak to you anywhere. He rousted me at the pool in Heaven this afternoon."

"Isn't that a bit disconcerting?"

"Scared the hell out of me."

Jillian chuckled as she finished her lasagna, then drained her wineglass. "What do I do about Pierce?"

"I guess you'll – oh shit."

"What?"

Aaron was staring over her shoulder. "Jergan Angst just cleared the lock and he's headed for our table."

🐾 🐾 🐾

Without speaking, Jergan pulled out a chair and sat down. His uniform was splashed with mud dried by the blower into slate-gray patches. He studied them for a long moment.

"Where the hell have you been, Trout?"

Aaron bristled at the hostility in Jergan's voice. "I'm off duty. Why?"

"God, Trout, are you always the last to know?"

"Usually. What happened?"

"Only the total collapse of the coffer dam around Bore 19. Everything flooded. Three dead, five injured so far. I keep thinking about the cold terror that must have surged through those poor bastards as they watched those barriers collapse and saw that wall of swamp water pour down on them."

Jillian shook her head. "Oh, dear God."

Aaron glanced at Jillian. She had gone perfectly still and the color had drained from her face.

He felt the heat rise in the back of his neck as he turned to Jergan. "You needn't be quite so graphic. We get the point."

Jergan signaled for a waitress, ordered a beer then turned to Aaron. "I've been out there all morning working my ass off and you're sitting in here drinking coffee. If I were running Trail Patrol, I'd have cancelled leave and recalled all off-duty personnel."

Aaron snorted. "If you were running Trail Patrol, I'd quit."

"You wouldn't have to. I'd fire your ass. By the way, you haven't introduced me to your guest."

Aaron turned to Jillian. Her eyes were moist and her breathing uneven. "Jergan Angst, meet Dr. Jillian Rozner."

Jergan stared at Jillian. Aaron took his shot. "Close your mouth, Angst. You look like a swamp frog."

"I…. I'm pleased to meet you. I didn't know. I…. Well, Aaron and I work together."

Jillian nodded. "I assumed as much. How many are missing? Do they know yet?"

Jergan paused for a moment obviously considering his answer carefully. "One hundred and seventeen men and women were down there when it collapsed. It will take several days, maybe weeks to reach all the escape chambers. We won't know any more until we get to them."

Jillian placed her hand on Jergan's arm. "Is there any hope of saving them?"

He looked down at her hand and spoke softly. "There may be if they managed to get to the escape rooms and from there to the relief shafts. Those doors can be sealed from the inside in a nanosecond. We don't dare open the surface hatches until we know that the pressure has been equalized. The rescue team was working on it when I left."

Jillian looked away from Jergan and focused on Aaron. "I have to go out there."

"That's crazy. You'd only be in the way. Do you have any idea how dangerous it is?"

"No, but I think I should be there. Will you take me?"

"Only if I can't talk you out of it."

"You can't."

Jergan started to say something, then settled back in his chair and took a swallow of beer.

Aaron glanced across the table. "Tell us what it was like when you left."

Jergan leaned forward. "The shaft is about fifty yards off the main trail. A trestle leads to the site. Most of that has been torn away. The rescue team managed to sink pylons and place a temporary cofferdam around the mine entrance. When I left, they were pumping water out of the shaft. The bodies of the three miners lay on the ground pending identification. The team is hoping to recover others before dark."

Aaron took over. "Bore 19 is about forty kilometers out. There is no way we can get there before nightfall, even in a skimmer. Let me go investigate and report back to you."

"No. It's important that I be at the scene. If I'm eventually going to run this corporation, the men need to know that I'm concerned for their welfare."

She glanced at each of them and spoke quietly. "What would my grandfather have done?"

Aaron shook his head conceding defeat. He knew the answer.

Jillian looked directly at him. "He'd already be there."

She stood and both men rose with her. Aaron dropped a handful of credits on the table. "You'll need to suit up again."

Jergan touched her sleeve. "Be careful."

She smiled. "Thanks. You better get some rest."

They left Jergan to his beer, climbed back into their foul weather gear, and passed through the air lock into the wind and driving rain of the compound. Aaron shouted over the storm. "We'll never commandeer a skimmer. They will all have been pressed into rescue service. Can we use Alice?"

"I think she'll cooperate, but you'll have to speak kindly. She's not too sure about you."

Aaron chuckled as he took Jillian's elbow and guided her across the open courtyard toward her building. "Alice may be an excellent judge of character."

When they reached her complex, Jillian placed her palm on the door panel. The door slid open and she headed directly to the garage. "Wake up, Alice. We have work to do."

The aircar slowly came to life. Panels began to glow in the cockpit and external running lights winked on. The entire front of the vehicle lifted allowing access to the pilot's couch. Jillian strapped herself in and gestured for Aaron to do likewise.

Alice activated her cabin-heating blowers. "Where are we going, Jillian?"

"To Bore 19, Alice. The landing pad should be in your chart reference."

"I have located it. Are we under any time constraints?"

"No, but we do need to go directly there."

Aaron was charmed by the muted, feminine voice of the aircar's computer.

As Alice opened the garage door, she hesitated before lifting off. "Who is your passenger, Jillian?"

"Lieutenant Aaron Trout of the Trail Patrol."

"I remember Lieutenant Trout from our mishap in the swamp. He can be quite irritating."

"Alice, watch your manners. Lieutenant Trout is our guest."

"I apologize. I will be courteous, but he's still irritating, isn't he?"

Aaron watched the color rise along Jillian's neck and suppressed his laughter. "Alice appears to have my number."

Jillian raised her hand to her forehead. "I wish she weren't quite so candid."

Twelve minutes of hard travel through driving rainsqualls brought them to the mouth of Bore 19. In the deepening twilight, men and machines worked feverishly to rescue the trapped miners. Giant ion lights flooded the site with a blue-white glow. Jillian studied the tableau from the hovering aircar, then spoke to Alice.

"Put us down as close to the entrance as possible. I need to talk to the leader of the rescue team."

Alice hesitated. "This is not wise, Jillian."

"I didn't ask for your opinion, just put us on the ground."

"As you wish."

Aaron studied the scene, below. "Alice may have a point."

"I don't care. I want to talk to the foreman."

The bright red aircar settled onto the solid landing pad north of the shaft. Several of the men stopped to glance at the vehicle, then resumed their task. Aaron watched as the entire transparent front of Alice tilted up providing a rain shield for the cabin as Jillian stepped from the comfort of the interior into the downpour. She fought her way through the storm to a large man who was directing the rescue effort.

Aaron followed but stood to one side giving them their privacy. Water cascaded off their rain gear as their animated gestures punctuated their conversation. After a while Jillian hung her head and turned her back to the waiting aircar.

When Alice opened the door for her. Aaron could see the consternation on her face in the light. "What did he say?"

"He said they've got most of the water out of the mine, but they haven't found any additional bodies. He's hoping that the men are in the relief chambers. He also said that Bore 19 is one of the most prolific sources of nodules. They're very anxious to get it back on line."

Aaron used his hand to wipe the condensation off the windshield. Alice immediately activated the circuits that heated the material and dried the surface.

"Does he know what happened?"

"Only that the cofferdam collapsed. He says that they're inspected once a week. This is the first one to fail. It doesn't make any sense."

As Aaron turned to study the wrecked bridge east of the site, an enormous bellow echoed through the swamp, overpowering the wind and rain. Jillian grabbed his arm.

"Solomon?"

"No."

"Did you recognize it"

"No, but I think it's the same one we heard earlier."

Jillian stared out the windshield. "You may think I'm losing my mind, but I'm beginning to discern different emotions in the gator's voices. The one we heard on the bridge sounded angry."

Aaron studied her closely. "And this one?"

"Triumphant."

– 9 –

Solomon glided through the swamp using broad sweeps of his great tail to propel himself toward his lair. Periodically, he stopped to sniff the damp air above the water and listen to the rustle of leaves in the canopy. No foreign scents filled his nostrils; no strange sounds assaulted his ears. Swimming in a slow circle, he tried to identify the source of his uneasiness, but could not. A great calamity had taken place. No, not quite right, it was about to take place.

Solomon turned at the sound of the rushing water. He raised his massive head and listened. Strong waves of terror from the man-creatures washed over him. He could feel the anguish from the digging place. Shortly after he could sense the urgency of the rescuers rushing to the scene. Not since the great starship exploded had he experienced such pain. He tipped back his head and unleashed an anguished bellow that shook the trees around him.

Slowly, he settled back into the water, turned for home. As he approached the forked tree, he dove beneath its protruding roots and navigated the narrow, underwater passage that led to his cave.

Solomon surfaced in the inner pool and saw Sheeba raise her head from the ledge where she lay guarding the nodules. Daylight streamed through the opening at the top of the dome and illuminated her resting-place.

She queried him silently.

I felt the pain, Solomon. Men have died.

Yes.

Was yours one who was extinguished?

No, my love.

Sheeba slid forward until her snout touched him as he lay in the water directly below her.

That which keeps the water out of their digging place has failed, has it not?

It has.

Did they not strongly build it?

They did.

I do not understand.

Solomon heaved himself onto the ledge and stretched out beside her. He rested his snout on her shoulder and looked around the interior of the great cave. Water dripped from the dome and plinked into the pool.

I fear the others.

He felt Sheeba tense.

Would even they do this thing?

The stakes are high.

Does the woman-king know of this?

She does.

Sheeba shuffled around until she could look into his eyes.

It has begun, has it not, my love?

I fear it. He who was cast out is moving among us.

Sheeba lowered her head, resting her jaw on the rock and whispered the unholy name.

Joshua.

Jillian lay on a lounge chair staring up through the dome of Heaven, fascinated by the tiny white threads of cirrus clouds against the bright blue sky. Perhaps the sunlight could dispel the horror of the mine disaster.

Why hadn't she been up here before? It might not be La Jolla, but it offered sunshine and clear skies. Her soul needed the warmth and brightness. She vowed to make this a habit.

In the pool, a lone figure swam easy laps. The plop, plop of his cupped hands striking the water and quiet splashing of his feet echoed in the domed space. He never seemed to tire. She didn't know him but he was certainly in excellent condition.

Several couples talked quietly in the restaurant area enjoying the varied foods and each other's company.

Across the pool, a petite blond woman, completely nude, dozed on a floor mat. Not until the woman rose and raised her face to the light before slipping into the pool could Jillian be sure that it was Alice's friend, Shelly LaCoste, chief mechanic for the Rozner Corporation. Alice spoke warmly of her.

Shelly floated on her back, slowly fluttering her arms and legs to propel her body gently through the water. When she reached Jillian's end of the pool, she stood in the shallow water and brushed her wet hair back with her hands.

Jillian took the initiative. "Good afternoon, Shelly."

Shelly looked up and took a moment to recognize her. She seemed embarrassed. "Good afternoon, Dr. Rozner. I didn't know you came up here."

"My first time. I miss the sun in La Jolla, and call me Jillian."

Shelly smiled. "That's a beautiful suit, Jillian."

Jillian glanced down. "Thank you. I'm afraid I haven't gotten used to public nudity. I've always been a bit modest."

"It grows on you. Pretty soon you'll think nothing of it. I wouldn't be comfortable just anywhere, but in Heaven everyone respects your privacy."

Jillian smiled. "Or they get tossed?"

"Or they get tossed."

Shelly tipped her head back and let the sun shine fully on her face. "I come up here any time I can get away. It refreshes my heart and eases my soul."

"From what Alice tells me, you don't get away often. She says you work much too hard."

Shelly walked up the steps at the corner of the pool, retrieved her towel and came to rest on the lounge next to Jillian's. "I'm afraid Alice has exaggerated ideas of my efforts."

"Alice may be your biggest fan. She says nobody understands her circuitry like you do."

Shelly laughed. "I had to find some very old manuals to trace some of her internals. They no longer even make parts for many of her components."

"Well, we both appreciate your efforts."

Shelly glanced around. "I was just going to wander over to the snack bar for some lunch. Would you care to join me?"

The invitation caught Jillian by surprise. "I'd like that very much."

Shelly stopped to pick up her cover from a poolside table and slipped it on over her head. They chose a table in the shaded portion of the eating area each having received her quota of ultraviolet for the day.

After an excellent lunch of fresh fish and samples of several different salads, they lingered over tea and delicate pastries, talking about the families they grew up with and trading stories of Earth.

Jillian sipped her tea. "How did you get away for a whole afternoon?"

Shelly laughed easily. "My crew threw me out. They said I was becoming impossible to live with and demanded that I leave. They rebel every so often."

Jillian poured fresh tea for both. "Every report I've seen on your shop is highly laudatory. They praise your efficiency and thoroughness. The morale rating is sky high. You should be very proud."

A faint pink glow flushed the chief mechanic's cheeks. "Thank you. We all work very hard but I try to make sure we have a good time as well."

Shelly remained quiet for several minutes but glanced up often to study Jillian's face. Her battle with herself was nearly comical.

Finally, Jillian couldn't watch her suffer any longer. "What's on your mind, Shelly?"

Shelly fidgeted. "I know this is impertinent and I'm not certain I should bring it up, but well, we're all wondering how long you're going to let Pierce sit in your office before you fight back."

Jillian sat back in her chair and took a moment to compose herself. "What would you have me do?"

"I don't know, but it was an honor to work for your grandfather. He could be ruthless but we all knew that if we needed anything, and I mean anything, all we had to do was ask. We loved him and his choice of you to succeed him was well received. I've always felt Pierce could not be trusted."

Jillian stared into her teacup deciding how to respond. The old knot of anger roiled just beneath her breastbone. "I'm working on some things."

"Well, don't wait too long. The natives are getting restless. Speaking of restless, I'd better get back to the shop. If I'm gone too long, they may discover they can survive without me."

"I wouldn't worry too much about that."

Shelly smiled as she rose and gathered her things. "Thank you for a lovely lunch, Jillian. I'm so glad we spent some time together. Let's do it again."

She suddenly grew quite serious. "If you need help, you just call anyone in Shuttle Repair. You'll get it."

Jillian could only nod as Shelly turned away and headed for the dressing rooms.

🐊　🐊　🐊

Daniel lay in the tall grass across the channel from the entrance to Solomon's lair. As the patriarch departed at dawn on his morning patrol, he passed within a tail's length of the younger gator's hiding place. Daniel held his breath and remained motionless, terrified that his pounding heart would give him away. Solomon cruised by without glancing in his direction.

The protégé had lain awake the entire night hatching his audacious plan. He well understood that what he was about to do could end his life, but he had to know. His young mind fixated on the only creature who could answer his burning question and she lay inside Solomon's lair. He listened to the birds flitting through the bushes at the shoreline and felt the breeze shift to the East promising rain. Still, he remained motionless until he calculated that his mentor neared the most distant point of his circuit, then he rose onto his six stocky legs and slipped into the channel. Each sweep of his tail brought him closer to his master's cave.

He paused only momentarily before diving for the underwater entrance. Deeper than he had calculated, the cleft in the rock expanded into an underwater channel cut through solid rock. The tight passage opened into a large underground pool. Daniel surfaced.

Immediately he spotted Sheeba standing on her ledge staring straight at him. She had sensed his presence, probably while he was still outside. All of his well-rehearsed queries turned to swamp moss in his mouth. The huge female hissed and showed her teeth.

How dare you invade the lair of Solomon.

Daniel turned to dive for the entrance then remembered the gravity of his mission. Summoning all of his courage, he swam slowly toward her.

**Forgive me, Great Mother. I had to come.
I must commune with you. I am Daniel, ward
of Solomon.**

Sheeba glowered at the young gator then settled onto her ledge, still wary, but apparently more at ease. She studied the intruder lying in the water.

I know you, my son. What do you want?

Daniel took a moment to organize his thoughts.

I have come for the truth. You, alone may enlighten me.

There are many truths. Which do you seek?

The young gator swam a little closer. He tried to recall his carefully practiced lines. They wouldn't come. Anguish erupted from his soul.

Why me?

The massive female huffed then let silence hang in the cave. Daniel heard the waves lap against the rock walls and watched light streaming through the opening at the top of the dome play on the ripples around him. The great mother would speak when she was ready.

She rested her massive jaw on the stone ledge.

I believe I know what is in your heart. These questions are more properly addressed to Solomon. He is your master.

Daniel felt the knot tighten in his belly. His daring adventure had come to nothing. Solomon would be returning shortly.

I fear him.

As well you should, my young friend, but if you are to be a worthy successor, you must find the courage to confront that which terrifies you.

His spirit sank like a stone in the pool but he spoke calmly.

You will not help me. Solomon is so powerful. I fear I can never live up to his expectations.

He turned to depart. As he was about to dive, she spoke.

Daniel.

He turned back toward her. Her eyes softened and she raised her head.

Solomon chose you because you are worthy. You are courageous and your heart is true. You are brave. Did you not come here?

Ɓe would not tell you this, but he sees a younger Solomon in you. Go in peace, my son. All is as it should be.

Daniel released the breath he had not realized he'd been holding.

Thank you, Great Mother.

He turned to leave.

Daniel.

He froze.

I never said these things. You must not tell Solomon you were here. Now go.

Daniel dove for the entrance and swam hard until he could surface in the channel beyond the rocks. When he reached the opposite shore, he climbed onto the bank and lay pondering her words.

🦅 🦅 🦅

Alone in his office, Adak Pierce pored over the latest reports of Rozner Corporation nodule production illuminating the huge screen on the opposite wall. Long columns of complex numbers marched down from ceiling to floor. All appeared to be in order except....

He picked up his mug and took a long draw of the sweet, dark coffee Janice had prepared for him. The warm liquid slid down his throat, leaving an aftertaste of smoky Venutian beans. Glancing back at the document, he set down the mug, then waved his hand to flip back through the previous screens. Reclining in his chair, he closed his eyes. Adak's breathing slowed and his bearded chin dropped to his chest. Remaining in this near comatose posture for several minutes, he visualized the columns of numbers trying to sense where the discrepancy lay. Something was wrong.

Suddenly, he jerked his head up and, leaning forward, stared at the report. Scanning the fifth screen he ran his eye down the far-right column.

"Impossible."

Adak hefted his huge bulk from the chair, walked around the desk and gestured to the wall connecting to his secretary's office. A portal irised open and he stepped through.

"Janice, tell Wiggins I want to see him now."

"Yes, Mr. Pierce."

"And tell him to bring the latest lab tests."

"Yes, Sir. Is something wrong?"

"Wrong? You're damn right, something's wrong."

Janice studied his face. "Can I help?"

"No. Just get Wiggins in here."

"Yes, Sir."

Adak returned to his office, picked up his coffee, then set it down without drinking. He began to pace before the large window that looked out on the swamp. Rain pounded on the marshlands bending the foliage toward the ground.

He turned as the portal opened and Wiggins entered carrying a data cube. His hands trembled as he stopped just inside the doorway.

"You wanted to see me, Sir?"

"Yes, Wiggins. Are those the latest test results?"

"Yes, Sir. I ran them myself, this morning."

"Deposit the cube in the desk receptacle."

Wiggins placed the data in the reader and faced Adak. "Is something wrong, Sir?"

Adak didn't answer, but crossed the room and sat at the desk. When he had perused the reports glowing on the opposite wall, he focused on Wiggins.

"Do you notice anything unusual in these results?"

"No, Sir."

"Well, you damned well should. Look at that far-right column, the one labeled Beta 2. Is that not a measure of the change in potency of the nodules after suffusion?"

Wiggins leaned forward to examine the report. Tiny beads of perspiration appeared on his upper lip. "It is."

"Does anything strike you about those numbers?"

Wiggins glanced from area to area on the massive screen, then gestured with his hand to arrange the images so they overlapped, exposing only the right-hand column of each. When he glanced at Adak, his face was white.

"They're deteriorating."

Pierce slammed his fist down on the desk. The shock bounced his coffee mug, nearly toppling it. "Yes, Wiggins. They're slowly eroding. Each new batch of nodules is less potent than its predecessor. Why?"

"I don't know, Sir. We have changed nothing. All of the procedures are being performed precisely as Dr. Rozner stipulated. You can see that all of the readings in the other columns are constant."

"Why didn't the computers pick it up? They're programmed to track anomalies, aren't they?"

Wiggins' started biting his lip. "Apparently not this one."

Adak rose from his chair and began to pace. "Who's in charge of the mercury suffusion process?"

"I am. As head of production, I oversee that myself."

"Well damn it, man, can't you adjust it?"

Wiggins leaned over and placed his hands on the desk. He took a deep breath and looked directly at Pierce who had halted behind his chair. "Infusion occurs after the chamber is sealed. The entire process is, or rather was, known only to Dr. Rozner. Any attempt to tamper with it automatically initiates the destruction sequence. Believe me, we've looked and there is no way to disengage the failsafe. The knowledge died with him."

Adak closed his eyes and drew in a deep breath. "The bastard. I knew Rozner. He was far too good a scientist to destroy his work. There's a record somewhere or somebody knows the entire process. Who would he have told?"

Wiggins glanced down at his feet. "As chief of production, I would have been the logical choice. He didn't tell me."

Adak walked over to the window and stared into the rain. As he watched, the downpour let up and the sky lightened. Slowly he raised his head, and glared out at the swamp.

"I've been a fool. I know who has the formula."

Dr. Wiggins strode quickly back to his office and secured the door. He sat behind his desk and tried to slow his heart rate. When he thought he could control his voice, he spoke.

"Communications. Contact Dr. Jillian Rozner."

"Located. Dr. Rozner will receive your call."

After a short delay, the screen resolved into an image of Jillian seated on the large sofa in her apartment. "Hello Dr. Wiggins. How nice of you to call."

He took a deep breath. "I'm afraid it's not a social contact. I think that Pierce has deduced that you have the Rozner process. I've called to tell you to be careful."

Jillian leaned back against the cushions. "Well, we knew he'd work it out eventually. You don't think he'd actually harm me?"

"I don't know."

She appeared to concentrate for a moment then glanced back at the screen. "Thank you for calling. I'll try to stay out of dark alleys. Good night, Chet."

"Good night, Jillian."

Joshua lay in the tall swamp grass with only the tip of his snout protruding into the open pool of brackish water. The remainder of his enormous body reclined, half submerged, in green and yellow vegetation. Periodically, his eyelids blinked to lubricate black and gold eyes.

Across the water man-creatures worked feverishly around the entrance to the digging place. Through rain-filtered daylight he could see the urgency in their actions. The rumble of great machines spewing massive geysers of water into the late afternoon air, pounded against his ears, and acrid smells of overheated machinery filled his nostrils. An occasional shout pierced the background din.

He raised his huge reptilian head and turned to see what had disturbed the grass near the bank. A smaller gator eased his way into the marsh and glided toward him. Joshua studied the newcomer for a moment, then turned to refocus on the rescue effort. Gideon swam silently into position beside him and focused on the mine entrance. He felt the pressure of the young one's mind but closed the channel.

Now that the battle has begun, if you wish to commune, you must reach out to me in the language of the infidels. I do not like it but the ancients have decreed. We must prepare ourselves.

He felt the lash of his rebuke strike Gideon. The younger gator remained silent for a moment.

I beg your forgiveness. Have we succeeded, Joshua?

It is uncertain. The man-creatures attempt to rescue their companions. How are the others?

All are exhausted. Some are injured, but none seriously. They await your assessment.

The rain intensified, bouncing off Joshua's huge, armored body. It was harder now to see what the man-creatures were doing. Joshua turned to study his lieutenant. The eagerness in the young one's eyes nearly made him smile.

Tell them they have done well. Say we have dashed them in pieces like the fragile eggs of the marsh birds. Tell them that the man-creatures no longer remove the nodules from the tomb.

When Gideon did not depart immediately, Joshua turned back to study the activity at the mine, waiting for the young one to gather his courage. He could clearly remember the anxiety of broaching a difficult subject with an elder. He heard the intake of breath beside him.

The infidel, Solomon, communes with one of the man-creatures, does he not?

He does.

How?

The simple, one-word question burned in Joshua's ears. It reverberated in his brain where it had seared for weeks. He swung his head around to focus on Gideon, then turned forward and lay his massive jaw on the water.

I know not.

A hideously loud shriek of rending metal echoed across the swamp. Joshua watched the twisted girders of the trestle leading to Bore 19 tumble into the water. Two man-creatures extinguished their torches and stepped back onto the bank.

Gideon raised his head further to see through the grass.

They are destroying that which they built.

Only that part which is unwhole.

What does this mean?

Joshua stared at the frantic activity, then heaved a huge sigh.

They will make it whole again.

The young one remained silent for a time.

If they make it whole, will they not again seek the sacred nodules?

They will.

Then we have failed.

Joshua turned to study the young one's face. All of the excitement had drained from his countenance.

Remember, life's journey is not a single sweep of the tail.

Gideon raised his head and studied the activity on the distant shore.

We must try again.

Yes, my son.

Across the water, Solomon lay hidden in tall rushes. He had been here for several hours. A bright red bird landed on the branch above his head, chattering noisily. He watched it for a moment then returned his attention to the young gator approaching Joshua and strained to intercept their conversation. They were communicating employing very little energy and at this distance he could only catch an occasional word.

uncertain...rescue...nodules...done well...

It was enough. He closed his eyes. A great sadness filled his soul.

Oh Joshua. How could you?

Jillian lay with just her face exposed above the hot water in the deep bathing tub. The chill of the rain and wind slowly dissipated from her body. She and Aaron had spent the morning exploring the compound. Jillian wanted to know every centimeter of the place.

She sat up, lathered her hair, then rinsed it by tipping her head under the waterfall that cascaded into the shallow end of the bath. She ran her fingers through her short, dark hair.

"I didn't think I'd ever get warm again."

"Did you request something, Dr. Rozner?"

"No, Wilson. I was simply talking to myself."

Jillian settled back into the warm embrace of the bath water. She was definitely going to have to turn down the sensitivity on Wilson.

"Time."

"Six hours, twenty-eight minutes and fourteen seconds Past Midnight, Saturday, April 17th two-thousand-four-hundred and twenty-six, Earth registration."

"Jeez, I just wanted the local time."

She closed her eyes. "I've got to do something about that computer."

She relaxed. The images flowed through her mind. She could see Aaron standing on the bridge fiercely concentrating all of his attention on Solomon while the massive gator floated in the water, opening his enormous mouth. All those teeth. She could still feel the aftereffects of the pressure of the gator's thoughts in her head.

The scene shifted to visions of the mine entrance. The bodies and the frantic cries of the rescuers as they fought to save their companions all swirled in her brain.

"It's too much."

"The water is too deep?"

"No, Wilson, it's okay."

"I can reduce the level."

"The water's fine.

Jillian groaned as she stood up and stepped out of the pool. She was definitely going to have to reset that thing.

"Air."

Blasts of warm air struck her body from all angles drying her. She slipped on her dressing gown, padded to the main house panel and located the controls for the household computer. She passed her hand in front of the screen setting personality to zero then proceeded to the service area and requested tea. A steaming mug appeared in the glass enclosure on the counter. She retrieved it and sipped the hot liquid as she dressed.

Images of Aaron donning rain gear or eating at the table in Sanctuary flashed through her mind. She heard the deep baritone of his laugh as Alice delivered her candid assessment of him. She felt the warm comfort of his embrace and smelled his rain-soaked jacket, as she cried on him after Solomon had spoken to her.

She laughed and shook her head. How far she'd come. A date in La Jolla required a new sundress revealing bare shoulders and jewelry. Here, she needed a full-body rain suit with only her face exposed. The only "jewelry" was the laser weapon Aaron insisted she carry.

🐊 🐊 🐊

Shelly LaCoste wiped off Alice's maintenance hatch and tucked the rag in the belt of her jumpsuit. "That does it Alice. You're as tuned as modern science can make you."

"Thank you, Shelly. Everything feels wonderful."

Shelly glanced around the cavernous space of Shuttle repair and sighed. Through the open hanger door, she watched the late-afternoon rain fall nearly straight down. It hissed against the hard pad of the entry ramp.

In the middle of the room, a full crew slaved over an enormous ore carrier brought in by the guild. The muffled sound of their tools leaked out from the interior of the huge piece of equipment. As always, Shelly was fascinated by the odd shape of the vehicles designed to slip through the narrow corridors of safe passage. The craft's designers had taken advantage of every trick to fashion the largest possible capacity into a beast that could still maneuver safely inside the limits of the air channel.

Technically, these were not her responsibility, but Industrial Division was badly overbooked and she had reluctantly, perhaps unwisely, agreed to help out. How was she ever going to get all of these machines up and running before tomorrow morning?

"I guess I'll just have to call in the third shift."

"Were you speaking to me, Shelly?"

"No, Alice. I was thinking out loud."

"Jillian does that, too. I've often wondered if she gets satisfactory answers."

Shelly shook her head. "I hope she gets better ones than I do."

"Perhaps she gets better answers from the gators."

Shelly focused on the red aircar. "What do you mean?"

"When Solomon speaks to her, she gets very upset. I think it causes her pain."

Shelly stared at Alice. "You're not making any sense. Who's Solomon?"

"Solomon is the huge gator in the swamp that Jillian talks to. Aaron Trout introduced them."

Shelly glanced around for something to sit on. This was going to take some time to sort out. She found an empty parts crate, upended it and sat contemplating Jillian's aircar. "Are you telling me Jillian and Aaron carry on conversations with swamp gators?"

"Yes, but they only talk to Solomon."

Shelly shook her head, trying to clear the fog. "How do they do this, Alice?"

The aircar was silent for a long moment. When Alice had finally formulated her response she spoke. "They touch brains."

Shelly put her head in her hands. "I'm getting dizzy trying to follow this. What do you mean, they touch brains?"

Alice cogitated for a long moment. "They hear each other's thoughts."

"You mean like telepathy?"

"That word is in my data base. It seems to describe the transaction."

Shelly was fascinated. "What do they talk about?"

"Jillian didn't say. I just know that she leaned on Aaron Trout and cried."

Shelly shook her head. "This is very confusing."

A shout rang out from the other end of the shop. A large piece of canopy bounced on the floor but didn't break. Shelly watched for a moment to be certain her people had the situation under control then turned back to the aircar.

"Who have you told this to, Alice?"

"Anyone who would listen. I'm very proud of Jillian."

Shelly stood up and walked toward the aircar. "When did you begin telling everyone, Alice?"

"Three days ago."

Shelly drew in a deep breath and let it out slowly. "I'm not certain this is something Jillian would like widely known. Please don't tell anyone else."

Alice spoke softly. "If you think that's best, Shelly."

"I do"

"Shelly?"

"Yes, Alice."

"I trust you."

Gideon lay in the reeds watching bubbles appear as fish fed on insects that skimmed the water. He'd been brooding for several hours, gathering his courage to confront Joshua. A small fish broke the surface near his snout and he snapped at it without conviction. His mood broken, he turned and ambled up the bank. He knew where to find Joshua. In the late afternoon, the patriarch would be sunning himself on his favorite rock.

Several gators lay on the bank, dozing, communing, and tending young. As he passed Martha, she raised her head and huffed. He ignored her invitation and took the lower path that lead to Joshua's lair.

The alpha male lay on his rock, soaking up the last of the day's warmth. Gideon approached slowly, rattling a few stones to announce his presence. The patriarch spoke without lifting his head.

Why do you disturb me, Gideon?

I come seeking truth.

Joshua raised his head and turned to study his protégé.

Which truth do you require, and why do you assume I would dispense it?

Gideon summoned all his courage.

I would know the value of the nodules.

Joshua lay his head back on the rock and heaved a sigh.

Ah, so the time has finally come. Such truths are not borne lightly. Are you prepared to receive such a heavy burden?

I am.

Joshua studied the face of the younger gator, concentrating on the eyes.

Yes, I believe you are. Come around in front of me where I can more easily see you. These old bones hunger for the heat of this old rock. I prefer not to move.

Gideon sidled around until he faced Joshua directly, being careful not to cast his shadow on the ancient one. The patriarch stared out over the swamp for a long moment before he spoke.

I am tired, and my heart is heavy. The infidel, Solomon communes with the visitors and shares the sacred knowledge. This should not be. I do not believe the ancients intended us to use our gift to enlighten these lesser creatures. We must use our skills to banish the man-creatures. The ancients left us to guard the orbs, not to give away their secrets. It is the reason for our creation. Solomon blasphemes.

Gideon stirred, settling into the muddy bank.

I don't understand. What are the nodules that we should die to protect them?

Ah, my son, that is not so easily answered. The nodules are many things. Before men walked this world, before their ships filled our skies, before the devil, Kozner, worked his alchemy, we guarded the nodules and we waited.

Waited for what?

Joshua lifted his head and stared at the first stars twinkling in the twilight sky.

For their return.

The ancient ones?

Yes, our creators.

Gideon remained silent, organizing his mind as Joshua had taught him. The evening breeze rattled the reeds behind him. No logical line of inquiry presented itself.

I don't understand.

Joshua stared directly at him.

It is most difficult.

They remained silent for several minutes. When Joshua spoke, his voice echoed as if coming from a great distance.

Many generations back, our creators arrived aboard great cities, filled with light, that traveled through the heavens for many lifetimes. They explored untold worlds, colonizing some and ignoring others. Here, they found wealth worthy of protection.

Gideon made the leap.

The nodules.

Joshua rose on his six stubby legs and thrust his head toward Gideon. His eyes blazed with rage.

The nodules. Their power is nearly limitless. We were created to guard that power. We live and die to keep faith. We have not the right to reveal the secrets to lesser beings.

Rozner?

Rozner or any other.

Gideon glanced down to discover that he had retreated into the shallow water. The sheer force of Joshua's voice had propelled him backward. Badly shaken by the outburst, he finally found his courage.

I cannot believe your brother, Solomon, would do such a thing.

Joshua stood there, trembling, his breath coming in hissing gasps. Slowly, he regained control and sank to his belly on the rock. He lay staring into the twilight. When he spoke, profound sadness filled his voice.

He is my brother no longer. We have taken separate paths.

Deep in the swamp, a gator bellowed and night birds called to welcome the darkness. Joshua raised his enormous bulk and slid off his rock.

It is time to join the others.

Gideon followed, as he still had many questions. He hurried to catch up with his mentor.

These nodules that we guard, they are more than a source of energy, are they not?

Joshua halted and swung his massive head to confront his student. His eyes blazed with the heat of his anger.

Whose council have you sought? How dare you inquire into the ancient mysteries?

Gideon shrank into the grass as he lowered himself into the submissive pose struck before superiors.

I have consulted no one. I came to you.

Joshua grunted and started to turn away. Gideon couldn't let it pass.

The nodules are more, are they not?

The ancient gator wheeled to face his underling.

As the sun is more than a candle flame, young Gideon. You have not yet glimpsed their power nor have the man-creatures.

The ancient gator turned and shuffled toward the encampment, leaving Gideon to stare after him.

— 10 —

az had been searching for his partner since dinner. Aaron had not shown up at their usual table and his absence had been pounced on as license to talk about him. Some of his fellow patrol officers were sarcastic; others were actually sympathetic. But, of course, no one believed he talked to gators.

Laz checked their hut, the registry for Heaven, and then had a brainstorm. He smiled as he located a terminal and placed the call. He knew where his partner was. "Dr. Jillian Rozner's residence, please."

"One moment. Dr. Rozner will receive your call."

The screen filled with an enormous panorama of a sunlit ocean beach on Earth. At first Laz thought he had a wrong connection. He was about to try again when Jillian stepped into the picture. "Good evening, Lieutenant. May I help you?"

"I'm sorry. I'm a little confused. Where are you?"

Jillian looked puzzled, then glanced over her shoulder and laughed. "Don't let that fool you. It's a pictowall of my beach at La Jolla. Isn't it wonderful?"

"It certainly is. Uh, is Aaron there?"

"Aaron? No. Why would he be here?"

"Oh, I . . . well, I just thought . . . ."

Jilllian's warm smile sparkled with playfulness. "I do believe you're blushing, Lieutenant but to answer your question, I haven't seen him all day. Is it important?"

"No. I'll find him. I'm sorry to have disturbed you."

"Anytime, Lieutenant."

The screen darkened.

Laz stood befuddled. He had no other ideas. Where could his partner be? Then it hit him. "Oh, no. He wouldn't."

He stepped away from the terminal and strode toward the trailhead. As he stopped to check his gear, Aaron cleared the portal, walking toward him.

"Where the hell have you been Trout? I've been looking all over for you."

Aaron looked down. "Solomon summoned me."

"Jesus, Aaron, you have to tell me when you're going out there. You know it's against regs to go alone. I'd go with you."

Aaron kicked at the mud with his toe. "Yeah, I know you would but I didn't want to drag you any farther into this."

Laz heaved a huge sigh. "Look, Aaron. We've got to talk. Who have you told about the gators?"

Aaron glanced back over his shoulder as if a gator might appear behind him.

"No one. Only you. Oh, and Jillian, of course, but Solomon directed me to summon her. You know that."

Laz studied Aaron for a long moment. "Well, old friend, it was the only topic of conversation at dinner tonight. They all think you're nuts."

Aaron raised the corners of his mouth in a sad smile. "I am and so is Jillian, but at least we're going crazy together."

Laz reached out and grabbed his partner's shoulders. "Damn it, Aaron. This isn't funny. It could cost you your job."

"Well, I was unemployed when I found this one."

Laz started to retort then conceded defeat. "You're hopeless. Let's go home."

🐾 🐾 🐾

After seeing his partner safely in bed, Laz settled down with his personal viewing screen to watch the latest Chaps

Henry vid. He lay on his bunk with the small screen propped up against his knees.

No one could explain the resurgence of interest in films about the United States Old West, but competition for the vids was fierce. He'd been lucky to snag this one from the library at Salvation.

Laz had his own theory. He reasoned that people hungered for a simpler time when good and evil were clearly identifiable and all a man needed was a good horse, a fast gun and unflinching courage. Chaps Henry never had to deal with telepathic gators and complicated space drives. All he had to do was rescue the girl from the clutches of Black Bart and recover the deed to the ranch. There was something very appealing in that.

As Chaps strolled out of the saloon and reached for his horses' reins, Laz's guardian beeped. "Oh, hell. Now what?"

He suspended the adventure and answered the device. "Lazarus."

The gentle voice on the other end melted his anger. "Laz. This is Shelly LaCoste. Did I catch you at a bad time?"

"No, you got me before Chaps Henry rode off to save the girl in distress."

"I beg your pardon. Oh, you have the new cowboy film. I'd like to lay claim to it when you finish."

"I'll save it for you."

Laz waited for her to continue but there was only silence. She hadn't activated video so he had no idea what she was doing. Finally, she spoke. "Laz, we need to meet and talk."

"Now?"

"I think it would be best."

Laz glanced around the room, locating various pieces of his uniform. He hadn't bothered to hang them up. "What did you have in mind?"

"I thought we could meet at Salvation as soon as you can get there."

He caught the note of urgency in her voice. "This is serious, isn't it?"

"I'm afraid it is."

"I can be there in ten minutes." Laz cut the connection and deactivated the lapvid. Chaps would have to wait.

As he cleared the air lock from the dryer and strolled into Salvation, he scanned the room for Shelly. She waved at him from a small table along the west wall. He smiled as he crossed the room to her. He wasn't quite certain why he was short of breath but then he really didn't want to know.

She smiled a warm greeting. "Good evening, Lieutenant. Thank you for meeting me on such short notice."

"My pleasure. Would you like something to drink?"

She nodded. "A Bull Gator would be nice."

Laz flagged a passing waitress, ordered two beers then turned back to Shelly. "To what do I owe the honor of your invitation?"

Shelly frowned and the small lines between her eyes deepened. "I'm worried about Aaron and Jillian."

"So am I."

The beer arrived and Shelly pushed her glass around on the table without drinking. "Do you really think the gators talk to them?"

He leaned back in his chair and held the stein in both hands. "I don't know but it's clear that Aaron and Jillian think so. If it were only Aaron, I'd be less inclined to believe it."

"Me, too. But with both of them insisting that they have periodic conversations with those awful beasts, I just don't know what to make of it."

Laz watched the light play on the surface of the table, then glanced up into Shelly's eyes. Why did they have to be so blue?

"How did you find out about the gators, Shelly?"

"Alice told me. She's been telling anyone who would listen. I convinced her to stop but it's probably too late."

Laz took a long, slow drink of his beer. "Aaron didn't show for dinner. No one could talk about anything except this gator business. I'm afraid it could cost him his job."

"What does he say?"

"He doesn't seem to care."

Shelly laughed. "Well, if you're having cosmic conversations with swamp creatures, I guess everything else seems trivial."

"I guess."

She leaned forward and rested her arms on the table. "What do you think we should do?"

"I don't see that there's anything we can do except to be there if they need us."

Her smile was warm. "You're a good friend, Winton Lazarus. Aaron is very lucky to have you as his partner."

He could feel the heat rising in his cheeks. "Thank you."

They sat for a moment smiling at each other. Laz had to know. "Are you involved with anyone?"

Her eyes widened. "You mean like a life partner?"

"Yes."

She let the silence hang in the air for a moment longer than necessary. "No."

Laz released a pent up breath. "Good."

She waited. "Good? That's it?"

He didn't know how to react. He thought of several snappy comebacks he'd often used with other women, but they all felt wrong. Finally he shook his head.

"Good."

The *Windflower Vagabond* had been decelerating steadily since her mid-course correction. Following the dictates of the Rozner Constant, she had been halving her velocity every S.T.U. At forty-four thousand kilometers per hour, she had one more deceleration to make before achieving her orbiting speed of twenty-two. The massive intergalactic ship would not actually land on Rozner's world, but achieve a parking orbit four hundred kilometers above the surface. After taking on a cargo of nodules and newly built Rozner Drives, she would depart for other ports of call.

On the bridge, Captain Wyman scanned the six-tiered instrument panel, fully prepared to abort orbital insertion if any portion of the Rozner Drive system deviated from the norm. The fate of the *Majestic Vagabond* was much on her mind. Perhaps they would never know what had happened since the needed data had burned up with the craft. On her left, her communications officer, Major Jac Sabot, conferred with Rozner traffic control.

Portions of the blue-green world below them revolved into view before being supplanted by entire regions shrouded in a nearly permanent, dense gray fog. Through the intense magnification of the down-looking scope, she could make out some surface details.

In one of the cloud-covered areas, a tall recreation tower pierced the saturated atmosphere into brilliant sunlight that glistened off its transparent dome. Suzanne rubbed the back of her neck, remembering the truly magnificent spa at the apex of the tower. Her captain's bars granted her automatic access to the hedonistic pleasures; the best being unlimited hot water. What a luxury.

"Captain, traffic control is inquiring if we wish to establish parking orbit."

She glanced at her communications officer. "Confirm."

"They're asking if we will need drive maintenance."

"Confirm that we will need a complete overhaul of the Rozner units before we can accept additional cargo. I don't want to block the escape routes through the forward bays until I know that our Rozners are tuned."

"Aye, Captain."

Suzanne glanced around the bridge, noting the relaxed demeanor of her officers. This crew had been together for several trips and responded to each other instinctively. Orders were executed almost before they were given. She felt a strong attachment to these people.

"Captain. Traffic control instructs us to establish orbit at five hundred kilometers. They're anticipating a small passenger liner they intend to insert at four hundred. They want to unload her first."

Suzanne grinned and her eyes sparkled with mischief. "Damned right, they do. She'll have a supply of Galian wine aboard, probably the Coastal Chardonnay. Tell them that we graciously defer to the liner, but that I intend to be loaded and away in seventy-two hours. And request an audience for me with the captain of the liner. Let's see if we can't horse trade him out of a few cases."

Jac turned back to his panel and repeated her instructions before signing off, then spoke in a perfectly flat voice. "Begging the Captain's pardon, Sir, but you are one sneaky mother."

"So noted."

On the other side of the bridge, the navigational officer, Lt. Carey Nighthawk straightened up without taking his eyes from his screen. "I have the liner on scope."

"Acknowledged. Helm, hold current course and speed. Communications to internal."

She paused for a moment composing her message to the crew. "Attention all hands. We are preparing for orbital insertion around Rozner's World. Liberty will be granted to all officers and crewmembers on the usual rotational basis. I know it's been a long trip, but let's try to remember that we are civilized custodians of a starship. I know that I can count on all of you to act accordingly. That is all."

In the pilot's chair, First Officer, Locke Martin snorted. "Sure you can."

Sheeba raised her head and glanced around her lair. Sunlight filtering through the small opening at the top of the dome reflected off the pool, casting flashes of brightness that flitted over the walls like illuminated butterflies. She listened, waiting for the sound that had disturbed her to be repeated. The quiet lapping of tiny wavelets against the base of her ledge reassured her and she settled again to wait for Solomon.

Her eyes opened and she huffed softly, rising to her feet. Some disturbance, some presence she could not identify had invaded her space. She opened her great maw and hissed, then snapped her jaws shut and sniffed. Only the familiar scents of her cave drifted on the moist air. She stood, motionless, all of her senses tuned to receive the faintest stimulus.

Nothing.

Slowly, she lowered her massive body and closed her eyes. Then she heard it. A steady hum like one of the man-creatures' machines. Very close. Very quiet. When she opened her eyes, a pale, blue-white glow filled the cave, seeping into rock crevices and blinking off the ripples in the pool.

Again, Sheeba stood. She raised her head and stared at the orifice in the dome, certain that the light and sound came from the sky. The steady tone increased in volume and the light brightened until its source was suddenly obvious. It came not from without, but from within. Both sound and light emanated from the mound of nodules beside her.

One nodule, slightly larger than the others, pulsated, casting a blue glow into the deep shadows of the cave. It lay on the backside of the pile, quietly humming. Sheeba watched as the intensity of the light increased.

Some ancient chemistry in her blood stirred. She nudged the nodule with her snout, sensing the rightness of the mystery. She felt no fear or even distress. All was unfolding properly. The light brightened until the cave revealed its most hidden recesses.

As the humming increased in volume, Sheeba gently closed her powerful jaws around the orb and lifted it from the pile. She set it down on the ledge before her and took up her vigil.

The humming stopped. The nodule continued to give off intense blue-white light. As she watched a small hairline fissure appeared and a white flash shot from it like a searchlight. The beam of light intensified until she could no longer look directly at it.

Sheeba stepped back, still not alarmed but nervous. Yet, somehow she felt all was as it should be. As she watched, the fissure expanded. A tiny snout poked out of the crack, closely followed by the rest of a reptilian head. The nodule split in two in a brilliant flash of white energy and an infant gator tumbled onto the ledge. The light faded.

He lay for a moment gasping and gathering strength. The huge round eyes in his nodding head focused on her and he uttered a tiny squeak. Slowly, he struggled to his feet and immediately headed for the water. Sheeba started forward, but the infant had already jumped from the ledge into the pool.

He swam easily, bobbing on the wavelets. In the center of the pool, he snapped at a minnow and missed. His second attempt succeeded. Swallowing the fish whole, he turned for home.

Sheeba approached the remaining pile of nodules. Obeying instincts thousands of years old, she employed her great tail to sweep the entire mass into the water. They had fulfilled their purpose.

The infant gator scrabbled up the rocky base of the ledge and used his six tiny legs to pull himself onto the shelf. He staggered over to Sheeba, curled up in the crook of her fore-leg, and fell instantly asleep. Sheeba was at peace. Solomon had a son.

The late afternoon sun cast long shadows on the water as Solomon approached his lair. He raised his head and inhaled deeply, savoring the damp, earthy breeze. The tingling at the base of his skull had never failed him. Something had changed. He swam in a circle above the underwater entrance to his cave not wanting to alert an intruder to its location.

A presence, not necessarily threatening, but foreign, hovered nearby. Solomon circled the island with its massive gnarled tree that covered his lair and inspected the hidden rear passage. All appeared normal. Still uneasy, he returned to the main tunnel, dove and surfaced in the pool in the middle of the cave.

Sheeba lay on the ledge cradling a small object against her jaw. As he approached she glanced up, then nodded to a place beside her. Solomon scrabbled up the rock face and stood staring at the tiny creature nestled against his mate. The infant stirred, opened his eyes, and studied him.

A strange sense of peace settled over Solomon. He had anticipated this moment for many years. Now that the infant had arrived, he found he was not even surprised. Unbidden, the ancient words echoed in his mind.

Behold the one who comes unto you for he shall speak peace. Truth shall be in his eye and unbounded courage in his heart. You shall call his name Lucent for he is born of the light. For he is like a refiner's fire and he shall purify. His days shall be many and his wisdom great. You shall raise him in the old ways and tell no one.

Long have the stars burned in their heaven. Long have the moons shone on the water. Long have my people waited. Woe to one who would harm the infant.

He felt the warm pressure of Sheeba's mind.

Solomon, this is your son.

He nudged her with his head.

Mine and the ages. We shall call him Lucent.

She nodded. Solomon rested his jaw on the stone ledge with his snout nearly touching his son. Lucent stirred, yawned then toddled forward to inspect the obstacle. Solomon watched as Lucent, without making a sound, climbed the shallow valley between his nostrils, plodded up the long ridge of his snout and crawled up the steep cliff between his eyes to the top of Solomon's head. He felt the infant stand for a moment scanning the interior of the cave, then apparently satisfied, turn around twice, curl into a scaly ball, belch and fall promptly asleep.

Sheeba rested her head on Solomon's forearm.

Your son is adventurous.

My son needs training.

He scowled at Sheeba, but there was no reproach in it.

When the moons had set and the night birds called above the swamp, Sheeba gently plucked the sleeping infant from Solomon's head with her mouth and tucked him under her foreleg. Solomon stretched, then rose and slipped into the pool. Once outside, he marveled at the rare, clear air, then lay with his head resting on a floating log and watched the stars deep into the night.

🐊 🐊 🐊

Tiny lights blinked sporadically beside each touch sensitive pad. Six tiers of the two-centimeter circles ringed the interior of the clear, neural control cylinder that stood at the center of the bridge.

Captain Wyman swung aside the hinged section at the rear and stepped into the enclosure. It whispered closed behind her. She studied the displays before laying her hands on the third bank of circles. She rested each of her fingertips on one of the pads that provided a direct neural connection to some vital aspect of the huge craft. She could easily have delegated the task but she loved the sense of intimacy with the ship.

Closing her eyes to concentrate better, she felt the slight roughness in a water pump in hydroponics. She gently depressed her left ring finger and felt the vibration fade. She used her right little finger to lower the temperature in the larder three degrees.

Turning slowly, Suzanne let her hands drift across each of the six manuals, touching all four hundred and thirty-two circles, sensing anomalies and making changes where necessary.

Satisfied that the ship was tuned, Captain Wyman opened her eyes and leaned against the console, breathing rapidly. She willed her pulse to slow and tried to shake off the giddiness that always accompanied a neural session. When her heart rate returned to normal, she stepped out of the enclosure and took a slow turn around the bridge, pausing briefly at each station. Her last stop was navigation. "Have we established orbit, Carey?"

"Yes, Sir. Stable at five hundred above the planet."

"Very well."

She glanced at her second in command. "Lt. Martin, you have the helm. I'll be in my cabin."

"Aye, Captain, I have the helm."

As Suzanne approached her quarters she veered off into the passageway that led to the admiral's cabin. She paused before the portal and glanced back down the dimly lit causeway. A faint shadow flitted across the light. She froze, waiting for the intruder to reveal himself. A cleaning robot scurried into the pool of illumination, paused, turned left and retreated up the passage to the bridge. Suzanne released her breath and turned back to the doorway.

Normally vacant, unless the flag officer was aboard, the Admiral's cabin was occupied. Only Captain Wyman and three of her senior staff knew they had a guest, and only

Suzanne knew his identity. Confined to his cabin by his own demands for secrecy, the occupant had recently surfaced from one of several long periods of suspended animation. He'd spent the balance of the trip reading and watching vids, and had insisted on preparing his own meals in the small, attached galley.

Suzanne rested her hand on the entry panel and a soft chime sounded. When her palm print had been verified, the door was released from inside and irised silently open.

"Come in, Captain. I was about to pour tea. May I offer you a cup?"

She turned to see that the door had closed, then looked at the tall, silver-haired man before her. "Thank you, Your Honor, I could use it."

She settled onto the couch and watched him pour the tea. He carried two of the Admiral's China cups over from the galley.

"I came to tell you we're in orbit around Rozner's World."

"Excellent. Thank you for your generous hospitality."

Suzanne smiled. "We can transport you to the surface at your convenience."

"Good. I'm anxious to begin my inquiry."

Suzanne sipped her tea being careful not to burn her mouth on the hot liquid. "May I ask you a question, Sir?"

"You just did."

She glanced up at the kindly face. There was laughter in the eyes. "Why would the Chief Justice of the World Court alter his itinerary for a dispute over corporate ownership, and why the secrecy?"

"I believe that's two questions, Captain."

Suzanne chuckled. "So it is."

"I'm afraid I can't answer either. Let's just say I'm on sabbatical."

Suzanne swirled the remaining tea in her cup, watching the patterns created by the steam rising from the surface.

"I am the captain of this vessel."

"So you are. Does your inquiry stem from an officer's need to know, or simple curiosity?"

She glanced up, prepared to take offense, but the old man's eyes sparkled. "A little of both; but more of the latter. Anyone who commands a ship utilizing the Rozner Drive has to be concerned by recent events on the planet below us."

"As are we. The death of Dr. Rozner greatly complicates matters."

"I assume you're acting in your capacity as Chief Justice of the World Court."

He nodded.

Suzanne studied him for a moment. "Does the World Court have jurisdiction on Rozner's World?"

He inclined his head. "Ah, my dear, you have just put your finger precisely on the kernel of the problem. Do we, indeed?"

"What is your opinion?"

The judge set down his cup and steepled his fingers. "Rozner was originally a citizen of Earth. I know of no instance in which he renounced that citizenship. Yet he spent most of his life on the planet below us. I prefer to think of him as having been on a long business trip."

Suzanne crossed the room to the galley and retrieved the teapot. After filling the judge's cup she topped off her own. "Isn't Rozner a private company?"

The Judge sighed. "That's the problem. The Rozner Corporation is not just any company. As you know, virtually all space travel is dependent on the drives produced here. It is vitally important that nothing be allowed to interrupt the output of this facility. I wanted to arrive unannounced so that I might see the situation as it actually is, not after it's been whitewashed for my perusal. It's just too important."

"I agree but aren't we edging perilously close to the old discredited anti-trust laws? I thought all of that was settled shortly after the turn of the millennium."

"Perhaps, but we are not considering breaking up the company. Quite the contrary; we're trying to preserve it."

Suzanne studied his face. The eyes were devoid of any duplicity. "Why send you?"

"The court felt we should bring the full weight of the justice system to bear on the problem. I had the most gray hair."

Suzanne thought for a brief moment. "Does it make any difference what country Rozner was born in? Aren't national borders pretty much passé?"

"You're correct. The old concept of nation-states as legal entities died in the twenty-first century. Not, as some had predicted, by war, but by simply becoming irrelevant. Commercial sanctions are far more effective than bombs, and not nearly so messy."

"But there are still countries? I mean, we still identify areas by the original names."

The judge took a long sip of his tea before answering. "Oh, we still use the old labels, but really it's just a method for seeing that all areas are represented."

Suzanne set down her cup on the side table and rose. "But you're not going to tell me what you plan to do on Rozner's World, other than observe?"

"No, Captain. I'm not."

"Very well. Let me know when you wish to be ferried to the surface."

He stood and walked her to the door. As she reached the portal he placed a hand on her shoulder. "It was a valiant attempt, Captain. You'd make a great prosecuting attorney."

She studied his face, catching the twinkle in his eyes; wisdom and humor, what a grand combination.

The bright lights of Salvation glowed through the fog casting colored blossoms into the rain-soaked night. Periodic shouts of laughter penetrated the twelve-tone music reverberating around the interior of the huge recreational facility. It assaulted Aaron's ears.

He sat at a small table near the bar, huddled over a Bull Gator beer, recovering from a long day of patrolling. His soiled uniform stuck to his sweaty body and the old gator bite scar on his left thigh throbbed. As soon as he gathered sufficient strength, he intended to stagger across the compound to his quarters for a long, hot shower, then fall into bed.

Laz had abandoned him an hour ago to dress for a date with Shelly LaCoste. Aaron could not recall any specific woman in Laz's past; at least not one he had seemed to care deeply about. Laz just gathered women like some people collect mushrooms. Shelly seemed different.

A great shout from the other side of the room announced that the team from Cygnus II had scored again. The Galaxy Cup still had its followers.

At the bar, Jergan Angst was holding court, undoubtedly spreading his conspiracy theories about whatever issue currently occupied his attention. Aaron took a long drag on his beer. In light of recent events, maybe Jergan wasn't so far off the mark.

Aaron glanced at the lift that soared to Heaven and regretted that his credit balance precluded that pleasure.

He drained the last of his brew and pushed back his chair. As he reached for his tab, a hand descended and plucked it from the table. Aaron looked up into the eyes of a distinguished, gray-haired stranger.

"I'll take care of this, Lieutenant Trout."

Aaron studied the man, taking in the expensive Earth-style clothing and air of total confidence.

"Well, thank you. Have we met?"

"Not yet."

"How do you know my name?"

The elderly gentleman laughed; a warm genuine rumble that originated deep in his chest. "I know a great deal about you, Lieutenant. We have a mutual friend."

Aaron sat back down and gestured for his guest to do the same. "Who might that be?"

The gentleman smiled. "We'll get to that if we have time. Am I keeping you from something?"

"Only a hot shower and a cold bed."

"Have you had dinner?"

Aaron nudged the empty stein.

The old gentleman studied him for a moment, taking note of the soiled uniform and slumping shoulders. "If you have the strength to enjoy it, I would be delighted to buy you dinner. I understand the food here is excellent."

Aaron ran his hand through his soiled hair. "Who are you?"

The smile broadened. "Let's just say I'm an emissary."

"You mean, like an ambassador?"

"In a sense."

Aaron pushed his stein around in the damp puddle it had left on the table. "Well, Mr. Emissary, I never turn down a free meal and you've spiked my curiosity. I still don't know your name."

"Just call me John."

"Well, John, you have my full attention, or rather you will have after we order. I'm suddenly ravenous."

"Good, good. We'll have a hearty meal. We're going to need to be well fortified for our adventure."

Aaron handed the stein to the waitress who had appeared at his elbow. "Our adventure?"

John chuckled. "Oh, didn't I mention that? Well, never mind, we'll have plenty of time to discuss it over dinner."

After they had ordered, John pulled an ancient piece of parchment from his coat pocket. He gently unfolded it along well-creased lines and spread it out on the table, being careful to avoid any wet places. The edges of the parchment were rough and the printing faded. Symbols in red and green dyes highlighted certain features.

"Do you recognize this, Aaron? May I call you Aaron?"

"Aaron's fine. It looks like an old map."

"Very good. Actually it's a molecular reproduction of an old parchment. Do you recognize it?"

Aaron studied the lines and symbols that marched across the document in an apparently random pattern; something hauntingly familiar. Something he recognized on a gut level. He pointed at the map, tracing the lines across the surface.

"It's the trail network, but it's not quite right."

"Excellent, my friend. It is indeed, a map of the network on this planet, but this document is over three-hundred years old."

Aaron felt the air escape from his lungs. "But Rozner's mining operation has only been here about fifty years. Who built the trails?"

"Who, indeed?"

Aaron sat staring at the map, searching out familiar landmarks. Some of the features identified as bridges and spurs no longer existed. "Where did you get this?"

"I've had it for many years."

"That doesn't answer the question."

"No, it doesn't."

Aaron studied the man's face. "What do you want of me?"

Before John could answer, their meal arrived. He folded the parchment and tucked it into his coat pocket. Aaron ordered another beer. John requested coffee. The fish was steeped in wine and herbs, then lightly browned, a real treat.

John closed his eyes for a moment, savoring the delicacy. "Is this local?"

"It's taken from the open waters on the other side of the planet. I'm afraid it's normally beyond the budget of a patrol officer. Thank you."

"My pleasure."

Aaron finished his fish and drained the last of his beer. "You still haven't answered my question."

"You mean, what do I require of you?"

"Yes."

John reached into his coat and extracted the parchment. He folded it to reveal the quadrant nearest Salvation, and handed it to Aaron. "Do you know this sector?"

Aaron glanced at the map. "I know it well."

"I want you to take me there."

"When?"

"As soon as we finish here."

Aaron set down the stein. "Tonight? Do you know how dark it is out there? You won't be able to see a thing. Can't it wait until morning?"

"No, it can't. First, this is a matter of some urgency. Second, you're on duty tomorrow. And most importantly, we're meeting someone."

"Who?"

"An old friend."

"In the swamp?"

John drained the last of his coffee and set the cup carefully in the saucer. "He lives there."

Aaron sat back. "You're talking about Solomon."

John just smiled.

The waitress approached the table and began clearing the dishes. "Will there be anything else for you gentlemen?"

John glanced at Aaron. "No, thank you. We need to leave."

He waved his hand over the sensor a few times. "I believe this will cover it."

She stared at the credits. "Oh, yes, Sir. That will certainly do. Thank you."

John started to rise. Aaron reached out and lay a restraining hand on his arm.

"Look, John. I appreciate this wonderful dinner, but I've been on duty all day. I'm dirty, I'm tired and I have no interest in going back into the swamp tonight. Frankly, I have no idea who you are, or what you want, and I don't even care who you intend to meet, Solomon or anybody else, but I'll be happy to discuss it in the morning. Right now, I'm going to my quarters for a hot shower and some sleep. And before you start, there really isn't anything you could say that would change my mind."

Without a backward glance, Aaron rose and headed for the weather lock. He'd taken three steps when John spoke.

"It could be worth some serious time in Heaven."

Aaron froze. He didn't intend to, his feet just stopped. He turned and stared at John. "How serious?"

"Oh, let's say sufficient credits in their computers for a hundred hours."

"Do I have time to go to the head before we leave?"

John laughed. "I think we can delay that long."

When they had suited up, Aaron crossed the compound to his quarters and retrieved a plasma light, not large, but very powerful. As they passed through the gateway to the trail network, John pointed to the sign Laz had hung last year after a full night of carousing at Salvation. "Abandon hope, all ye who enter here."

John chuckled. "I always liked Milton."

"Yeah, Laz reads too much."

They proceeded cautiously through the fog-shrouded night, Aaron leading. He kept the light focused on the path, occasionally shining it behind him to make certain that John was still tracking. Once they passed the outer marker, the trail lights were sufficient and he extinguished his hand-held device. Plaintive calls of night birds drifted on the heavy air and gator bellows punctuated their chorus.

At one point, Aaron thought he recognized the voice of one of the huge reptiles then dismissed the thought.

The bridge materialized out of the fog. John stopped and appeared to listen, then turned to Aaron. "I believe my friend will meet us at the bridge."

As they approached the structure, John took the lead. He proceeded to the center of the span, then leaned over the railing. "Good evening, Solomon."

The ancient gator lay in the water below.

Greetings, old friend. J was not certain that you would come. Thank you for bringing him, Aaron Trout.

Aaron struggled to find his voice. "My God. You really do know this gator."

John turned and smiled, his eyes twinkling in the glow of the bridge lights. "Solomon and I are old friends."

Aaron grabbed John by the shoulders and spun him around. "Who are you?"

Alice banked around the top of the tallest cypress tree and descended to a few meters above the swamp. Shafts of sunlight penetrated the fog, illuminating dark pools of stagnant water and floating vegetation. In Alice's comfortable cabin, Jillian sat watching the brightly colored birds flit through the mist.

"Jillian."

"Yes, Alice."

"Where are we going?"

"Nowhere. Just cruise around and let me think, but stay in the safe corridors."

"I have the proper charts loaded, Jillian."

They passed over a huge gator who raised his head and bellowed at the intruder. A smaller version of the creature cruised in his wake. Jillian wondered if the larger was Solomon as she resettled herself in the pilot's couch and wrapped her favorite comforter around her legs.

"I sense tension, Jillian. Are you troubled?"

"I'm calculating how to get the corporation back."

"Didn't you say the lawyer was coming?"

"Yes, but we can't wait that long. I have set other plans in motion and have discovered a surprising number of allies."

"You mean like Winton Lazarus and Shelly LaCoste?"

"Among others. I hear many of the miners are demanding new leadership."

They were silent for some time. Alice banked around trees and old stumps, following a flock of brightly-colored birds in their erratic flight.

"Alice."

"Yes, Jillian."

"You wouldn't be teasing your feathered friends, would you?"

"Me? I'm simply studying their flight patterns."

"Right."

Alice continued to soar over the treetops, but Jillian noticed that she stayed a respectable distance from the birds.

"Could your friend from the Trail Patrol help?"

"Aaron?"

"Yes, he seems quite capable."

"I thought you found him irritating."

"He grows on you."

Jillian sighed. "Yes, he does."

Alice swooped down toward the water, startling a flock of large sea birds. They exploded into the air, squawking indignation.

"Maybe the lawyer could tell you what to do with Aaron."

"I don't think so, Alice."

She was about to instruct Alice to overfly the site of the recent mine disaster, when the com link chimed. Jillian activated the unit with a casual wave of her hand. "Jillian Rozner".

"Dr. Rozner, this is Lewis."

It took her a moment to place the concierge from her building. A faint wave of irritation at being disturbed passed through her. "Yes, Lewis. What can I do for you?"

"You have a guest, a very distinguished gentleman. He did not wish to leave his name. I told him that I didn't know when you would return. He asked me to try to contact you and said he would wait in the lobby."

"Did he say what he wanted?"

"No. He simply said he would wait."

Jillian glanced down at the grid on the dash and saw that they were about twenty minutes out. "Tell him that I'll be there in half an hour."

She felt the aircar bank and knew Alice had anticipated her command and was already heading for home. As they swept over a particularly dense portion of the swamp, she saw a twisted mass of metal flash beneath them.

"Did you register that, Alice?"

"Yes, Jillian. I believe it was the wreckage of a shuttle vehicle."

"Can you tell if anyone is still in it? We should report the coordinates to Trail Patrol."

"There are no signs of life forms and I have already done so."

Jillian chuckled. "I should have known you'd be ahead of me, Alice."

Alice was silent for a moment.

"How can I be ahead of you if you are in my cabin? That would seem to be a physical impossibility. Dade's third law clearly states that objects proximal in space cannot...."

"It was a figure of speech, Alice."

"Oh, is it one of those things you say that doesn't make any sense?"

Jillian felt a small glow of affection for her logical companion. "Yes, Alice."

As they approached the complex, the garage door irised open and Alice slid gracefully into her home. Jillian could almost hear her sigh as the various systems shut down.

With Alice neatly tucked away in her garage, Jillian entered her apartment to freshen up before meeting her guest. The red light flashed on the communication center.

"Message, please."

"Dr. Rozner, this is Lawrence Stern. I was your grandfather's lead attorney. I understand that you were trying to contact me. My research will be delivered to you on Rozner's World by a trusted messenger sometime this week."

Jillian let out the breath she didn't realize she had been holding. The distinguished gentleman downstairs must be the courier with Stern's package.

"Now, we're getting somewhere."

Jillian grabbed a quick shower, ran a brush through her hair and donned a clean jump suit.

"Wilson?"

"Yes, Jillian."

"I'm going out for a while. Security on."

"Yes, Jillian."

As she entered the lobby of the apartment building, her visitor rose from the chair with surprising grace for a man of his age. Hair tousled from the dryer at the entrance, he still presented an imposing figure. His eyes sparkled with good humor. Silver hair crowned a large head atop his tall, well-proportioned frame.

"Good afternoon, Dr. Rozner. I'm John Marshall, Chief Justice of the World Court. I apologize for barging in on you like this, but we must talk."

Jillian took a moment to gather herself. "I was expecting a delivery."

"I'm afraid it won't be coming."

Jillian stared at him. "How do you know that?"

John glanced around the lobby. "Is there somewhere we can talk?"

"There's a small conference room through that door."

"Is it secure?"

"I'm sure it is. That room was designed for meetings with doctors and clergy. We could go up to my apartment if you wish."

"No. The conference room will do."

Jillian studied her guest. Her first impression of him was trustworthy, almost noble. She especially liked the laugh lines around his penetrating, gray eyes.

She nodded, coming to a decision "Excellent. Shall we?"

When they were comfortably seated at the round table that nearly filled the room, Jillian inclined her head toward the serving unit. "Can I offer you anything?"

"No, I'm fine."

She watched him fold his hands and heard a shallow sigh. A cold knot of foreboding formed in her chest. "I've never met Mr. Stern. He was Grandfather's lawyer, but I always assumed he was dependable. Why is his delivery not here?"

"Because he's dead."

The knot tightened. "But the message on my com center."

"That message was prepared some time ago for transmission last night. He said he didn't know when he would be able to get to a unit."

"How do you know all this?"

"Larry was my partner in the old firm before I ascended to the bench. He was also a superb attorney and one of my dearest friends. I'm proud to say your grandfather fell into that latter category, as well."

Jillian felt a brief touch of sadness. If Stern was a good friend of Grandfather's, she wished she had known him. She sat back in her chair. "How did he die?"

John raised his eyes and looked directly at her. "He fell from the roof of his building."

Jillian looked directly into Justice Marshall's eyes. "What was he doing on the roof?"

John dropped his gaze and stared down at his folded hands. "Excellent question."

She sat for a moment trying to take it all in. She felt somehow vaguely responsible even though she knew that was irrational. "What do the police say?"

"They've declared it an accident."

"And you don't buy that."

"Larry had no reason to be on the roof. He suffered from acrophobia. He'd never go up there."

A brightly-colored bird landed on the windowsill, cocked his head, tapped once on the glass and flew away. Jillian watched it disappear into the fog wishing she could take flight with it. This was all becoming more than she could handle.

She looked around the small room, taking in the lighted wall panels displaying scenes from Earth and the swamps of Rozner's World then refocused on Marshall. "Where does that leave me?"

John glanced at the refreshment center. "Maybe I will take you up on a cup of tea."

Jillian rose and walked to the wall unit. When the tea was ready, she set it in front of the judge. "Do you take anything in it?"

"No. This is fine, thank you."

Jillian sat in a conference chair and waited for him to speak. He watched the steam rise from the cup, then glanced up. "Dr. Rozner, I'm here in two capacities. First as an emissary of the World Court, and secondly, to offer my services to you in Larry's stead. The latter, while highly unusual, is not unethical. On rare occasions, I act in an advisory capacity. I'm still a member of the bar, and I can always recuse myself from the bench if necessary. Of course, if we ever actually went to trial, I'd have to bring in someone else. If you prefer another lawyer, I can help with the arrangements."

Jillian looked into his gray eyes and saw determination. "I would be honored to have you represent me. I assume you're talking about control of the Rozner Corporation."

"That and any other matter. Helen Anderson contacted me twice while I was aboard the *Windflower Vagabond*. The board of directors is having serious second thoughts about Pierce's appointment."

Jillian watched him sip his tea then set the cup down very gently. "Why would you do this?"

"Because there is no more important issue than control of this process."

They were silent for a moment while she considered this, then she returned to the refreshment unit and requested a hot herbal drink. "How can you help me retake Grandfather's company?"

"To be honest, I don't know, but we can't leave that madman in control of the source of power for virtually all star ships. Your grandfather served as a magnificent custodian of the resource he helped create. His appointment of you as successor was enlightened. I've looked into your background, Jillian. Your intelligence, education and temperament make you a worthy recipient of the trust."

Jillian felt the heat rise in her face. "I'm not certain I like being investigated."

Marshall settled back in his chair and stared up at the ceiling. When he looked at her again, his eyes were full of compassion. "There was nothing malevolent about it, Jillian. We had to know about his successor. Pierce is extremely dangerous. I've known him for years. There are also other considerations."

"Such as."

"The gators."

Jillian choked on her tea. "The gators? You know about the gators?"

"Solomon and I are old friends."

She fell back in her chair. "Am I the only one who doesn't know about those reptiles?"

The judge chuckled. "Very few people do. Until Solomon spoke to the Trail Patrolman . . . ."

"You mean, Aaron."

"Yes, Aaron Trout and then to you, I thought your grandfather and I had an exclusive."

Jillian stared into her teacup, watching the steam swirl across the surface of the hot liquid. This was all getting too confusing. "How do you know Solomon spoke to Aaron, or to me for that matter?"

"He told me."

Jillian gawked at the judge. "You mean you've been to see him since you arrived?"

"Actually, I have, but he contacted me at home and aboard the *Windflower Vagabond* and apprised me of the situation. That's why I'm here."

Jillian leaned back in her chair. "Are you telling me that Solomon can reach out across millions of kilometers of space and commune with you whenever he pleases?"

"Easily. He doesn't do it often, thank God, but he knows how to reach me if he wishes."

She set down her cup and closed her eyes. "This is too bizarre."

Marshall sat quietly for a moment then put down his tea, rose and began to pace. "Maybe all of this will make more sense if I give you a little history. Let me tell you a story."

"Many years ago, a brilliant young scientist needed capital to fund an independent line of research. He was convinced that he had conceived a process that would make man's dream of interstellar travel a reality. He was married to a lovely woman, a doctor, and had two small children - a boy and a girl. One autumn evening, he sent his wife out in their aircar to secure supplies for his project. He'd never done that before. Furthermore, he insisted that she take the children. Now, it's important to know that he'd spent most of the morning working on that aircar . . . something he never did.

Two thousand meters over the city, the radial converter failed. All three were killed."

Jillian stirred. Something about radial converter failure. Alice. Alice's radial converter had failed the day she crashed in the swamp. The judge was speaking again. She refocused.

"Pierce showed up at the funerals and played the role of the distraught mourner and in a strange way, I think he was. He did collect a huge life insurance policy on all three, triple indemnity."

Jillian sat in stunned silence, then found her voice. "Didn't the police investigate?"

"Of course. I'm certain they suspected foul play, but they couldn't prove anything. The insurance company finally paid off."

She watched him closely, seeing the flicker of anger flash in his eyes. "How do you know all this?"

He stopped and stared directly at her. "I was the prosecuting attorney at the time. We all knew what he'd done. We simply couldn't prove it." He chuckled softly. "So you see, Jillian, my motives for being here are not entirely altruistic."

"Why are you telling me this?"

He placed his hands on the arms of her chair and glared at her. "Because you must understand. This is a very dangerous man. He will bastardize your grandfather's dream. He is ruthless, avaricious and he feels he has been wronged. That is a very explosive combination. We're afraid that if he acquires the secret he will sell it to the highest bidder or worse yet, destroy it. Either would be disastrous."

"What do you mean?"

"Rozner Corp. has a total monopoly on space drives. The best we can hope for is a benevolent dictator to run the company. Your grandfather filled the role perfectly, but as with all such arrangements, the problem is succession."

Jillian considered this. "Why didn't the government simply nationalize it?"

"Which government? He was on a distant planet. That's why he spent much of his life preparing you to take over. Pierce will rape the corporation."

She stared at him, then glanced down at her tea. "I take your point."

He reached for his own cup. "I'm not entirely certain you do. At least not fully. There are many powerful interests whose very existence depends on ships driven by the Constant. If they feel threatened...."

Jillian felt a cold chill settle over her entire body. "What are you implying?"

"Interstellar war."

Cold water seeped through the neck seal of his rain gear and ran down his back. Aaron hunched his shoulders, attempting to refasten the collar. He stood with Laz in the downpour on the beginnings of the temporary bridge to Bore 19, watching the workman bring up the last of the bodies from the mine. He was dismayed at how long it had taken to recover the deceased. Several small collapses had delayed the efforts to reach the rescue chambers for almost two weeks. There had been little hope even before it was discovered the doors hadn't closed in time.

He turned to his partner and studied Laz's face. He'd only seen him in such pain once before. The death of his mother had devastated Laz. He'd been left nearly senseless by the news of the accident on Earth. Aaron had rushed over to Laz's home and found him wandering along the lake totally unaware of his surroundings. This was nearly as bad.

He reached out and grasped Laz's arm. "You knew someone in the mine accident, didn't you, Laz? Someone's name they just released. That's why you insisted on coming out here."

"This was no accident."

Aaron draped his arm around his friend. "How do you know, Laz?"

"I just know."

They stood silently watching the rescue team for several minutes. Aaron waited for Laz to organize his thoughts at his own pace. He'd speak when he was ready.

Mud-caked bodies were being gingerly lifted onto litters and placed aboard aircars. Additional vehicles circled in the rain overhead, waiting for clearance to set down on the narrow strip of dry land.

"My brother is down there."

Aaron froze. "Will?"

"Yes."

Aaron gripped Laz's shoulder.. "You never told me Will was on Rozner's World."

"I didn't know he was here until I saw the roster of the dead they just released. I don't think he wanted anyone to know where he was. He said he wanted a totally fresh start after the accident. Will still thinks it was his fault."

"I thought the tribunal cleared him."

"They did, but he still thinks he should have been able to save her."

"Jesus, Laz, you saw the vid. No one could have gotten through those flames."

Laz stared straight ahead. Tears ran down his cheeks and mingled with the rain.

"I think he always felt he should have tried."

Aaron felt his friend's pain burn into his own gut. Laz had always taken responsibility for his younger brother even though Will's recklessness had often placed them both in danger.

"Are you sure he's still down there? Maybe he lost his ID-card and came up earlier with the other survivors."

Laz shook his head. "All I can do now is watch for his body to be brought up."

"The last I heard, they still hadn't reached the escape chambers. He could still be alive."

Laz turned to his friend, a faint spark of hope kindling in his eyes. "He could, couldn't he?"

"Will's a tough kid, Laz." Aaron felt a small pang of guilt for offering what might be false hope.

Nearly exhausted rescue teams ascended from the shaft, bearing stretcher after stretcher. They rolled the dead gently onto the landing pad to be airlifted back to Sanctuary. Most of the victims were unrecognizable.

Some were missing arms or legs. Laz watched intently as each casualty was deposited.

The drumbeat of rain increased to a steady roar, drowning out the voices of the rescuers. Aaron started to reach for his friend, to guide him away from the carnage, when Laz stiffened. A shock of brilliant red hair escaped from under the watch cap of the most recently recovered corpse. Laz sank to his knees and huddled there, rocking slowly back and forth.

Aaron rested his hand on his friend's shoulder and tried to think of something comforting to say. Nothing came.

A great gator bellow shattered the drumbeat of the pounding rain, then dissipated, leaving only the hiss of raindrops on saturated leaves and swamp water.

Winton Lazarus lay on his back staring through the transparent ceiling dome into the dense fog. Half-seen branches swayed in the gentle breeze that was slowly clearing the waterlogged atmosphere as sunrise heated the upper layers. Laz had been awake for the past hour, remembering his brother and worrying about Aaron. The double burden was almost more than he could bear.

When it finally came, confirmation of Will's death at Bore 19 had been redundant. He had known the minute he had seen the red hair protruding from beneath the navy-blue watch cap. Now, unbidden tears flooded Laz's eyes and ran down his cheeks. Shelly stirred beside him, mumbled something and lay quietly again. He had come here to bury his pain in the willing body of this beautiful girl. For awhile, he had succeeded. She had welcomed him to her bed and given herself freely. Laz felt a twinge of guilt remembering how roughly he had used her.

While she had fallen almost instantly asleep, he had turned onto his side and stared at the wall. Finally, he wept, careful to smother his sobs in his pillow to avoid waking her.

She had reached out and touched his back. He turned to her and she took him in her arms and held him until his body no longer shook.

With daylight beginning to flood the room, Shelly stirred and raised up on one elbow, searching his face.

He wiped away his tears in a gesture he hoped appeared to be clearing sleep from his eyes. "Good morning, Shelly."

"Morning, Laz. Are you feeling any better?"

"Yes, but...." He couldn't think of whether to thank her or apologize for last night.

She pressed a finger to his lips and then moved it to kiss him lightly. "If you would be so kind as to request coffee and scones from the wall unit, I shall try to drag my tender body to the shower. You may join me there if you wish, but no fooling around. I have to be at Shuttle Repair in an hour."

Laz gave her his best indignant glance. "Would I do such a thing?"

She laughed. "Every chance you get and I know it."

He rolled out of bed, strolled to the terminal and requested black coffee and scones for two, then as an afterthought, added fresh orange juice. He carried the tray into the bath and was rewarded by the vision of Shelly under the shower that sprayed from three walls of the bathing enclosure. With her eyes closed, she scrubbed her short, blonde hair into a frothy lather that formed a halo of bubbles around her relaxed face. She really was a beautiful woman. The nearly perfect proportions of her diminutive body left him staring. She opened her eyes and smiled, clearly aware of the effect she was having.

"Are you going to join me?"

"I'm not sure I wouldn't rather just watch."

"Well, you'd better watch from in here, we don't have a great deal of time."

Laz stepped into the enclosure and gasped as the cool water hit him. "Damn, do you always bathe in ice water?"

"Oh, it's not that cold. I thought you were a big, tough patrol officer."

"Not that tough."

Shelly chuckled. "Computer, up ten degrees."

Immediately the water temperature raised to normal levels. Laz relaxed and let the spray pound on his body. When he glanced at Shelly, she was studying him closely.

"What happened last night?"

Laz took a step backward. "I was thinking about my brother."

"Your brother?"

He took a short, sharp breath, then let it out slowly. "He was killed in the Bore 19 accident. They just found him."

She reached up and touched his cheek. "I heard the reports. So that's what all the desperation was about last night. Well, I'm glad I could be here for you."

Laz captured her hand, drew it from his face and held it tightly. "I want to apologize if I was too rough. I needed... well, I just needed."

"I know."

She reached down and took his other hand by the wrist and placed his palm on her breast. Tilting her head she kissed him until his body responded. He tried to speak, but she inserted her tongue between his lips and pressed her hips against him. He finally succeeded in freeing his mouth. "I thought you were in a hurry."

"Shhh."

She led him to the nearest wall, leaned her back against it and pulled him to her. He tried to protest, but she put her fingertips on his lips, then dropped her hand to his erect member and massaged him until he gasped and released.

They stood for a moment, simply holding each other, gathering strength from tenderness. Then she placed both hands on his chest and pushed him away. "Now we're both late for work."

"You're right. I'm supposed to meet Aaron at supply."

Laz washed quickly and left the enclosure. Shelly stepped into the spray for a final rinse.

"How is Aaron?"

Something in her tone caused him to glance up. "Fine. He's just been a little preoccupied lately."

"With the gators?"

"Well, the gators are part of it."

"Your partner's conversation with those reptiles is the hot topic. Did you tell him about our conversation at Salvation? I mean about how everyone thinks he's mad."

"Yes. What do you think?"

Shelly smiled warmly. "I think you better take good care of your friend."

She stepped out of the shower, which detected her absence and shut down. As she dried her hair, she ran her fingers through her short, blond locks. "Have they ever spoken to you?"

"No, and I'm not sure I want them to. Scared the hell out of Aaron, particularly the first time"

She dried her legs with long slow strokes. "What do they talk about?"

"He won't say."

Laz accepted a towel from the wall dispenser and dried his body. Shelly crossed to the unit and retrieved a handful of body lotion. Laz watched her smooth it onto her legs. She spoke without looking up.

"Jergan Angst says Aaron goes out on the trails at night, alone. He says that's a violation of regs."

"He would."

"Could Aaron get into trouble?"

"If someone reports him."

She grimaced. "Someone like Angst."

"Precisely."

Laz watched her dress. Who else would wear fine lingerie beneath her mechanic's coveralls? She looked so tiny, so frail, like a songbird covering bright plumage with a winter coat of drab feathers. He felt a sudden urge to protect her. If he wasn't careful, she could destroy his reputation as a callous playboy. He shook his head, he no longer cared.

Why had he come here, last night? If sex was all he needed, he could have gone to any number of women, but Shelly offered something far more valuable. She offered comfort.

As they left her apartment, she took his hand. "We're having a small retirement party for our chief mechanic, tonight. We'll meet at Salvation about six. Why don't you join us? See if Aaron would like to come. I think Trail Patrol should be represented."

"Is that an official invitation?"

She grinned up at him. "Actually, it's a thinly disguised ruse to maneuver you into taking me to dinner afterward."

"Won't that be a little awkward for Aaron?"

She was beaming. "Not if I can pull this off. I've invited a special guest."

"Who?"

"Dr. Jillian Rozner."

— 12 —

Lucent lay on the ledge and watched as Sheeba circled the pool in their cave. She dove and remained submerged for several seconds, then resurfaced in front of him. She huffed and backed away, inviting him to join her in the water. He jumped from the ledge splashing down in front of his mother. Sheeba dove again and Lucent followed her into the murky depths.

This time she did not resurface as in their customary game but continued down to the floor of the pool before leveling off and heading for the East end of the cave. Lucent followed her.

They swam through a narrow opening in the rock wall, then glided upward surfacing beyond the root structure of the massive tree that guarded the entrance. Lucent blinked at the bright light, looked up, and for the first time, saw open sky. Storm clouds scuttled across the sun breaking the swamp into patches of darkness and light.

Where are we, Mother?

Outside, my son. There is much for you to explore beyond our cave.

Is this where Solomon goes when he leaves us?

Yes.

Lucent looked around, taking in the trees, the hanging moss, the dark waterways leading off in all directions.

Is outside a very big place?

Yes, my son, outside is very large. You can see only a small part of it from here.

Let's go see the rest.

Sheeba huffed.

In time, Lucent. In time.

A bull gator bellowed in the distance. Lucent raised his head and listened.

Was that Solomon?

No.

He climbed up on the log and strained to see down one of the waterways.

I like it outside. Why do we stay beneath the rocks?

Our cave is a place of safety. All creatures need a cave.

Solomon speaks of the man-creatures. Do they have caves?

Yes, Lucent. They build them on dry land and come into our world on raised pathways. Sometimes they fly.

He thought about this for a moment.

You mean like the birds that come into our cave through the light hole?

They fly in machines they make themselves. A few fly to distant stars in very big machines. Our nodules make this possible.

How can this be?

Sheeba sighed.

You must ask Solomon. I cannot answer all your questions.

Lucent walked down the log to stare directly into his mother's eyes.

Solomon is very wise. He knows many things. I want to be like him when I am larger. You shall be, my son. You shall be.

Aaron closed the cover on the amber light and straightened up from the crouching position that had cramped his back. "Try it now, Laz."

The light winked on with the rest of the system, glowing like a miniature sun through the dense fog. "That's got it. Any more on the list?"

"Nope. Last one. Why do we always draw light repair?"

"Because we're good at it."

"Yeah, right."

Laz gathered up his tools, clipping each to his belt then glanced at his wrist. "We're officially off duty. Let's head in. You going to the retirement party tonight?"

"I thought I might drop in. You're sure Shelly invited me?"

Laz nodded. "I'm under strict orders to bring you, and I never refuse a command from a superior officer."

Aaron glanced up from the power cable he was coiling. "She does outrank us, doesn't she? Is that ever a problem for you?"

"Not when she's out of uniform."

Aaron shook his head. "I wouldn't touch that one with shielded gloves. This is getting serious, isn't it?"

"Ah, you know me. I'm never serious."

"Uh huh. Well, we better head in and get cleaned up. I wouldn't want to be late for an affair thrown by this woman you're not serious about."

"Good idea."

Showers, shaves and clean uniforms refreshed them both. As they cleared the weather lock and entered Salvation, the full force of the music hit Aaron. Twelve-tone jazz had been abandoned in favor of something he didn't recognize. They found their group in the semi-private portion of Salvation. Shelly had arranged to have the area walled off from the rest of the cavernous space with portable room dividers. She led a cadre of revelers grouped in rows, like a cadet review. They were all moving in synchronization through complex patterns of steps. Aaron could only stare. Shelly spotted them and waved.

When the music stopped, she hurried over. She was perspiring lightly and grinning. "Welcome noble officers of the Trail Patrol. Grab a brew and join the party."

Aaron managed to find his voice. "What was that?"

"Line dancing. It's part of the nostalgia craze. The crew of the *Windflower Vagabond* brought it from Earth. The tall lady in the back row is her captain, Suzanne Wyman. She's an amazing dancer."

"Where did you get that music?"

"They brought that too. Late twentieth century. Something called country."

Laz had been studying the dancers. " It looks difficult."

She grabbed his hand and pulled him toward the dance floor. " It's not, really. You just have to memorize a pattern. I'll walk you through the next one."

He pulled back. " I think I'd better just watch."

She smiled broadly and the light danced in her eyes. "Don't be silly. There's nothing to it."

"That's what they said about quantum light theory."

By the time the music started again, Shelly had Laz at the end of the first row, walking him through an intricate series of steps. He looked like he'd rather be facing an enraged gator.

Aaron had just summoned the courage to join them, when he felt a hand on his shoulder.

"Good evening, Lieutenant"

He knew before he turned. That rich voice resonated in his spine.

She wore a peach-colored dress that draped across her body in graceful folds. The opal pendant at her throat caught the light of the room and danced with fire.

He stared, then found his voice. "Good evening, Dr. Rozner."

She smiled. "Hadn't we graduated to Aaron and Jillian?"

"Yes, of course. I'd ask you to dance, but I have no idea what they're doing out there."

Her laughter sparkled above the din. "This was all the rage at the turn of the millennium. It was making a comeback when I left La Jolla."

Aaron spotted a table by the wall. "Please, sit down. Can I get you something to drink?"

"If they have any of the Chardonnay from Gallia, that would be nice."

As he made his way to the private bar Shelly had set up for the occasion, he tried to center himself. Of course, he was surprised to see Jillian here. She was obviously an invited guest, as was he. Aaron checked his appearance in the mirror behind the bar and smoothed his hair. His hand shook a bit as he picked up the wineglass. "This is silly."

"Is there a problem with the wine, Sir?"

"No, it's okay. The wine is fine. I was thinking about something else."

"Of course, Sir."

When he handed Jillian her Chardonnay, she smiled and lifted her glass. "To country music."

"And to line dancing."

They sat sipping their wine and watching the dancers. Jillian set down her wineglass and ran her fingers up and down the stem. Aaron watched her slender hand, enjoying the graceful arch of her wrist. She glanced up as if to speak then let her gaze drop again.

"What are you thinking, Jillian?"

She focused on him. "Aaron, has our mutual friend spoken to you, lately?"

He glanced at her and smiled. "Solomon?"

"Yes. I'm almost afraid to speak his name. I haven't been contacted since our night on the bridge. How about you?"

"Once."

"When?"

Aaron sipped his wine then set the glass down. "I'm not certain that I should say."

"Why not?"

"It involves another."

"John Marshall?"

Aaron glanced up in time to catch the fleeting smile that tweaked the corners of her mouth. "How did you know?"

"Just a wild guess."

"Some guess. He told you, didn't he?"

Her smile brightened. "Only that he and Solomon were old friends. I deduced the rest."

Aaron shifted in his chair. "Remind me not to try to keep any secrets from you."

"Good plan. What did they talk about?"

"Not much. I think they were just getting reacquainted."

Jillian studied the dancers. Aaron watched her, enjoying the rapt attention she paid to the step patterns. Maybe he could try it. Better have another glass of wine first. This didn't look like something you could do stone sober.

He rose from his chair and turned toward the bar. Jergan Angst stepped in his way, swaying drunkenly. He'd crashed the party along with a few of the bolder Trail Patrol officers and spent some serious time imbibing.

"Talked to any gators lately, Trout? I hear the little lady's hallucinating, too."

Aaron pushed down the wave of anger that boiled up from the pit of his stomach. He glanced back at Jillian who sat watching them, but he was certain she could not hear their conversation over the music. "No, Jergan, I haven't and it might behoove you to remember that the 'little lady' as you call her, is a ranking officer in the corporation that employs you."

Jergan's lop-sided grin twisted into a sneer. "She's just a figurehead, sport. The men have taken over. She's a fish doctor who's been beached. Not bad legs, though. Maybe I'll take a run at her myself."

"I wouldn't advise it. She prefers human companions."

A flash of pure hatred sparked in Jergan's eyes then dissipated so quickly that Aaron wasn't certain he'd seen it. "I'll bet she's a yeller, Trout, or does she just moan and thrash around. Pretty good ride, is she?"

Later, Aaron had no recollection of swinging, but his hand ached. Jergan lay on the floor, a tiny stream of blood trickling from the corner of his mouth. He wasn't moving. The manager arrived on the scene almost immediately, and confronted Aaron.

"What's going on here?"

Jillian rose from the table. "I believe that man slipped on spilled beer. Please wipe up the floor. I'm certain you don't want any further accidents."

He stared at her for a long moment obviously not buying the explanation but reluctant to go through the hassle of pressing charges.

"Yeah, well, okay. If you say so. Charlie, get a towel and wipe down this area."

Jergan turned his head slowly from side to side, then levered himself onto one elbow. He sat up, glaring at Aaron. "This isn't over, Trout. I'll find you when you don't have the little lady to protect you."

"Anytime."

Eventually, he staggered to his feet and headed toward the bar, never glancing at them. The bartender approached with two fresh glasses of wine.

"These are on the house. Several of us have wanted to do that for a long time."

Aaron accepted the glasses. "Thank you, but I'm not very proud of myself."

Jillian glanced over the rim of her glass. "What did Jergan have to say?"

"Oh, nothing. He's just a little drunk. Jergan's okay most of the time. He does get mean when he's had too much alcohol. Talks trash about Trail Patrol."

She set down her glass and studied him. Laughter danced in her eyes. "I would never have guessed that you were so protective of the service."

Aaron rubbed his right hand with his left. The knuckles hurt like hell. Jillian caught the motion and smiled. "Jergan has a hard head."

"Very."

"Better let me see your hand."

"It's okay."

She reached across the table with her palm up. "Come on, tough guy, let me see."

He placed his hand in hers. The knuckles were red and swollen. Jillian used her other hand to massage his. At first, the experience was quite painful. Then he began to relax. Her touch was gentle and cool. Her long, delicate fingers probed the tender places between his knuckles and gently eased his pain. When she finished, he knew he should withdraw his hand, but he didn't want to. They sat holding hands and not speaking.

A shout from the floor signaled the end of a line dance. Shelly had Laz twisted into a nearly impossible position, but a wide smile lit his face. Jillian laughed. "Your friend is enjoying himself."

"Laz can have fun on a forced march."

Her eyes sparkled. "Not a bad trait to have."

Aaron glanced away for a moment. The intensity growing between them was as exiting as it was uncomfortable. He noticed Jergan leaning against the portable bar alone, pursuing his drink. Jillian squeezed his hand lightly, calling his attention back to their table. She was also staring at Jergan.

"Why does he dislike you?"

"I don't think Jergan likes anybody. He's not a very happy man. He can't stand to see anyone else enjoying himself."

"Not a very pleasant way to go through life."

"Not as pleasant as this."

A smile played around the corners of her mouth again. Shelly approached their table with Laz in tow.

"You two going to sit here all evening? There's serious dancing to be done."

Laz pulled over a chair. "Done is the operative word. I'm through."

He reached behind Shelly and placed the chair against the back of her legs. She laughed. "Is that a hint?"

"Hint, hell. It's a declaration of surrender."

She sat and he retrieved a chair for himself and pointed at Jillian's glass. "What are you drinking, Doctor?"

"Galian Chardonnay. It's really quite lovely."

"Shelly?"

"I'll try that."

Laz headed for the bar. Jillian watched him go then turned to Shelly. "Laz is a good sport."

Shelly smiled. "And a good friend."

In the moment of silence that followed, Aaron felt that something profound passed between the two women, but he had no idea what. Somehow, it involved Laz. This was far more treacherous ground than the swamp at night.

Laz returned with a bottle of the Galian white and two glasses. He topped off Jillian's and Aaron's, then poured wine for Shelly and himself. He raised his glass in a toast. "To clear skies and good company."

🦅 🦅 🦅

Adak held the flask containing the orchid seedling up to the light. The tiny plant reclined limply against the agar. The latest cymbidia crosses were not thriving. He might have suspected fusilarium wilt, but the entire greenhouse had been sterilized. He gently set it back in the growing rack. None of its peers were doing any better.

The cattleya hybrids on the other side of the room were in full bloom. They covered the entire wall with a spectacular display of color. On the south wall, the pure white butterfly orchids illuminated their five-tiered bench. He heaved a huge sigh and stood absorbing their translucent beauty. Retrieving his mug from the workbench and taking a long drag of the coffee, he glanced up at the control panel in the west wall.

"Computer, set misting cycle for meridian plus two. Repeat at four and six."

"Acknowledged."

Adak placed his mug in the wall unit and watched it fill before recovering it. He was ready for the unpleasant task.

"Communications. Locate Sherm Ellis."

"Mr. Ellis is in his law office in Seattle, on Earth."

"Contact."

"Connecting."

After a slight pause, a cultured feminine voice responded. "Williamson & Ellis."

Adak set down his mug. "Sherman Ellis, please."

The delay created by the vast distance made it appear as if the receptionist were trying to decide whether to respond. Adak knew this wasn't true, but he still took it as a personal affront. His irritation grew with each passing moment.

Finally, the lawyer's personal secretary answered. "Mr. Ellis is preparing for court and cannot be disturbed. May I have him return your call?"

"This is Adak Pierce. Tell him to open the God damned com link."

After a longer pause than might have been expected from the communication connection, a brusque male voice responded. "Sherman Ellis, may I help you?"

"Don't give me that shit, Sherm. You knew damned well who was on the line. Are you alone?"

"Yes."

"Secure your end."

"The link is secure. What do you want?"

"I want what I pay you for. That Rozner bitch is still here, and she's imported some high-powered legal talent. It took me a while to get a fix on this turkey but my people have identified him as John Marshall. That mean anything in particular to you?"

After a short pause, Adak heard the sudden intake of breath on the other end. Then Ellis responded. "The John Marshall?"

"What the hell do you mean, The John Marshall? How many are there?"

"One is quite enough, Adak. John Marshall is the Chief Justice of the World Court. What's he doing there?"

"Obviously assisting the Rozner brat. I don't want him poking around in my affairs. See that he's called off."

"Jesus, Adak, I may have some pull in legal circles, but you don't just recall the Chief Justice like some law clerk. What do you propose I do?"

"That's your problem. Just get him off Rozner's World, or need I remind you that you're the one who drew up the phony buy-sell agreement in the first place. What if he traces that?"

The pauses were getting longer. "That could be a problem."

"Of course it could. How long do you think your handiwork would stand up under intense scrutiny?"

"Not indefinitely."

Adak picked up his mug and drained the last of the coffee. He needed something stronger. Across the room, the cattleyas swayed in a well-choreographed ballet as the ventilation system initiated.

"Anybody asking about Stern?"

"No. It's being accepted as a suicide. There were questions about why he was on the roof of his building, but we leaked a story that he was adding floors and needed to check out the possibility. The information he had will never be delivered."

"How about our other little project?"

"You mean the aircar?"

"Of course I mean the aircar. Do we have a third one I don't know about?"

Ellis sighed. "My inside operative waylaid the welcome package before it could be delivered to her apartment. She never got the maps of the safe corridors. She did go down in the swamp. Dr. Rozner managed to survive the crash."

"Ellis, you have a genius for the obvious. Of course she survived. Why else would we be having this friendly little conversation. Listen, Sherm, I want that meddling woman eliminated. Arrange another accident. Only this time, make it count. And don't forget, you're the first worm they'll encounter if they start turning over rocks."

Adak broke the connection.

Lucent woke from his nap and lay on the ledge beside his mother, listening to her deep breathing. Sheeba often dozed in the afternoon and Lucent knew she expected him to do the same. Solomon had been gone since sunrise.

He watched the light play on the water in the cave and heard the wind blow across the opening in the dome. A minnow surfaced a meter from his nose and he watched the ripples expand across the surface. The young gator closed his eyes and tried to sleep but it was no use. He was awake.

A bright red bird landed in the bush that partially covered the opening at the top of the cave. It twittered once and flew away. Lucent wondered where the bird had gone. Did it go to find the rest of outside?

He watched Sheeba breathe, trying to determine how soundly she slept. He scuttled sideways away from her body. She didn't stir. Quietly, he slipped into the water and dove following the line taken by his mother when she had led him out of the cave. It took him a moment to find the underwater passage but once he'd located the opening, he hesitated only a moment before swimming through.

Surfacing in the broad channel east of the island, Lucent stared in wide-eyed wonder at the huge trees. A fresh scent filled his nostrils sweeping away the staleness of the cave. Off to the west, a gator bellowed. He shivered. Could it be Solomon? Perhaps he could find his sire. Solomon would be proud.

He swam a short distance then halted, raised his head and peered around. Outside was so big. A small prickle of fear ran down his back. He lowered his head, resolutely pointed his snout westward and propelled himself up the channel with determined sweeps of his tail. A large fish rolled a few meters in front of him but he paid no attention. When he reached a fork in the waterway, he arbitrarily chose a channel and redoubled his effort. All his muscles began to tire, but he pressed onward.

After several minutes, he knew he had to stop and rest. Silently, he floated in mid-channel letting his legs dangle into the black water. At first he thought minnows were jumping. When he felt a rhythmic pounding on his back, he looked up into the drops of water falling steadily from the gray sky. Is this what Sheeba called rain?

Now it was hard to see. The bull gator bellowed again, this time much nearer. Solomon must be just ahead. In the next roar of the adult, Lucent detected an unfamiliar note.

Gathering his strength, he began to swim again. As he rounded a bend in the channel, it widened into a broad pool. At its center, an enormous gator lay watching the far bank. Lucent couldn't see what held his attention, but something in the adult's posture urged caution. He floated silently watching the other gator. Rain pounded on the surface of the pool and hissed in the leaves overhead.

Without warning, the huge male turned and charged across the water toward him. Lucent had no idea how he'd given himself away or why the bull appeared hostile. He turned and fled up the channel. He could hear the splashing of the male grow louder and knew he was gaining. Terror gripped him and he thrashed his tail wildly from side to side. He heard huge jaws snap closed directly behind him. Lucent projected the only image that filled his mind.

Solomon.

As he passed an intersecting waterway, a massive bow wave flooded out of it followed by a scarred snout and enormous body. Solomon rushed in behind Lucent and confronted his pursuer. His bellow shook the trees. Lucent turned to see the other male splash to a halt, turn and flee.

When he could catch his breath and slow his heart, Lucent swam back to Solomon who lay watching his adversary cross the deep pool and climb up on the opposite bank. Solomon spun around to confront him.

Why are you outside? Where is Sheeba?

Lucent was startled by his sire's anger.

She sleeps.

Why are you here?

Lucent paddled backward.

I came seeking you. Do you not know that I must do the bidding of the ancients?

Solomon lay perfectly still studying his son. Birds flitted in the trees overhead and fish surfaced nearby. Still the great gator remained motionless. Then he reached with his powerful jaws, plucked Lucent from the water and deposited the infant on his broad back. Lucent settled between the parallel ridges that ran the length of the adult gator. Solomon slowly cruised up the channel.

As they approached their lair, Sheeba emerged, swimming rapidly. She halted when she saw them. Solomon glided up to her.

Why were you not watching our son?

She swished her tail.

Even I must rest. Your son is precocious.
My son needs discipline. He nearly provided
sustenance for another.

Sheeba turned and swam for home. Solomon and Lucent followed. As Solomon dove for the entrance, Lucent floated free and followed his sire into their lair. The adult gators climbed up on the ledge and lay quietly exchanging thoughts too softly for Lucent to detect. He wasn't certain how to respond. Why was Solomon angry with Sheeba?

When he thought they had finished, the young gator crawled out of the water, curled up against his mother's side and fell asleep. Dreams of huge trees and water falling from gray skies filled his slumber.

Shelly LaCoste held the ancient part up to the light. She could see the seared interior and black flash marks around the top.

"I don't know, Alice, this geo transponder is pretty far gone. Is this the original unit?"

"Yes, Shelly, the aft array was replaced when we arrived on Rozner's World, but that one has never been unseated."

"Well, we'll have to do something about it. This unit's shot." Shelly straightened up from her crouching position and kneaded the small of her back with both hands. She glanced around the vast, brightly-lit interior of shuttle repair as if expecting a new transponder to drop from the ceiling. Twenty-eight vehicles in various stages of tear down and reassembly filled the work area nearly to capacity.

"Where are your people, Shelly?"

For a moment, Shelly thought Alice was referring to her ancestors then realized that the ancient aircar had detected the absence of other mechanics in the building.

"This is rest day. We're closed."

"Then, why are you here?"

Shelly sat on an upturned parts crate. "Good question, Alice. Actually, I'm here as a favor to Jillian. I promised her I would have you ready for tomorrow."

Alice concentrated for a moment. "That's not all of the reason. I sense you are not being fully truthful."

"Jeez, Alice, you don't allow a girl any secrets, do you?"

"Have I probed where I shouldn't? Jillian says I do that."

Shelly stood up and retrieved the integrity scanner from Alice's rear deck. She glanced at the meter, shook her head and clipped the unit to her belt. "No, Alice, I don't mind telling you. I wanted to work on you, myself. Many of your systems are not even in the newer databases. Most of them are quite delicate. My people are very skilled, but you're special. You're extremely important to Jillian and she's my friend."

"Jillian says it's good to have friends. I think Lt. Aaron Trout is Jillian's friend, too."

"Yes, I believe he is."

"Why do her systems overload when he approaches?"

Shelly's laughter echoed about the hanger. "Do they, Alice?"

"Oh, yes. Her temperature rises and her breathing becomes more rapid. If he touches her, Jillian's pulse quickens. I thought she was malfunctioning."

"No, Alice. Jillian's fine, but you're right about Lt. Trout."

"Is he your friend, too, Shelly?"

"Yes."

"Does he cause you to malfunction?"

"No, Alice."

They remained quiet for some time while Shelly made various adjustments to Alice's circuitry. She was lying on Alice's rear deck with her head and shoulders buried in the propulsion compartment. Periodically, she reached up and groped around for a specific tool, once barking a knuckle on the edge of the hatch.

"Shelly."

"Yes, Alice."

"Do the gators talk to you?"

"No, only to Aaron and Jillian as far as I know."

"Why?"

"You'd have to ask the gators."

"I did. They won't answer me. Do you really think they talk to Aaron and Jillian?"

Shelly raised herself out of the propulsion compartment. "They're convinced that they do."

"Maybe that's why Jillian malfunctions around him. Sometimes if you share something important with someone, you become special to each other - like Jillian and I have."

"Alice, you're far too wise for a mere machine."

Shelly closed the rear hatch and walked around to the front. She passed a meter over the nose of the aircar, then nodded and returned the instrument to her belt. It began to beep and she retrieved it. She held the sensor against Alice and watched the needle gyrate wildly. "What is it, Alice? You seem agitated."

"I found something."

"What do you mean, you found something?"

"I have been probing the memory banks of some of the other aircars in the shop. I got bored. A male voice in one of the computers spoke of Jillian."

"What did he say?"

"He said they were going to kill the bitch."

Shelly stood perfectly still. When she became aware that she was not breathing, she drew in a sharp breath. "Are you certain that's what he said?"

"Yes."

Shelly laid her hand on the shiny surface of the aircar. "Sometimes people say things they don't really mean, Alice."

"Like when Jillian tells Aaron she's not too tired to go for a walk but she really is."

"Something like that."

"Oh."

– 13 –

"Wake up, Alice. We have places to go."

The lights on the control panel began to brighten as Jillian approached the aircar. "Where are we going, Jillian?"

"I'm told that there are phosphorescent eels migrating into the shallows of the marsh behind Bore 19. I want to see them."

"At night?"

"That's the only time I can see them. They glow like lasers. You can pick them up on your sensors in daylight, but I don't have your talents."

Jillian slid into the cockpit and strapped on the flight harness. "Door please, Alice."

The front of the aircar swung down and settled into place, neatly enclosing the pilot's compartment. The garage door irised open and Alice began to glide forward.

The sharp contrast between the brilliantly lit garage and the velvet darkness of the sleeping corporate campus muted as the household computer faded the lights of Alice's garage.

"Since we're going out this evening, it's a good thing that nice young man was here this afternoon, isn't it, Jillian?"

"What nice, young man, Alice?"

"The one with the warm hands who worked on my attitude control circuits."

Jillian slammed the kill switch with the palm of her hand. Alice dropped a few centimeters to the garage floor with a solid thump, her nose protruding into space through the open doorway.

"Why did you do that, Jillian?"

Jillian needed a minute to get air into her lungs. Only part of her breathlessness resulted from the sudden impact with the floor. " Tell me about your visitor, Alice."

"He was the mechanic from shuttle repair that you ordered."

"What did he do?"

"If you'll turn my power back on, I'll bring up a schematic on the dash vid and show you."

Jillian's hand was shaking and she couldn't slow her breathing to a normal rate. She took a deep breath. "Okay, Alice, but just the panel. I don't want to move until I know what's been done."

Alice called up the proper diagram. "He only did what you asked him to, Jillian."

"Listen, Alice. I didn't send anybody to work on you. Whoever was here came for his own reasons."

Jillian studied the schematic, carefully tracing each circuit that related to attitude control. All appeared to be normal. Then she saw it. The hot lead and the ground had been reversed on the high-velocity pitch thrusters. It would have no effect at cruising speed, but when she called for climbing acceleration, as she would over open water, Alice would dive into the swamp.

She leaned back into the pilot's couch and tried to think. She couldn't stop shaking. "Didn't this change strike you as unusual, Alice? Why didn't you tell me?"

"I thought it peculiar, but he insisted that this is what you ordered. If he was following your instructions, you obviously knew about it. He had warm hands."

Jillian sighed. "Now listen very carefully, Alice. I'm going to manually feed power to your bow thrusters. I want you to apply just enough force to slide us back into the garage. Do you understand?"

"Yes, Jillian."

Harsh rasping noises welled up from the floor as Alice slid back into position. The glowing ceiling of the garage brightened. "Have I done something wrong, Jillian?"

"No, but we need to talk. Listen very carefully. From now on, no one is to work on you unless you and I have discussed it beforehand. If you ever have any questions, you call me. Someone is trying to hurt us. Do you understand?"

"Yes, Jillian, but who would want to cause us harm?"

"I have my suspicions, Alice."

Alice was quiet for a moment. Lights flickered across her dash. "Did you not charge me with protecting you?"

"Yes, Alice."

"Then I have been unsuccessful."

"I have not been injured. You haven't failed." She couldn't tell if this appeased Alice or not. The aircar remained silent.

Jillian climbed out of the cockpit and walked around to the rear panel. She unlatched the cover and set it on the floor. The circuits she needed were directly beneath the opening. She reversed the connections, replaced the panel and returned to the cockpit. The dash display showed everything in proper order.

"Does that feel better, Alice."

"It feels familiar. The other didn't."

"Did he change anything else?"

"No Jillian, just the one circuit."

They were quiet for a moment while Jillian tried to decide if she still wanted to go see the eels. Alice broke the silence.

"He had nice, warm hands."

In the Admiral's suite aboard the *Windflower Vagabond*, Chief Justice Marshall half-listened to the arguments being presented by his peers on the trans-galactic conference call. He couldn't get the news of the tampering with Alice three days ago out of his mind. Jillian should have informed him immediately although he had no idea what he could have done about it.

When the legal debate petered out, he cleared the screen. He stood considering the relative merits of a drink versus a shower when the decision was taken out of his hands. A soft chime sounded. He glanced up at the entry screen and saw Captain Wyman waiting beyond the portal.

"Open."

When the door had irised, he greeted his guest.

"Good evening, Captain."

"Good evening, Your Honor. I was wondering if the Admiral had any more of the Galian White he might be willing to share with an overworked ship's captain."

A broad grin spread across the old man's face. "I detect treachery in your simple request. You anticipate that any shortage in the Admiral's stores will be blamed on the current resident of his quarters. Well, my shoulders are broad. Let's raid the cellar."

When he had poured out the wine, he proposed a toast. "To this sound ship and her noble captain."

"Thank you."

"Is this a social visit or is there something on your mind?"

Suzanne smiled over the rim of her glass. "Am I really that transparent?"

"You could easily have detected that the communications link from this cabin has been busy for the better part of an hour. I suspect that it's no coincidence that you appear on my doorstep just as the connection closes."

Suzanne set her wineglass on the low table between them and reached for a cracker. When she had liberally spread it with cheese, she glanced up at the judge. "Are you making any headway?"

He swirled the brilliant white wine around in his glass and took a sip. "I believe we're making some progress."

"Anything you'd care to talk about?"

"No." He glanced up at her. "I'm not being intentionally difficult, Captain. It's just that everything is so nebulous at the moment that I wouldn't know how to explain."

"Can you wrest control from Pierce?"

He stared into his glass, watching the light play on the surface of the liquid. "I don't know."

Suzanne finished her wine and stood. "I really must get back to the bridge. Is there anything I can get for you?"

"No. Your crew has seen to all my needs, and Captain, I will tell you everything as soon as I can."

She stood watching him for a moment. "Thank you, and thank you for the wine."

Jillian couldn't get the eels out of her mind. She also missed the exhilaration of flight. The first night Alice was home after Shelly had thoroughly gone over the aircar, Jillian seized the opportunity to investigate.

Alice slipped out of her garage, soared over the compound and trailhead then banked left and climbed over the treetops at Bore 19. Her infrared sensors guided her flawlessly around obstacles. In the moonless dark, she was as comfortable as in brilliant sunshine. Jillian reclined in the pilot's chair allowing Alice to set her own course. A warm, orange glow colored the horizon.

"How are you feeling, Alice?"

"Very well, thank you. I'm certain that we got all of my circuits reordered properly. How are you feeling, Jillian? Are your circuits properly aligned?"

"I'm fine. Are we getting close?"

"We'll be coming up on the eel pod momentarily. Would you like me to descend to ten meters?"

"Yes." The glow in the water intensified as they approached the surface. A writhing mass of orange, florescent light shimmered beneath them. It filled the bay behind the Bore 19 site. As Jillian watched, the entire school shifted to florescent green, then back to brilliant orange.

Her voice was little more than a whisper. "The patterns in the water are so beautiful."

"Why do they change color, Jillian?"

"I don't know, Alice. Maybe it's a normal response."

A series of lights flashed on Alice's dash. "My sensors are detecting a great release of energy. The eels are very excited. I think they're mating."

"That would make sense. They probably come to this shallow bay for that purpose, then return to open water."

"Is that why you get into your big soaking tub, Jillian? Is that your shallow bay?"

"Uh, no, Alice, although the idea has occurred to me. It just feels good."

"Doesn't mating feel good, Jillian?"

"Yes, it does. Can't we talk about something else?"

"I'll bet that nice patrol officer from Shelly's party would get into your soaking tub with you. You said he treated you well."

"Alice."

"Yes, Jillian"

"Let's see if we can get closer to the eels."

They descended five meters and leveled off. At this altitude, individual fish could be detected. Clearly they had paired off and were performing a ritual older than time. At the height of their excitement, they flashed brilliant green, then resumed their orange glow. Shortly after the climax, they drifted apart and rebonded with other animals. Then the ritual was repeated. Jillian was fascinated by the synchronization of their activity. How did they all peak together? She knew of no other species that did.

"How many are there, Alice?"

Alice paused to cogitate. "I sampled a square meter, then extrapolated the count over the surface of the inlet. I calculate a minimum of three million, but then I'm assuming that they are only one layer deep."

"You're probably right. They're so beautiful. From up here, they appear similar to the fresh-water eels found in the northern lakes of the African continent but these are much larger. I wonder where they go when they're not mating."

Jillian leaned back in the pilot's couch and heaved a huge sigh. "We can return home anytime, Alice. I've seen what I came to see."

Alice turned to port and climbed. "Are you planning to get in your soaking tub, Jillian? I could call that patrol officer and invite him over."

"Leave it alone, Alice."

Jillian finished her morning shower, dressed in a casual, blue-green jumpsuit, and strolled into the kitchen.

"Wilson."

"Yes."

"Casaba juice, coffee, three eggs, side of salt pork and four slices of toast with peanut butter."

The household computer hesitated only a moment before it set about the appointed tasks.

Moments later, a tray slid out of the wall onto the counter. All of the requested items were present.

When she had devoured everything including all of the toast with extra servings of peanut butter, she returned to the bath, cleaned her teeth and began to wander around her quarters. She straightened the throw pillows, moved small pieces of statuary, and ran her hands along flat surfaces, checking for any dust left by the cleaning robots.

Finally she dropped into her favorite chair. "Vid, please."

Jillian watched a portion of an insipid news broadcast. The woman reporter on the screen was interviewing a specialist on mold control. "Suspend."

She rose from the chair and headed purposefully for the utility area. After donning her foul-weather gear, she entered the garage and flipped on the light. "Wake up, Alice."

Tiny lights began to glow on Alice's control panel. "Are we going somewhere, Jillian?"

"I want you to put me down near the bridge where Aaron and I met Solomon."

Alice brought up a map of the site on her dash screen. "This is a restricted area, Jillian. You will need an escort."

"You'll be my escort, Alice."

"I don't think that's what it means. Shall I locate Lt. Trout?"

Jillian flushed. "No. I specifically do not want Aaron."

Alice completed her preflight check and opened the garage door. "Is Lt. Trout no longer your friend?"

"He's still my friend. I just have to do this alone."

"You won't be alone, Jillian. I'll be with you."

"Yes, Alice."

Alice lifted off and glided out of her garage into the falling rain. A steady blast of air from vents beneath her bubble canopy kept the clear surface water free. She banked over the courtyard and headed over the swamp. "Jillian."

"Yes."

"I miss La Jolla."

"Me too, Alice. Do you miss the sunshine?"

"I don't like all this rain. We have had precisely 6.72385 cumulative hours of sunlight since we arrived. The only time we get sun is when we fly above the atmosphere. My circuits are soggy. Are your circuits soggy, Jillian?"

"Yes, Alice."

After several minutes, Alice hovered. "We're over the bridge. Do you wish to descend?"

Jillian leaned forward and peered through the windshield. "I can't see a thing through the rain. Descend, but don't land."

They settled gently until Alice announced, "We're a meter above the railing. I'm too wide to fit on the bridge deck."

"Back off and land on the dike."

Alice shifted position then landed easily. "We're three meters east of the bridge. Are you getting out?"

"Yes. Can you give me some light."

Alice's brilliant searchlights flashed through the downpour. Anything beyond several meters was lost in the falling sheets of water. "Any wind, Alice?"

"South southeast at 1.2 kilometers."

"Good."

"Are you sure this is wise, Jillian?"

"No, but I have to be certain."

Lights flashed on the control panel as Alice ran through her post-landing checklist. "Do you wish me to locate Solomon?"

Jillian shuddered - almost a sob. "I have to know."

"Do you wish me to find him?"

"Yes."

Three minutes later, Alice displayed a map on the panel. A tiny red dot pulsed in the upper right quadrant. "I scanned for body mass. Solomon is the largest creature out here. He's laying six hundred yards northwest of us."

Jillian heaved a huge sigh. "Open."

The control panel retracted into the floor and the clear front of the aircar lifted providing a canopy to keep out the rain. Jillian released the safety straps and stepped out under its extended protection. She hesitated only a moment before venturing into the downpour. Rain pounded on the hood of her weather suit, masking any other sound. She followed the course lit by Alice until the beams of the powerful searchlights dissolved into the storm. Jillian activated the canister light on her hip and cautiously felt her way along the dike to the bridge.

Grasping the railing, she pulled herself to the center of the span. As she summoned her courage to contact Solomon, the shadows shifted at the end of the bridge. Something or someone had partially blocked the light from

Alice. As she stared into the rain, the shadows changed again. A cold chill ran down her spine.

Jillian summoned all her courage. "Who's there?"

No answer, but the shadow moved, this time gliding from left to right. "Who's there? Identify yourself."

The pounding of the rain on her hood broke the hiss of the torrent. As she stared, the figure advanced and Jillian realized only the bottom portion of the light was interrupted. Whatever shared her bridge was built low to the ground. Truth came with a rush of adrenaline. Gator.

She closed her eyes and concentrated. "Solomon."

No response.

"Solomon, Is that you?"

A long snout poked out of the curtain of rain as the creature advanced. It bore no scar. Jillian began to tremble. She glanced over her shoulder toward the other end of the bridge. All she could see was a veil of falling water. As she turned to run, a second unscarred snout pierced the wall of rain in front of her. They had her trapped.

She froze. There was nowhere to go. Both gators continued their slow steady advance from opposing ends of the span; their heads swinging from side to side. The knot of fear in her gut nearly doubled her over. She closed her eyes and concentrated. "Can either of you hear me?"

No answer. They simply kept plodding toward her. In unison, they opened their massive jaws and hissed. Row upon row of glistening teeth filled each maw. First one snapped shut, then the other. Jillian tasted the bile that rose in the back of her throat. Now, over the sound of the rain, she could hear their claws scraping on the wooden bridge deck. She closed her eyes and tried to silently yell. "Solomon."

I come.

She heard the rush of water as an enormous body crashed out of the swamp, splintered a section of railing and landed on the deck of the bridge. The entire span shuddered with the impact. A deafening bellow echoed through the heavy air, and an answering voice was choked off in mid cry. Jillian turned back to the east end. The first gator continued his unhurried advance.

She felt the bridge tremble as a massive body thundered toward her from the West. She leaped for the railing, in time to avoid the charging reptile that flashed past. Through the driving rain she could detect the dark jagged scar across the broad nose.

Solomon ripped into the remaining adversary. Now Jillian could see the great difference in mass. Solomon was at least three times the size of his opponent. It was over in a moment. Her guardian pushed the carcass over the side. It dropped a meter to the water and made a dull splash, then drifted beside the bridge.

Jillian gingerly eased down from the railing. When her feet struck the deck, her legs collapsed and she dropped to her knees. She gripped the lowest bar for support.

Solomon turned and sidled toward her.

Why are you out here, alone, Jillian? Where is Aaron Trout?

She tried to speak, but emitted only a hoarse squeak. Then she remembered whom she was addressing and concentrated on projecting her thoughts. "I don't know. I didn't tell him I was coming. This was something I had to do by myself. I had to know."

Could he not have escorted you? I have instructed him to protect you. It is why I revealed myself to the man-creature.

"I didn't want to put him in danger."

Solomon thrashed his tail from side to side.

You are not being truthful with me.

Jillian shook her head and her shoulders slumped. "I couldn't be certain that he wasn't, in some way, influencing me. I had to eliminate as many variables as possible."

Am I real, Dr. Rozner?

"Oh, yes. You're real and I think I am crazy."

I assure you, Jillian, you have not lost control of your mind.

Jillian glanced at the floating carcass. "Why did your friends attack me?"

Solomon stepped forward and Jillian leaped to her feet, relieved that her legs would support her. She backed away and Solomon stopped.

They intended to extinguish your light as I have theirs, and they are not my friends. Not all of us welcome your presence, Dr. Rozner. These are disciples of Joshua.

"Who's Joshua?"

Solomon swished his tail. It made faint rasping noises on the boards of the bridge decking.

Who, indeed? One who brands me a traitor for revealing our secrets to lesser beings. Joshua would have extinguished your grandsire's light if he could have reached him, as he would mine. It is why you must never come here alone.

Jillian stared at the huge gator, seeing him in a new light. What formed in her mind was nearly unthinkable. "Are you in danger, Solomon?"

Perhaps.

He yawned and Jillian realized that she had approached the gator while he spoke. She stepped back several paces. Solomon lifted his head as she retreated.

I, too, have been cast out by my own.

She felt a sudden kinship for the great creature. She thought for a moment. "Can I communicate with you if I'm not on the bridge?"

Easily. You need only summon me from wherever you are. Now you must go.

Jillian glanced toward the end of the bridge and realized that she could see Alice. The rain had stopped. The aircar had shut down her intense beams and displayed only parking lights. Looking up, Jillian could see patches of brightness in the solid cloud cover. Water dripped from dense foliage into the dark pools. She turned to leave then looked back at her protector.

"Do you think there will be other attempts on my life?"

I am certain of it. Your friends may also be in danger. The stakes are very high.

Jillian shuddered, feeling a chill start at the base of her spine and spread upward. She could think of nothing else to communicate.

Solomon slipped over the side and lay in the black water. Small ripples expanded outward from his huge body. Jillian waited until he drifted away from the bridge before easing past. She stopped at the end of the span.

"I still don't know what I'm supposed to do."

In time, my child. In time.

Alice waited patiently, her canopy open to receive her master. Jillian climbed in and settled into the pilot's couch.

"You're trembling, Jillian. Are you alright?"

"I think so, Alice, but let's go home."

As Alice lifted off, Jillian could see Solomon lying in black water watching their departure. She felt a childish impulse to wave.

Alice banked left and gained altitude. "I wanted to help but I have no weapons. Maybe we should ask Shelly to add some."

"I'll think about it, Alice."

As she broke out above the cloud cover, sunshine flooded the cabin. Alice began to hum. Jillian recognized her little tune of contentment. The humming stopped and lights rippled across the control panel. Alice was deep in thought.

"Why did Solomon deactivate his friends?"

"They were not friends, Alice. They follow someone named Joshua."

"Is Joshua powerful, like Solomon?"

"I don't know, but I'm afraid he might be."

Alice remained quiet as she soared over the treetops toward the compound. Jillian waited for her to speak. "When you returned from the bridge, you were frightened, Jillian. The last time I sensed such fear was just before we crashed on the dike. Were Joshua's friends trying to deactivate you?"

"Yes, Alice."

"I wouldn't like that."

Jillian laughed and heard the shakiness in her voice. "I wouldn't be too wild about it either."

Alice slid into the garage and rotated until her nose pointed outward. The door irised shut as bright lights illuminated the space. Alice raised the canopy and ran through her postflight sequence. Jillian headed straight for the bath. She peeled off the soiled jump suit and dumped it into the cleaning chute in the dressing room wall.

"Wilson?"

"Yes, Jillian."

"Shower. My usual settings."

She heard the water come on in the three-sided enclosure, waited for a moment for the household computer to adjust the temperature, then stepped around the corner into the unit. After washing her hair and thoroughly scrubbing her body, she reached for a towel, then changed her mind.

"Wilson?"

"Yes, Jillian."

"Draw bath."

She could hear the water cascading into the bathing pool. She crossed to the kitchen, leaving wet footprints and retrieved the remainder of the exotic Chilean Cabernet. The rare Earth wine had mysteriously appeared with her name on it, in the lobby of her building. At first, she couldn't imagine who had sent it. Her first impulse had been Aaron. It was such a romantic notion, but a Trail Patrolman's salary would hardly support such a lavish gesture.

It could be a trap. More than one unsuspecting recipient of a gift bottle had been poisoned. She had examined the seal. Then she had found the small card taped to the back. "Enjoy. John Marshall."

That hadn't precluded the possibility of treachery but it did lessen the odds. What the hell. There were worse ways to go and today she felt fine.

"Jillian, your bath is ready."

"Thank you, Wilson."

Gideon lay hidden in the tall grass above Joshua's rock. He could see the patriarch basking in the late afternoon sun. The storm had abated as suddenly as it had struck, and bright flashes of sunlight danced on the water in the cove.

Gideon knew that Joshua had seized these few precious minutes of heat to bake his ancient bones, and would not welcome interruption. Still, there was little choice. Summoning his courage, he rose and began to sidle down the slope toward the water.

As he approached the massive boulder, Joshua spoke without lifting his head.

Why do you disturb me, Gideon?

How did you know it was I, Sir?

Joshua turned his head and fixed the younger gator with a penetrating glare.

Do you think I have not been aware of you hiding in the tall grass like a cowering female? What is so urgent that it cannot wait until I am ready to receive underlings?

Gideon shuffled around in front of the master.

Two of the younger bulls trapped the
Rozner woman on the bridge.

Joshua rose up on all six legs, fully alert.

I gave no such orders. Did they extinguish
her light?

No, my Lord. As they were about to divide
her between themselves, Solomon crashed
over the side of the bridge.

Joshua lay back down and rested his jaw on his front legs.

Where are their bodies?

How do you know they are no more?

My son, sending two young ones against
Solomon is like casting swamp flowers into
the howling winds of winter. Where are they?

Gideon gazed out over the water.

Floating in the swamp, near the bridge.

Leave them. They shall provide a lesson for
impetuous fools. What of the woman? I need to
know if we are to mount a proper attack.

She escaped in her flying vehicle, the one
like no other.

Then we have lost our opportunity.

Gideon didn't answer, but stood staring into the shallow
water. Dark clouds began to drift over the sun, throwing the
swamp into shadows. He waited for Joshua to speak again,
but when it became apparent that the interview was over, he
turned and headed up the path.

Gideon.

Yes, Joshua.

You have done well to bring me this news.

A strange warmth spread through him as if the sun
had reappeared. Praise from the Ancient One did not come
frequently. As he passed the nesting ground, Martha raised
her head and huffed. This time he turned off the path
toward her bed. Perhaps the day could yet improve.

🐊 🐊 🐊

"Have you got your end secured, Laz?"

"I think so. What the hell did this?"

Aaron set the butt of the timber in place and drove a titanium fastener through the bridge railing into the upright with his belt tool. "Probably a gator, but it was a big bastard."

"Solomon?"

"Perhaps."

Laz stepped back and studied their handiwork. "Why would a gator attack the railing. Looks like he came right through it."

"Obviously, there was something on the bridge that he wanted very badly."

Laz shivered and looked around. "We're not missing any patrol officers, are we?"

Aaron shrugged. "Not that I know."

They gathered up their equipment and started for the next reported problem. Aaron glanced back, admiring the fruits of their labor. Something in the water arrested his eye. "Hold it, Laz. There's something floating against the bushes on the north side of the bridge."

Laz checked where his partner pointed. "It's just a log."

"I don't think so."

Aaron started back across the span, stopping when he drew parallel with the object. "It's a dead gator, Laz, and there's another one over there."

Laz joined him on the bridge. "What the hell happened here?"

"I have no idea, but it cost those two their lives."

Laz stood staring at his friend until Aaron became self-conscious.

"What?"

"I was just thinking that maybe Solomon would know. Why don't you ask him?"

Aaron stood staring into the swamp for a long moment. Laz waited patiently. Finally, Aaron turned to him. "I'm not sure I should."

Laz leaned against the newly repaired railing. "Aren't you curious?"

Aaron rested his left foot on the lower railing. "Sure, but I don't want to contact him for trivial reasons."

"Those two floaters look trivial to you?" Laz punched him in the shoulder. "Give it a shot, sport."

Aaron could already feel the tension building at the back of his neck. He closed his eyes, and projected. "Solomon."

I am here.

Aaron searched the water in all directions, but could detect nothing. "Are you close."

No, Lt. Trout. I am... I am away.

Aaron closed his eyes and focused all his energy trying to project a great distance. "We are at the bridge."

You do not need to shout, Lieutenant.

"Sorry. What happened at the bridge where you and I met."

I had to intervene on that which you refer to as a bridge.

"Why? What happened?"

There was a long pause before Solomon responded. Aaron wasn't certain he hadn't been abandoned. He glanced at Laz and shrugged his shoulders. As he was about to tell Laz what had transpired, Solomon spoke.

Dr. Jillian Rozner foolishly came to the marsh alone. Two of Joshua's disciples attacked her where you now stand. I extinguished their light. It gave me no pleasure.

Aaron felt his entire body chill. "Where is Jillian? Is she alright?"

Dr. Rozner is in perfect health. I believe she has returned to her lair.

"Why did she come out here alone?"

Did you not do likewise after we first communicated?

Aaron chuckled. "I did, didn't I?"

Hear me Aaron Trout. Jillian Rozner and I are leaving parallel wakes. She, also, seeks restoration born of honor.

Laz had been waiting patiently. Now he shook Aaron's shoulder. "What's he telling you?"

Aaron turned toward his friend, holding tightly to the railing for support. His eyes slowly focused. He'd forgotten Laz was with him. "He's told me that Jillian was here. These two tried to kill her."

"Is she okay?"

"She's safe."

Laz glanced at the carcasses then stared at Aaron. "Jillian came out here, alone?"

"Yeah."

"Jesus. She could have been killed."

"I know. Solomon intervened. Oh God, Laz if anything had happened to her...."

Laz rested his hand on Aaron's shoulder. "Solomon said she's all right, didn't he?"

"Yeah."

Laz glanced down at the dead gators again. "Did he kill these two?"

"Yes. They tried to trap Jillian on the bridge. They are followers of someone called Joshua."

"Who's Joshua?"

"I don't know. I'll ask."

Aaron turned back to gaze over the water. "Solomon?"

I am here.

"Who is Joshua?"

One who does not approve of my act of sharing the secret of the nodules with Doctor

Rozner or his offspring. Joshua has many followers. He believes he is right. There is no more formidable adversary than one who has the truth.

Aaron concentrated for a moment. "Is he dangerous?"

Extremely.

"Can you handle him?"

Another long moment of silence passed while Solomon formulated his answer. Aaron was beginning to recognize the pattern.

I know not.

− 14 −

Jillian had finished her bath without falling asleep and felt refreshed. As she sat drying her hair, Wilson intruded.

"Jillian, there's a call for you."

She realized that she hadn't bothered to put on her robe. "Audio only, Wilson."

"Hello, Jillian."

She recognized the voice immediately and felt her breath catch in her throat. "Good evening, Aaron."

"Laz and I have been on duty. We had to repair a bridge railing that had been shattered by a mutual friend of ours. You wouldn't know anything about that, would you?"

Jillian took a deep breath. "You've been talking to Solomon."

She could almost see Aaron wrinkling his brow. His voice was strained. "You could have been killed."

"The thought has occurred to me."

"Listen, Jillian. Promise me you won't go out there alone. If you need an escort, call me."

Was his concern personal or professional? "Yes, Lieutenant."

She set aside the hairbrush down and stood to reach for her clothes. "Really, Aaron, I assure you I'm quite alright. I had Alice with me."

His bark of laughter echoed in her ears. "Oh, and is Alice heavily armed?"

"No."

"I didn't think so."

She slipped into her blouse. "Look, Aaron. I didn't want to drag you into this."

"You don't get to vote. I'm already in. Promise me, Jillian."

"I promise. And Aaron?"

"Yes?"

"Thanks for caring."

Chester Wiggins tucked his pen back into the pocket of his white lab coat and made one final adjustment to the instrument panel on the test desk. Jim checked all gauges to be certain that they were now in normal ranges. Beyond the clear wall in front of them, the massive Rozner Constant engine sat on its trolley, awaiting activation. Nearly thirty meters long, the huge power plant filled the entire test chamber at the south end of the lab.

Chester stepped behind the desk and palmed the red button that sounded the klaxon warning for a test firing, then gave the command.

"Start engine."

Jim waved his hand over the control, then waited. At first, nothing seemed to happen. Only the slight vibration of the floor indicated any response from the space drive. As the interior of the engine heated, the mercury vapor-suffused nodules gave off steadily increasing energy. In total silence the aft end of the Rozner Constant drive glowed white hot.

Jim glanced at the panel. "Ten percent power, Sir."

Chester never took his eyes off the drive. "Hold it there, Jim. What's she putting out?"

"940."

"That's it? 940?"

"I'm afraid so, Sir."

Chester rose from his chair, skirted the control desk, and approached the window. "What's wrong? At ten percent, you should be at 1000."

He turned to the technician. "Take her up a little, Jim. I want to know what it takes to get to 975. We should be alright for a short run."

"Yes, Sir."

Chester could feel the light vibration increase normally as he carried out the order.

Jim tapped a gauge. "She's at 975."

"What's your power reading?"

"Twelve percent."

Beyond the glass, the huge engine glowed in a halo of blue light. Chester waved his hand. "Okay. Shut her down."

Jim ran the sequence as they watched the power plant revert to inert machinery, then crossed the room to stand by his boss. "What do you make of it, Sir?"

"Damned if I know. We're obviously losing integrity. Each drive we produce is less efficient than the last. When Pierce took over six months ago, ten-percent power equaled 1000."

"What does the old man say?"

"He's furious, but Dr. Pierce can't explain it either."

Jim studied the resting engine. "If we could only open one of these beasts up, maybe we could figure it out."

Chester passed his hand through his hair. "God knows we've tried but you saw the failsafes. I, for one, do not feel the need to die."

He crossed the room and poured a cup of coffee, then raised it to Jim in silent inquiry. Jim nodded and Chester poured a second cup.

Jim took a sip and turned back to the drive. "Some have speculated that the crew attempted to crack the Rozner unit on the *Majestic Vagabond*. I have a friend who swears that's why she blew."

"You'll hear all kinds of rumors, Jim. I wouldn't pay a lot of attention to any of them, but your friend's theory would explain a great deal. But our worry is the engine." What Jim didn't know couldn't hurt him.

Jim cocked his head toward the Rozner Constant drive. "You gonna tell the boss?"

"I don't have any choice. He wanted to see the latest test fire data as soon as we had it."

"Is your will current?"

"Yeah."

"Well, don't leave until I find the silver platter."

"Silver platter?"

Jim chuckled. "To bring your head back on, Sir."

Chester laughed. "Hopefully it won't come to that."

🗟 🗟 🗟

Winton Lazarus caught the cypress branch he had just lasered off the tree growing beside the dike. He tossed it into the swamp and turned to locate his partner. "Aaron?"

"Yeah."

"Where are you?"

"Down the bank on the other side. Come hold this damned thing for me while I trim it."

Laz vaulted the railing and half-walked, half-slid down the embankment to meet his partner. "What are you doing down here? I thought we were just supposed to trim the branches that overhang the trail."

"We are, but this sucker connects clear down here. Hold it for me."

Laz grabbed the branch and steadied it while Aaron sliced through the six-centimeter limb with his laser knife. A faint aroma of burned wood wafted on the damp air.

Aaron holstered his tool. "This is not my favorite part of the job."

Laz grinned. "What is your favorite part?"

"Beer at Salvation when we finish."

"I'll drink to that."

A steady rain began to fall and both men raised their foul-weather hoods. They scrambled up the bank and climbed over the railing. Standing on the trail they surveyed their handiwork. Laz leaned against a support post. "I think we've about got this section, Aaron."

"Pretty much. There's that one patch on the other side of the bridge, but we can get it in the morning."

Aaron holstered his laser knife. "You seeing Shelly later?"

"Not for dinner. She has a meeting with her crew. We'll probably get together when she's through."

"You're spending a lot of time with her. I miss my old drinking buddy."

Laz shuffled his feet. "Yeah. It's starting to worry me, too."

Aaron snorted. "What happened to 'Love 'em and dump 'em Lazarus'? You've got a reputation to uphold. We mere mortals have come to expect certain standards. If this icon falls, what can a guy believe in?"

"Jesus, Aaron. It's not funny. I'm scared to death."

Aaron put his left foot on the lower railing and stared into the swamp. "You really care for her, don't you?"

Laz turned to gaze out over the dark water. "I don't want to see anybody else. I just want to go home and share my day with her."

Aaron nodded. "I can understand that."

Laz glanced at his friend. "Don't you want to tell somebody what you did today? How about that branch that turned out to be a snake? That would make pretty good dinner conversation."

Aaron chuckled. "It would have to be somebody with a sense of humor."

"What about Jillian?"

"She's our employer, Laz. We're friends."

Laz studied him for a long moment and decided not to push it. "What am I going to do, Aaron?"

"Let it run its course. It's like swamp fever. Ten days, max."

"I don't think so. Sometimes we don't even have to talk to understand each other."

Aaron stared at his friend. "How does that feel?"

Laz felt the heat rise in his cheeks. "It's wonderful. It's like finding the other half of yourself."

"I can't even imagine what that would feel like."

They gathered up their tools and started the long walk back to the compound. The sun was setting behind broken rain clouds as they reached the bridge. A gator bellowed in the distance. Laz glanced toward the sound. "That your friend, Aaron?"

"No."

"How do you know?"

Aaron stopped and considered the question. "I just know."

"What does Solomon expect of you?"

Aaron started walking. "Originally, I thought he just wanted me to bring him Jillian, and I've done that. Now that there have been two attempts on her life, I think he expects me to protect her. I don't know if I can do that and it scares the hell out of me."

"Somehow, I don't think you ever get off easily with old Solomon. I'll bet he has other plans."

Aaron glanced over his shoulder. "Like what?"

"How should I know? You're the one he talks to."

As they cleared the weather lock into Salvation, Aaron spotted Jillian and Shelly seated at a back table. They had their heads together. Jillian glanced up and waved. As the men approached the table, Shelly rose and kissed Laz on the cheek. "Save my place, Big Boy, I've got a meeting. See ya, Aaron."

She scampered across the floor and disappeared into the lock without a backward glance, her short, blond hair bouncing over her collar. Aaron watched her go, then dropped into a chair beside Jillian. "That was a rather abrupt exit."

Jillian smiled. "She's late for her meeting. She'll be back afterward."

Laz flagged down a passing waitress, ordered three Bull Gator beers, slid onto Shelly's vacant chair and sighed. "It's still warm."

Aaron rolled his eyes. "Oh, for God's sake, Laz."

Jillian sat, a faint smile on her lips and said nothing. Aaron leaned toward her. "If I ever get that silly, smack me."

Garrett McPhee lowered the ultrasonic mining tool and studied the cavity he had gouged out of the ancient sediment. A jet-black nodule protruded from the side of the cut like the yolk of a fried egg. Years of experience told him that several more of the precious orbs would lie in a cluster with this one, possibly as many as thirty. He clipped his tool to his belt and reached for his canteen, savoring the moment of discovery.

Standing three hundred meters below the surface, where the new Bore 20 bottomed out in a large excavated cavern, he poured water down his parched throat, and listened to his crew working in the tunnels that branched off in all directions. Relying on an earlier molecular scan, he'd decided to work the north wall of the central receiving room and hit paydirt.

Three days ago, the exploratory team, following the dictates of the geologists, had sunk the shaft, opened up the receiving room and installed the elevator, lights and life support systems required by the miners. Their job completed, they had moved on to the next site. Now Garrett and his men braved the depths to search for the precious nodules.

He shook his head. It should be so easy to extract the rare orbs with heavy equipment but over the years, many had tried to automate the mining process with the latest technology. It simply didn't work on a planet where emissions from entire areas of the swamp negated the energy of most equipment. Nobody could explain why. In the end, a crew of twelve with sealed-beam, phased-ion hand tools still proved to be the most efficient method of extracting the power sources.

Garrett clamped his canteen back on his belt and poked his glowstick into the niche. The partially exposed nodule shone like polished obsidian. He retrieved his cutter from its holster and excised the sphere from its nest. As it tumbled into his hand, he again marveled at the weight of these rocks. It had the mass of a much larger stone. Placing the nodule in his pack, he returned his attention to the alcove he had carved out of the sediment.

Yes. There was another behind the one he'd extracted. Garrett hooted. As foreman, it was always good to make a strike to show to his men. Occasional cries from the tunnels announced that the crew was also hitting pay dirt. Their share of the profits would keep them in beer at Salvation for some time. As he worked to remove the remaining orbs, he wondered for the hundredth time about the clustering of the nodules. Geologists had speculated that they were fossilized eggs gathered in nests by some ancient reptile. This explanation struck Garrett as reasonable. He knew enough basic geology to recognize the sandstone cradling the nodules as the sedimentary bottom of an ancient sea. Millions of years of settling debris had tamped down the detritus of the swamp until the original sea floor lay far underground.

As he continued to add nodules to his pack, the weight became uncomfortable. Garrett glanced around for a place to set his burden. A small alcove chiseled out of the sandstone by the set-up crew provided the perfect resting-place. He had just straightened up when Jeremy Swent entered the room and set his own nearly-full pack beside Garrett's.

"We're making quite a haul back there, Boss. Look's like you struck pretty good yourself."

"Well, occasionally the old man gets lucky. I'll buy the first round when we get in."

"Okay, I'll get the next one."

Jeremy pushed a rock around with his boot. "You thought any more about taking the men's concerns to management?"

"I'll go see Pierce in the morning, but I'm not sure what I can accomplish."

Jeremy leaned against the wall. "Seems to me the first thing is to get better medical help. If we have an injury, it takes forever to get someone down here. We nearly lost Henshew last month with that arm laceration. Old man Rozner would never have allowed that to happen. And what about the food they send down here? The quality's really deteriorating, Garrett."

"Yeah, I know. I'll bring up all our grievances."

Jeremy stood quietly for a moment. "I've got to ask, Garrett. Do you think there's anything to the rumors?"

"I don't know, but if the newer engines are less efficient, the solution might be more nodules in each one. That should increase demand and therefore the value of these rocks."

"The guys will demand a cut of that."

Garrett took a long drag from his water bottle. "I think we have to be a little careful with this, Jeremy. Pierce is not Rozner. The old man would have automatically raised our payout. Pierce is likely to blame us for delivering inferior rocks."

"That's bullshit."

"I know, but Pierce isn't the kind of man who accepts responsibility. He'll want somebody to blame. My guess is that he'll insist on reducing our commission."

Jeremy stared into his foreman's eyes. "We'll strike. The guild will demand it."

Garrett rested his hand on Jeremy's shoulder. "We have to see that they don't do anything rash, at least until we can find out what kind of backlog the corporation has on hand. We might have to hold out for months. Are you prepared to do that?"

Jeremy's shoulders slumped and he released a deep sigh. "We're barely making it as it is."

"Look, Jeremy. It isn't like these guys can go to work for the competition. This is the only job on this planet many of them can do. Sure, Pierce is a prick, but where else can they find employment. Damned few of them have the credits to go anywhere else. If we're going to threaten their livelihood, we better be certain we know what we're doing."

"Yeah, you're right."

A loud whoop echoed through the mine. Jeremy grinned. "Sounds like the Indian hit pay dirt."

"Yeah. Listen, Jeremy. Let me talk to Pierce before you stir things up. If I can't negotiate a reasonable settlement, I'll lead you out myself."

"Fair enough. But don't be too long at it. The men are getting restless. What are you hearing from the other crews?"

"We have a meeting of the foremen scheduled for tonight at Salvation. They're worried and angry."

"Strike a blow for labor, Boss."

Garrett watched thirteen men gather around the large table at the rear of Salvation's main lounge. All were burly specimens, with rough hands. Each was presented with a large Bull Gator brew and an agenda of the meeting. Garrett kicked it off.

"First, I want to thank you all for coming on short notice. I know you had other plans."

Thornton interrupted. "Yeah, I planned to get laid."

When the laughter died down, Garrett continued. "Later, Thornton. First I need your attention. Each of you represents your crew, either as foreman or elected delegate. I hope you'll take anything that comes out of this evening back to your men. The document in front of you is a compilation of notes from several meetings that I've had with Adak Pierce and his corporate thugs. The top sheet is from today's conference. It speaks for itself. Please take a moment to read it."

While they read, Garrett watched the evening crowd filter into Salvation. Each group congregated at their accustomed tables; Trail Patrol near the bar, shuttle repair near the food service and the miners where they could get a good view of the huge holographic vid screen that dominated the west wall. The system currently displayed the rugby finals from New Zealand, on Earth.

Jon Tilly finished first. "This is outrageous. He's blaming us for the declining power of his damned engines."

Jeremy shook his head. "You called it, Garrett."

Winslow did the math. "This works out to a cut in pay. He actually expects us to deliver more nodules for fewer credits. As far as I'm concerned, he can stuff his nodules up any available orifice."

Hanshew slammed his mug down. "There's nothing wrong with them nodules. He's just fucking incompetent. Rozner never had any complaints about our work. I'll bet this arrogant bastard don't even know how the Rozner Constant works."

"Easy, Charlie. Nobody knows how it works. Rozner took the secret to his grave."

At the far end of the table, Samson Agee leaned back in his chair. "Don't be too certain of that."

Jeremy leaned forward so he could see who'd spoken. "What do you mean, Sam?"

"I hear things."

"What things?"

"Just things what make you wonder."

As the clamor rose around the table, Garrett pounded his mug on the surface and waited for the din to subside. "What Sam's referring to is gossip. Some think that the old boy passed the knowledge on to his granddaughter before he died."

Charlie Henshew made the connection. "Jillian Rozner. She knows."

Tilly was having trouble making the leap. He grabbed a huge paw full of Morvian peanuts from the bowl in the center of the table then halted with his fist halfway to his mouth.

"Why don't she tell Pierce? Then we could all just go back to work and get paid."

Sam glared at him. "Would you?"

"Me? I wouldn't tell that bastard he was on fire if I could see the flames."

The barmaid arrived with two pitchers of beer and deposited one at each end of the table. Garrett signaled her to bring two more. The men were silent while they filled their glasses.

The Indian hadn't said a word all evening. Now he lifted his mug to request the floor. Garrett nodded acknowledgement and the Indian rose to his feet. He towered over the table. "Dr. Rozner knows many things. She hears the wind and talks to the gators. They tell her their secrets."

Tilly interrupted. "Bullshit. The damned gators don't talk to no one. They just bite your fool head off."

The Indian raised his chin. "I am not so certain. Maybe we should talk to her."

"Oh, hell. What's she gonna do?"

"Perhaps she could talk to the gators for us. They know many things."

Tilly lost it. "Sit down. We're not talking to no gators. Jesus, somebody pour him another beer."

A boisterous shout erupted on the other side of the room from the group in front of the vid. Garrett looked over to discover that the Brits had scored. Two to one, England.

The barmaid arrived with more pitchers. When she was gone, Sam spoke. "We could strike."

His words hung in the air. Each man took them in and absorbed their impact. Before they could react, Garrett waded in. He didn't want to let this go too far. "That's one alternative Sam, but we don't know how long Pierce can hold out on what he's got stockpiled."

"Maybe we could find out." Sam nodded toward the weather lock where Dr. Rozner and Aaron Trout had just entered.

Tilly looked up to see whom Sam had indicated. "Christ, Sam. I told you that's all bullshit. She don't know squat. She's just a dippy broad that happens to be Rozner's granddaughter. So she inherited the corporation, what good did that do her? Pierce has it now."

Sam raised his stein toward Tilly. "She's not so bad. I've talked to her. It might be a good idea to see if she could help."

The Indian muttered something. Garrett waved his hand to indicate that he should speak up. The Indian looked directly at him.

"She knows."

Sam mused aloud. "She's always hanging around with that patrol guy, but if we could isolate her...."

Garrett held up his hand to ward off the suggestion. "No rough stuff, if that's what you're thinking."

Sam glanced up, his face full of confusion. "Jesus, Garrett, I'm not suggesting anything violent. I just thought we might get her to tell us what she knows. Invite her to dinner or something. Maybe take her on a tour of the mine."

The Indian leaned back in his chair. "She talks to the gators. You be careful with that one."

Tilly's grin spread across his whole face. "What's she going to do, Indian, sic the entire swamp on us?"

"You laugh because you don't understand these things."

Tilly refilled his glass. "So who's going to approach her?"

After a pregnant silence, Sam spoke up. "We could all draw lots."

Across the room, Jillian and the patrol officer seated themselves at a small table and conversed with their heads nearly touching. The officer threw his head back and laughed at something she had said, then took a long drag of his brew. Jillian sat serenely watching him enjoy his beer.

Garrett made up his mind. "I'll do it."

"Jillian."

"Yes, Alice."

"When are you going to proceed?"

"Proceed with what, Alice?"

Alice was silent for a moment. Jillian sensed she was composing a reply and waited patiently. Beneath the aircar, treetops flashed past and sunlight glistened off white-capped water. She had used this rare sunlit afternoon to explore the area beyond Bore 20.

"How long can you allow this to go on, Jillian? You know you must act."

Jillian released a huge sigh. "I give up, Alice. What are we talking about?"

"Your grandsire, of course."

"My grandfather is dead."

"But his dream is not."

Jillian stared at the instrument panel. Alice was reaching new heights of creative thought. "What do you mean?"

"Did not your grandsire leave his life's work in your hands when he ceased to be?"

"Yes."

"Whose hands is it in now?"

Jillian squirmed on the seat. This conversation had taken a decidedly uncomfortable turn. "Dr. Pierce is in control."

"Is this what your grandsire instructed?"

"No."

On the horizon, storm clouds rolled in from the west. Their sunny afternoon was about to end. A flock of water birds flashed across their course, silver wings glistening in the sun as they banked left then right. Alice didn't react. Jillian realized that Alice not giving chase indicated how absorbed she was in their conversation.

"Has the Holy One from Earth offered a solution?"

"The Holy One?"

"The one you call Chief Justice. I consulted my sources. Great men of dignity who wear robes when they work are called Priests and addressed as Holy Father."

"Uh, I think there's a little confusion here, Alice. The Chief Justice is a legal, not a religious scholar. He reads the law, not scriptures."

"Are not many of the scriptures considered law? Do they not refer to the Law of Moses?"

"Whoa, Alice. You're in pretty deep here. Where are you getting this stuff?"

Alice was silent for a moment. "I get bored. I've been studying."

"No kidding."

"What does the Holy One advise?"

Jillian shrugged. It might be easier to leave Alice to her logic. "He is preparing a case to be brought before the Galactic Supreme Court. It could well establish a legal precedent."

"You mean validating the supremacy of post-mortem instructions in a will versus prior contractual obligations with a third party?"

"Alice."

"I got that one from *Wade versus The State of New York*. Law records are fascinating. I can tap into the electronic archives of any jurisdiction on Earth and a few on other planets, but they're not nearly as complete."

"Well, granting for a moment your vast legal scholarship, Chief Justice Marshall is actually attempting to extend Earth contractual and estate law to Rozner's World. It's a question of jurisdiction."

The lights on Alice's dash twinkled as she combed her memory banks. "Much like *Creston versus the United Nations* extending jurisdiction to the Moon in 2046."

"Christ, Alice. I can't keep up with you."

"Few can. I'm going to be a legal beagle."

"Don't you mean legal eagle?"

"Birds, dogs, who cares?"

Jillian sat back. "You're certainly in a breezy mood."

"It's the sunlight. I've missed it so."

"I have too. Sometimes I think I'll never be dry again."

They were silent for a time as she watched the approaching storm, realizing their holiday could end abruptly. She was about to order Alice home when the aircar spoke. "You haven't answered my question, Jillian."

"I know."

"Has the Reverend Justice given you any encouragement?"

Jillian took a moment to absorb Reverend Justice; quite a concept.

"Justice Marshall feels he can garner support for his position among the other members of the Court."

Alice pondered this for some time before responding. Jillian stole a glance at the incoming front but they still had a few minutes.

"Jillian."

"Yes, Alice."

"What if the court rules in your favor, but Dr. Pierce refuses to abdicate? How will you enforce the decree?"

Jillian heaved a huge sigh. "I don't know, Alice, but I've been thinking I could enlist the miners."

"You mean like soldiers? Are you fomenting a revolution?"

Jillian twisted in her seat. "I haven't thought it through yet."

"Perhaps you should. Maybe Aaron could help. He wears a uniform like a soldier and he's terribly bright."

Jillian bristled. "Lt. Aaron Trout is not the answer to all of my problems."

"Perhaps not, but I'll bet he could relieve your sexual tension. Then you could think better."

"Alice."

The storm broke just as they reached Alice's garage. Booming thunder rolled through the heavens and vast sheets of rain deluged the Rozner compound. Workers gathered up picnic supplies and ran for shelter. Jillian stood in the open garage doorway and watched. Behind her, Alice ran through her post-flight checklist, then shut down. Jillian listened to the rain hiss on the walkways and considered her aircar's earlier suggestion.

Alice could be right. Maybe Aaron could help. He's certainly intelligent and he knows Rozner's World far better than Jillian herself.

She wondered if he could act as liaison to the miners. He would certainly have a better rapport with them. After all, he's out there on the trails every day. They must all know him. It's an idea worth pursuing.

− 15 −

hief Justice John Marshall signed off the vid conference and closed the folder on his desk. He glanced around the Admiral's quarters aboard the *Windflower Vagabond* and heaved a sigh. "That's it, then. I've done all I can."

He rubbed his hand across his tired eyes and slowly rose from the chair. The next step would be the most difficult. He needed to relax first.

Standing in the shower, allowing the searing water to burn away the tension of the past few hours, he outlined his presentation to Jillian. No matter how he organized the data, the conclusion remained preposterous.

After shaving and donning fresh clothes, he settled into the lounger with a cup of tea on the end table and ordered his notes on his lap. Should he proceed from the general to the specific, present the facts in chronological order, or open with a philosophical overview? Which would best ease the blow?

Finally, he discarded all these scenarios, tossed the papers on the floor, leaned back against the headrest and heaved a huge sigh.

"Computer."

"Yes, Sir."

"What time of day is it at Salvation on Rozner's World?"

"Early evening. 7:52 PM."

"Communications."

"Yes, Justice Marshall."

"Open a channel to Dr. Jillian Rozner on Rozner's World."

"Searching . . . connecting . . . Dr. Rozner has accepted your call."

The screen flickered then resolved into an image of neatly kept living quarters with Jillian seated comfortably on a broad couch; her feet tucked up under her. She held a steaming mug in her right hand.

"Good evening, Justice Marshall. Nice to hear from you."

"Good evening, Jillian. I trust you are well."

"Very well, thank you. How is your inquiry coming?"

Marshall leaned forward and folded his hands in his lap. "That's what I wanted to speak with you about. Do you have a few minutes?"

"Of course."

He leaned over and reached for the stack of papers, changed his mind, sat back and allowed his hands to return to his lap. "You must understand. The issues involved are quite complicated. We're attempting to extend a system of laws, developed for a specific nation-state, then expanded to all of Earth and finally to galactic societies in cultural dark ages."

Jillian didn't respond.

Marshall shifted in his chair. "I think I should come down there and speak with you directly."

"Well, you're certainly welcome to do so, but I'm not sure it's necessary."

"Jillian, this is very difficult."

To his utter amazement, she flashed him a dazzling smile. "Let me see if I can help you out. There is no legal way to extract Pierce from the chairmanship of the Rozner Corporation. Correct?"

"It's not that simple. There are enormously complicated jurisdictional questions involved. I have been consulting with the best legal minds available, and we have finally reached a consensus."

"But the bottom line is that we've been shafted."

Marshall couldn't help smiling. "That is technically not the legal term, but I'm afraid it is quite accurate. The extension of criminal law into far flung colonies is pretty well established, but civil and contractual jurisprudence is a much fuzzier matter."

"You mean that if he'd put a gun to my head and forced me to sign over the corporation, we could do something about it, but the discovery of a questionable claim leaves us helpless."

Marshall sighed. "That about covers it. I'm now totally convinced that the document Pierce used to gain control is fake but you're going to have to prove it. You need to dig into the background of the corporation's attorney, Sherman Ellis. He has an excellent reputation, but I think Pierce got to him. I don't know how.

"Have someone on Earth check the court records of every transaction he's ever brokered for Pierce. Push Ellis hard. He's not acting right. I think he's terrified. I think he'll fold."

Jillian leaned back against the cushions. "Is this something you can handle?"

Marshall felt the energy drain from his body. This was the question he'd been dreading. "I've gone as far as I can go without compromising my position with the court. Oh, let's face it. I've gone way beyond that point, but I can recommend someone if you like."

Again, she startled him with a brilliant smile. "Well, don't worry too much about it, Your Honor. I don't think that will be necessary. I've set other plans in motion."

"Other plans?"

Jillian took a long sip of her tea. "The law is only one tool for dealing with scoundrels. Do you think I've spent all this time just flitting around the planet observing swamp creatures and basking at the pool in Heaven?"

Marshall leaned forward. "I guess I hadn't really thought about it. What have you been doing?"

She hesitated as if deciding how much to tell him. "I think it's best if I not reveal everything to an officer of the court. I wouldn't want to place you in an awkward position."

Marshall felt a cold draft on the back of his neck as if someone had opened a window. "I hope you haven't done anything foolish. I consider you a friend."

"Nothing to concern you, Sir, and I truly appreciate your efforts on my behalf. I hope you'll come down before you leave. I'd be delighted to treat you to dinner."

Marshall stared at the screen for a long moment. "I'm afraid I'll be leaving with Captain Wyman and the *Windflower Vagabond* in the morning. My presence is required elsewhere. I do wish you well, and I hope you are successful in your efforts."

"Goodbye, Justice Marshall."

"Goodbye, Jillian."

Chester Wiggins rose from the cot at the rear of the lab he sometimes used during heavy work schedules. He made his way silently to the test instrument console without activating the lights. From his breast pocket he took a tiny laser light and shone the narrow beam on the control panel.

All was as he had left it after this afternoon's static test of the new Rozner drive. The massive engine rested like a sleeping animal on its stand. It awaited tomorrow's final firing in the sealed room beyond the clear glass wall.

Chester glanced around the control room and listened for any sound that would indicate another's presence. Satisfied that he was alone, he knelt down and activated the sequence that opened the panel in the base of the test-instrument housing. He turned a small knob a single degree to the right and sighed when it hit the stop. He closed the panel and retreated to his bed, wondering what he was going to do next.

Adak Pierce lay watching the gray, pre-dawn light brighten his bedroom window. Birds chattered and deep in the swamp, gators bellowed their greeting to the new day. As the foliage on the trees became more distinct he levered his huge frame out of bed and headed for the shower. This morning, he could not afford to be late.

Tanya had left after midnight. Their weekly tryst had settled his nerves and left him tired but refreshed. He whistled as he headed for the kitchen.

After a hasty breakfast and three cups of strong Cirran coffee, he poured a fourth and carried it to the greenhouse to check on the orchids. The cymbidia appeared to be thriving, but the cattleya seedlings lay wilted against the interior of their glass containers. This strain would never make it in the swamp. Back to square one.

"Time."

"Six-forty-two AM."

He drained the last of the coffee and set the cup on the workbench. With the test firing set for seven, he had no time to waste. Glancing at the white butterfly orchids on the window shelf, he heaved a sigh, then took the steps two at a time. Pierce carefully punched in the code that sealed the entrance to the greenhouse. He entered the garage, settled into his new aircar and headed for Rozner Corporate headquarters.

The logo on the roof disturbed him. Better see what Ellis would need to change it to Pierce Corporation. That had a cleaner sound as it rolled off the tongue.

Chester Wiggins was in the test chamber preparing the drive for activation when Adak Pierce entered. Chet left the Bach playing softly knowing it would irritate the man.

Pierce strode over until he was looming over Chester's shoulder. "Is she ready?"

He turned to confront the large man. "Almost, I have two more settings to check. Give me five minutes." It had been ready for the last hour but he knew Adak would hate the delay.

Pierce jerked him around by the shoulder and glared down at him. "This one better be right, Wiggins."

"Yes, Sir." Chester turned back to the drive as calmly as he could when Adak headed for the control room where Jim was already at the panel.

"Good morning, Dr. Pierce." Jim glanced through the glass. "You about ready in there, Boss?"

"In a minute. I want to be certain we have negative flux."

"I'm showing negative here."

Wiggins straightened up, closed the hatch on the port side of the drive and joined the other men.

"Ready when you are, Jim."

Behind the tempered glass, the massive Rozner drive lay firmly secured to its cradle offering no hint of the incredible power it contained.

Chet palmed the klaxon button. "Ignition."

Jim waved his hand over a sensor.

Nothing happened, but then it never did in the early stages of the sequence. Slowly the aft end began to glow. A halo of white light surrounded the stern.

He walked toward the transparent wall. "Where are we, Jim?"

"Five percent."

"What's your reading."

"310."

"Take her up."

He watched Pierce step around to where he could see the panel. Slowly the digital displays began to rise. Eight percent power. 746. The numbers in the display climbed. Nine percent. 852.

"Ten percent, Boss."

Chester nodded. "What have you got?"

"927."

"Damn."

Pierce leaned over the console. "Increase power."

Jim turned to face him. "Sir, ten percent is all we've ever tried in the lab."

"More power." Adak snarled.

Chester nodded for him to continue.

"Yes, Sir."

The dials began to climb. "That's twelve percent, Sir. Dial reads 953. We're showing a magnetic flux three percent out of the norm, Dr. Wiggins."

"I want to know what it takes to get to 1000." Pierce placed his hand on the back of Jim's chair. The menace in the gesture was clear. "More power."

At thirteen percent the reading settled in at 976. Chester could see the indicator his assistant was pointing to, eight percent field increase where there wasn't supposed to be any. The blue glow around the huge engine appeared distinctly misshapen.

Jim glanced nervously at him. "Doctor. We could lose the whole . . . ."

Chester cut him off. "Just follow your orders." It hurt to see the boy's look of betrayal. He had never overridden one of Jim's recommendations without explanation before. And the boy had no idea how much danger they were in.

Adak hand tightened on Jim's chair. "Take her up two percent."

Jim hesitated for a moment then hung his head and nudged the controls. "Up two percent."

The drives were silent. "What have you got?"

"993."

"Up one percent."

Jim paled. "Sir, I don't dare. I can't explain this flux."

He rested a hand on the Jim's shoulder. "Go ahead. Take her to sixteen."

Jim passed a trembling hand over the panel. The display changed.

He gasped. "That's 1000, Sir. Shall I shut her down?"

An arm of the flux ripped away from the side of the engine in a great blue arc. It swung like a living thing and vaporized a jagged hole in the south wall of the lab.

Chester slammed his hand down on the emergency scramble praying that it would cut the arc before it could whip their way. Or before it blew them all to hell.

He turned away from the dozens of alarms flashing across the control panel and looked at Pierce.

"This drive tests at sixteen percent power to achieve an output of 1000. However, there appears to be a new instability. I believe we have now recreated the problem that destroyed the *Majestic Vagabond*. We've just put Rozner's World and everyone on her in similar danger. I don't think it's safe to test any more drives until we understand what has just happened here."

He thought Adak was going to hit him. The man simply stood there shaking, the tension in his shoulders revealing his barely contained rage.

He glared through the glass at the drive. "You bastard. What's wrong with you?"

He whirled on Chester. "Why can't you people build a decent drive? It took sixteen-percent power to generate a thousand. Last month we did it at ten. That's a forty-percent decay. At this rate, we'll be out of business in a year. You damned well better find the problem."

He stormed out of the room.

Chester dropped into the chair beside his assistant who was still trembling. "That was a close one, kid. Very close."

🦅 🦅 🦅

Jillian sipped her tea then headed for the food service area. She paused for a moment to watch the night rain pound against the clear wall of the sitting area. Her body craved protein and fat. Peanut butter would do nicely. Spread on hot toast, it would complement the tea. As she reached the doorway, Wilson interrupted. "You have an incoming call, Jillian."

"Identify."

"The caller is Garrett McPhee."

Jillian hesitated. "The name is familiar."

"Garrett McPhee is the head of the mining section of Rozner Corporation. He is downstairs requesting entrance."

Jillian glanced up at the wall screen. "Thank you, Wilson. Video, please."

A tall, rugged looking man with a huge dark red beard filled the frame. Water dripped from his weather gear and drained away through the floor grating. Jillian took a deep breath. "May I help you?"

He glanced up at the two-way. "I'm sorry to disturb you at home, Dr. Rozner, but I urgently need to speak with you."

She studied him for a moment, and despite tiny nigglings of apprehension, made her decision. "Come up, please."

Moments later, Wilson announced her guest's arrival. Jillian smoothed her skirt.

"Enter."

The door irised open and Jillian involuntarily stepped back. Garrett had to duck his head to clear the doorway. His shoulders brushed the sides of the portal. He was easily as tall and muscular as Aaron and Laz combined. Jillian stared at the huge figure and failed to find her voice.

"Forgive me for calling so late, but my business can't wait for morning."

Jillian gestured toward the seating area. "Please be seated, Mr. McPhee. May I offer you some tea, or something more substantial?"

"Actually, a cold beer would be greatly appreciated."

"Wilson, beer for our guest."

"Immediately."

Jillian retrieved the beverage from the wall server and carried it to Garrett. He thanked her and waited for her to seat herself before dropping into the largest lounger. He looked like an adult on a child's chair.

"Dr. Rozner..."

"Call me Jillian."

He took a long drag on his beer then rested the glass on his knee and studied her. "Jillian, I'm here to represent the miners. We are deeply concerned. Frankly, this visit is a last ditch attempt to head off a strike."

Jillian fidgeted. "I'm not certain I understand. What is your grievance and why would you bring this to me? Dr. Pierce is currently in control of the Rozner Corporation."

Mcphee swirled the amber liquid around in his glass then glanced up. "May I be perfectly candid with you, Jillian? Frankly, we don't have time for anything else."

"Of course."

"Your grandfather was a great man, a visionary who built a vast empire based on a brilliant dream and solid science. He created an industry that employs thousands of people. The Rozner Corporation has always treated its miners fairly, even generously. There isn't a man among us who would have denied Rozner anything he asked."

He glanced down at his glass. From the swamp, the bellow of a male gator dropped into the silence. Garrett refocused on Jillian.

"We tend to be a fairly basic lot. Not many of us are well educated. Only a few have degrees. I act as foreman and spokesman simply because I have the best credentials."

His blue eyes twinkled. "The less generous among us say it's because I talk too much."

Jillian leaned forward and smiled. "I think you're doing fine, but I still don't understand why you've come to me."

Mcphee drained the last of his beer. "The mining guild has never accepted Pierce's authority. We don't understand why he's there. We thought that Rozner had named you as his successor, and frankly, from what we've observed since you've been on Rozner's World, he made a very wise choice."

Jillian nodded. "Thank you, but I'm not in control."

Mcphee slammed the glass down on his knee. "Damn it, woman, why aren't you in control? How did that bastard take over your grandfather's position? I can tell you that the miners will never accept him."

The tension around his pale, blue eyes drained away and he took a deep breath. "I'm sorry. I got carried away, but we feel very strongly about this."

Jillian leaned back on the couch. "I'm flattered by your loyalty, but Dr. Pierce is in office on the strength of a legal document he claims was executed by my grandfather, many years ago. I'm working on the problem with my lawyers but I'm not certain that I can hold out much hope."

Mcphee slumped in his chair. When he spoke his voice was much softer. "Do you know what's going on in the mines?"

"I have no idea."

"Well, you should. Let me tell you."

Jillian peered into the full-length mirror and ran her hands down the tailored dress. The slim skirt accented her long legs. She'd planned this meeting for days and needed to establish just the right tone. She only hoped she could control her anger.

She adjusted the right side of her hair with her hand and studied the effect. It would have to do.

She entered the garage. "Wake up, Alice."

Lights began to blink on her dash panel as Alice started the warm-up sequence. "Where are we going, Jillian?"

"To Rozner Corporation headquarters. I want to see Adak."

"Will Dr. Pierce receive you?"

"I have an appointment."

Jillian climbed into the pilot's couch. "How's that new radial converter working, Alice?"

"Fine, Jillian. I think it's stronger than my old one. Why are we going to his office? Is not Dr. Pierce hostile toward us?"

"That's why we're going."

Alice cogitated for a moment. "I do not understand."

"That's alright. You don't need to."

"What do you hope to accomplish?"

Jillian hesitated. "I'm not sure, Alice. I just want to try a few things. Maybe we can rattle him a little."

"Will that do any good?"

Jillian laughed. "Maybe none at all, but it might make me feel better."

The garage door closed behind them as they soared out into the heavy air. Gray clouds hung over the compound but the rain had stopped and the gleaming corporate compound spread out beneath them. Alice banked right.

"I'm going to approach from the South. We have competing traffic inbound from the West."

"Okay."

Alice slid right and deftly settled onto her usual landing pad. "How long will you be, Jillian?"

"I'm not sure. Why?"

"I need to recycle my navigation module. It will take twenty-three minutes."

Jillian smiled. "I think I'll be at least that long."

As she entered the corporate offices, she felt the receptionist studying her. This was not Theresa who normally occupied the desk. Jillian smiled sweetly.

"Dr. Jillian Rozner to see Adak Pierce."

"Dr. Pierce is expecting you."

"I should think he would expect all who have appointments."

The receptionist started to speak then changed her mind. She obviously didn't know how to take Jillian's comment. It wouldn't hurt to keep her off balance.

"Come this way, please."

Jillian followed her across the lobby and waited for her to open the door to the President's office, neatly handing her off to Pierce's secretary.

"Dr. Jillian Rozner to see Dr. Pierce."

Janice Smally didn't bother to stand. She simply gestured toward the door with her hand. "Go right in." She returned to her work.

Jillian made a mental note to dismiss the woman when she regained control of the corporation, it would be her first act.

Pierce rose from behind the ancient desk and strode forward to greet her. "Welcome, Jillian. So nice of you to come. May I get you something to drink?"

"Coffee, please. Black."

Jillian watched as Pierce stepped around her to the office door.

"For two please, Janice, then we wish not to be disturbed."

When refreshments had arrived and they had settled into chairs in the small conversation area near the window, Pierce fired the first salvo. He glanced at the tray.

"I love the new corporate napkins. You're doing a great job."

Jillian reined in the wave of anger that rose from her chest. "Thank you, I liked them."

He added sugar to his coffee stirring exactly three times, took a long sip of the hot liquid then looked directly at her. "I understand you've engaged legal council."

"It seemed prudent."

Pierce studied her for a moment. "What is it you hope to accomplish?"

She looked squarely at him. "I intend to recover my corporation."

"Your corporation?"

"My grandfather left it to me."

Pierce took a long sip of his coffee. "I thought we'd settled all of that to everyone's satisfaction."

"To yours, perhaps. Certainly not to mine and not to the court's."

"The courts have no jurisdiction in this matter."

Jillian allowed a faint smile to touch the corners of her mouth. "That remains to be seen, Dr. Pierce."

Jillian shifted her position in her chair. "How are things going in assembly?"

Jillian caught the momentary furrowing of his brow.

"Fine. Fine. We're right on schedule to fulfill all of our contracts."

She let that pass. "I understand the miners are restless."

He leaned back in his chair, his great bulk nearly toppling it. "Where did you hear that?"

Jillian just smiled.

Pierce waved it away. "You know how these laborers are. Always complaining about pay or working conditions. I've had to crack down on them."

Jillian took a long slow drink of her coffee. It tasted of darkly roasted beans and burning autumn leaves. "I'm hearing rumors of a strike."

He laughed, a deep rumbling sound that echoed in the spacious office. "They can't strike. They haven't the resources. They'd starve in a week. Even if they walked, they could never hold out."

She leveled a steady gaze at him. "Unless they had outside help."

"Where would they get help? Who's going to finance a labor action by a bunch of ignorant minors on a backwater planet?"

Jillian said nothing. She simply let the silence build in the room.

He sat forward nearly spilling his coffee. "You?"

Jillian smiled sweetly and remained silent.

Pierce glared at her. "Who's going to advance funds against stock that's in dispute. I control the corporation."

Her smile broadened. "Do you, Adak?"

He watched her, clearly uncertain what cards she held. "Would you really support those damned miners?"

"I believe that was your suggestion. It is an intriguing idea."

Pierce clenched his fists. She could see the muscles in his jaw tighten. He stood and began to pace. "Just why did you come here, today?"

"I just wanted to see how things were going. I'm pleased to hear that it's all running so smoothly."

She set her cup on the low table beside her chair and rose, extending her hand to her adversary. "Thank you for the coffee, Adak. I really must be going."

He reluctantly shook her hand and watched as she strolled toward the door.

When she was halfway out of the office, she turned and smiled at him. "I hear you're losing integrity with each new drive. That must be quite distressing."

She heard him gasp as the door closed behind her.

In the pre-dawn glow that filtered through the small window beside his bunk, Aaron lay listening to the sounds of the awakening swamp. A particularly hearty gator bellow roused him from his reverie and he raised up on one elbow to watch the compound come to life.

Across the way, Salvation lay in the subdued quiet like a sated lover. Most of the night's revelers had retreated to their beds for a brief rest before reporting to work. Aaron shook his head. "I'm too old for that shit."

Laz stirred on the other side of the enclosure. "You say something, Aaron?"

"No. Go back to sleep. I'm just talking to myself."

He glanced at the ceiling display. Five-twenty-one. No need to stir. This was their rest day. So why couldn't he rest? He'd lain awake most of the night, nagged by an overheard conversation in the bar. Three miners were griping about wages and working conditions. That was not particularly noteworthy. Indeed, he'd have paid no attention had not Jillian's name peppered the conversation.

The tallest one had drained his glass. "Pierce is a greedy bastard. I tell you, he will starve us out."

The bald miner had nodded his head in agreement. "It's that woman's fault. How'd she let him take over? If she had any balls, she'd run him out."

"If she had balls, she'd be her grandfather. Now there was a man."

"Amen to that."

Gray beard at the end of the table had not contributed to the conversation. He'd finally leaned forward and lowered his voice so that Aaron had to strain to hear. "Maybe Pierce could have an accident. Something that would include that woman as well. Let me work on it."

Obviously they didn't know about the documents Pierce had produced to assume control. Wasn't that what the Chief Justice was working on? Aaron didn't understand all the legal niceties, but he could smell rebellion. He thought of Jillian's request to help with the miners. He wasn't at all certain they would receive him.

These miners were tough men, hardened by years of physical labor. If they revolted, who would be the target of their anger? How could he protect Jillian? Why wasn't she doing something to resolve the situation?

Aaron tossed his bedding aside and reached for his clothes. If he couldn't sleep, there was no point in keeping

Laz awake. Outside the cool moist air erased the last traces of drowsiness from his eyes. No fog this morning. He headed for Salvation and hot coffee.

The day shift rattled dishes as they prepared for the onslaught of breakfast eaters. Aaron slid onto a stool at the long counter that covered one entire wall. He watched, fascinated as always, by the staff preparing and serving food. Computerized vendors could easily have accomplished all of this, but the human touch was desperately needed in this galactic backwater. The Rozner Corporation psychologists had insisted on it. Aaron liked the homeness of it.

"Can I help you, Lieutenant?"

Aaron glanced up to find a tall, red-haired waitress before him. "Coffee, please."

"Anything else?"

"No. Wait, I'll have toast and juice and some of those berry preserves the *Windflower Vagabond* brought up. They're a treat."

She smiled. "They are, indeed. We don't get anything like that very often."

She hesitated for a moment, studying him. "Aren't you Winton Lazarus' partner?"

He nodded. "Aaron Trout."

"I thought so. We miss him. I heard Shelly LaCoste roped him."

Aaron laughed. "Well, I wouldn't put it quite that way, but they do seem to care for each other."

"Damned shame. They always take the good ones out of circulation. Laz is special."

Aaron grinned. "I'll tell him you said so."

– 16 –

The evening crowd at Salvation buzzed with the usual mixture of earnest conversation and laughter as Aaron slid onto the chair opposite Jillian. He studied her.

"Okay, what's this planet shattering secret you're dying not to tell me?"

"You'll see. Wait for it."

"What am I waiting for?"

The amusement that played around the corners of her mouth bloomed into a full-blown, grin. "You'll know when it happens. In the meantime, perhaps you'd buy the lady a glass of the Galian White."

Aaron watched her, trying to decide if there was any point in pushing the inquiry, and decided there wasn't. She wasn't going to give. "I'll be right back."

As he headed for the bar, Laz and Shelly strolled through the inner lock and headed for Jillian's table. Aaron changed his order mid-stride.

"Give me a bottle of the Galian White and four glasses."

At the table, Jillian threw her head back and laughed at something Laz had said; probably one of his latest jokes. He always had a new batch. Aaron could never remember the punch lines.

Returning to his seat, he set the bottle on the table and placed a glass in front of each of his friends. "Good evening, Laz, Shelly. Have some nectar of the gods."

Laz picked up the bottle and filled the glasses. "Thanks, Aaron. I'll get the next one."

"How many of these are we planning to go through, Laz?"

"How many have they got?"

Aaron glanced at Jillian for direction. She smiled broadly at him and waved her hand in dismissal. Aaron had the distinct feeling that he was a page behind. "Is something going on here, Laz? Shelly?"

They just grinned.

"Okay, what am I the last to know about this time?" Aaron looked at the two of them and laughed aloud. He knew the answer before Laz spoke.

Laz touched his glass to Shelly's. "We have agreed to be Life Partners. The rings are ordered. And you, my friend, you're going to need a new roommate."

🐊 🐊 🐊

Adak stood at the trailhead and stared into the fog. The notion that he would actually seek out this mythical creature nearly boggled his mind. But Ellis swore that the information came directly from Marshall. While the Chief Justice had not actually stated that the gators talked to him, Ellis had certainly gotten the impression that the senior reptile named Solomon had the truth. Whatever that was.

Pierce shook his head. Yet he was prepared to test the thesis. He really had no choice. His entire empire would crumble if he couldn't stop the deterioration of the drives.

He glanced furtively around, but everything beyond a meter lay shrouded in heavy fog. He needn't fear discovery. He might as well have been invisible. Adak knew these trails intimately from his forays into the swamp to place his beloved orchids in the rotting stumps of fallen cypress. He knew the precise location of the bridge in question.

Ellis had been quite specific. Lowering his head against the damp air, he stepped onto the well-worn path.

He counted the small flashing lights set along the edge of the trail. Their amber glow kept the fog-enshrouded wayfarer from straying over the edge. Number two hundred and ten should mark the bridge. After that, well, he'd just have to see what happened.

His greatest fear was meeting the Trail Patrol. While he was the head of the corporation and technically their boss, his presence could raise awkward questions. He thought he'd timed it to arrive between circuits, so that he could contact the beast and be back in the compound before their next patrol.

He stopped to rest, leaning over and placing his hands on his knees, his breathing labored. A tiny knot of fear began to build in his gut. He tried to label it. Fear of the gator? More likely, fear that the creature would not have the information or would not divulge it. He needed whatever the truth was to maintain his control over the corporation. The miners were near riot now.

The entire idea was so preposterous, yet the rumors were rampant. Was it really possible that a swamp gator named Solomon had the truth? Had Ellis lost his mind?

As a scientist, he was naturally skeptical but all of his informers insisted that Dr. Jillian Rozner and perhaps the patrolman, Aaron Trout, conversed with the huge gator.

Pierce straightened up and reached with his right hand to loosen the weapon on his hip. As soon as he had the particulars, he'd blow the damned beast to hell.

The bridge appeared out of the fog sooner than he'd expected. No, the light count was correct. Funny how distances appeared to change with weather conditions. He stepped onto the wooden surface and strode to the middle of the span listening to his boots echo off the boards.

Leaning against the low railing, he closed his eyes and concentrated. They said clear your mind and project what you wish to convey. Feeling more than a little ridiculous, he closed his eyes.

"Solomon?"

Silence. He opened his eyes and stared into the gray abyss. Small wind currents swirled the fog over the water. This was asinine.

"Solomon?"

Behold. I am here.

The deep bass thundered in Adak's head. He fell back against the opposite railing. An icy hand of sheer terror gripped his heart and squeezed. He couldn't catch his breath. Slowly he marshaled his courage and stumbled to the railing.

"Solomon?"

Look down.

Pierce allowed his gaze to drop toward the water. Directly beneath him, the massive gator lay swishing his tail. Too terrified to flee, Adak could only stare as the creature slowly opened his gaping maw and displayed row after row of huge teeth.

Why have you come?

Pierce knew this was his only chance. He plowed ahead.

"I require the details of the process known as Rozner's Constant. Without that knowledge, production will cease entirely."

You are not worthy.

Stunned, Pierce straightened up. Hot anger burned in his gut.

"What do you mean, I'm not worthy? I developed most of the science. Rozner stole my stuff. And who are you to tell me I'm unworthy?"

I, Solomon, am the keeper of the knowledge. I, Solomon, imparted that knowledge to the one you call Rozner. And I, Solomon, will decide who shall have that knowledge.

Pierce could only stare at the beast. The gator yawned then snapped his jaws closed.

The truth is not in you. You are not worthy.

His entire body trembled with rage. How dare a prehistoric lizard tell him he was unworthy? Pierce drew his weapon and leaned over the railing, pointing it at Solomon's head.

"You damned well will tell me or I'll blow your fucking head off."

Solomon studied the man on the bridge for a long moment, then began to speak in Pierce's mind.

Mercury suffusion commences with the pressurization of the chamber to two hundred atmospheres. The nodules are arranged so that none touches the others. At the precise moment of attaining the required compression, mercury vapor is injected through the side ports. Because the chamber is already pressurized, enormous force is required to overcome the internal pressure. Heat builds up to plasma levels.

As Solomon spoke, the strength of his voice began to fade. Pierce leaned over the railing as if proximity to the beast would clarify their communication. Solomon's voice in Pierce's mind became more faint.

The time required for each stage of compression varies in inverse proportion to the mass of the nodules present in the chamber.

The signal was now so weak that Pierce had to lean far out over the railing. His head remained poised only centimeters above the gator's. He kept the weapon pointed at Solomon.

"Speak up, damn you."

Solomon exploded from the water, clamped his jaws on Pierce's arm and yanked him over the railing. Sheer terror overcame pain as he plunged into the cold, dark water. Searing agony ripped through his forearm as the weapon fell into the depths.

Suddenly, the gator released him, then, almost gently; the massive jaws closed around his midsection and Solomon began to roll. With each revolution, Pierce caught flashes of the foggy atmosphere before being plunged beneath the surface once more. The pressure of the bite increased until the pain became unbearable. He tried to scream but only succeeded in filling his lungs with swamp water.

Nearly unconscious, he was only dimly aware that the rolling had ceased. He felt himself being carried down to bottom of the marsh. A rough object scraped his back and he felt his body being squeezed into a tight space.

In his last moments, Adak Pierce realized that the gator had stuffed him beneath an underwater cypress root. He was now in the beast's larder.

🐾 🐾 🐾

As the first, faint rays of dawn penetrated the swamp, Solomon raised his head from the log and stared into the heavy cover to the south. Some disturbance had awakened him. He lifted his snout and drew in a deep breath of fresh, morning air. Only the clean scent of rain-washed foliage filled his nostrils.

After a long moment, he laid his head back down on the log and closed his eyes, drifting in the peaceful state between sleep and consciousness. Sheeba and Lucent would awaken shortly. The young gator grew rapidly and demanded nearly all of her attention. With the Dark One eliminated, Solomon would have more time to spend with his son.

Again, he raised up, this time easing his massive body onto the log and from there ambled to the adjacent island that covered the entranced to his lair. There was a disturbance. But what had he heard? He paused to listen for alarming sounds from below but detected only peaceful silence.

Solomon remained still, waiting for the sound to come again. Swamp birds greeted the dawn with their incessant chatter and bullfrogs drummed at the shoreline. He turned his head from side to side attempting to home in on the source.

Finally, he realized that it was not a sound, but a presence that had alerted him. The pressure of a malevolent mind or rather many minds seeking to touch his own flowed through his body like a storm current.

Who is there?

When no response came, Solomon slipped into the water and silently swam southward. Whatever had disturbed him lay beyond the trees, near the bridge. He hugged the shoreline, working his way toward the source. As he cleared the point and entered the small bay spanned by the man-made structure, the pressure increased. A strange mixture of hostility and fear bombarded his senses.

Solomon stopped the rhythmic sweep of his great tail and let his momentum carry him forward. At the core of the signal lay a familiar spirit. He reached out to it.

Joshua?

I am here.

Why do you come in stealth, bringing your minions?

Joshua remained silent for a long moment, then Solomon felt the wave of hatred like a blast hot air.

You have betrayed our creators. You have betrayed our kind. You have brought shame on us all by revealing the ancient knowledge first to Rozner, then to the woman-child. You must die.

The sheer force of Joshua's rage stunned Solomon. He drifted in the black water, trying to comprehend.

What do you propose?

I propose nothing. I have come to extinguish your light.

And you brought your disciples to watch?

Scorn emanated from Joshua's spirit.

I have brought my followers not to observe but to assist. This is no ancient con-

test of noble gladiators. Together, we shall destroy you because you must be stopped.

Solomon scanned the surface of the water, attempting to locate his rival. Finally, he allowed his mind to home in on the source of the energy and located Joshua under the bridge. Three smaller but seasoned veterans lay beside him. Solomon could not resist.

Are you certain you brought sufficient help? I can wait while you send for reinforcements.

Joshua's rage washed over him.

These will do.

The unholy quartet glided from under the bridge and fanned out into an attack formation. Solomon waited. When the gap had closed to a few yards, he began to advance, sizing up his adversaries, and knowing full well that he could not survive the encounter. He had just decided to take the gator on the left, first, when he heard splashing behind him. He turned in time to see a young gator flash past him and tear into the opponent he had selected for himself. The markings were distinctive; Daniel.

All three of Joshua's disciples immediately swarmed on Daniel making it impossible to determine the course of battle. The water churned with flailing legs and tails. Solomon bellowed and lunged at Joshua catching him by surprise. He managed to get a solid grip on his opponent's foreleg and clamped down with all the strength of his massive jaws. He felt, rather than heard the bone break and sensed the shock and searing pain of his opponent.

Joshua gnawed at the back of his neck, attempting to get a solid bite, but Solomon's broad back and iron-tough hide forced Joshua's teeth to scrape along the surface doing no harm.

A quick glance revealed that Daniel still struggled with the three smaller gators. Solomon feared for him but could do nothing to help. Joshua finally succeeded in getting a grip at the base of Solomon's neck and locked together they rolled, throwing great geysers of water into the morning air.

Solomon felt one of Joshua's hind feet scrape with razor-sharp claws down his belly but couldn't tell how seriously he had been wounded. He knew that breaking Joshua's leg was insufficient. He released his bite and struggled to get a new purchase on Joshua's throat for the kill but couldn't reach it. He had to break Joshua's ever-tightening grip on the back of his neck.

Solomon suddenly felt something strike him on the back and for a moment, thought it was another gator. Then he realized that their struggle had carried them under the bridge. He'd bumped into a piling.

He waited until their rolling twisted Joshua's body so that their bellies nearly met. When Joshua's back was to the pillar, he drew up his middle legs, and thrust both feet into Joshua's midsection with all of his remaining strength.

He felt the powerful shock as Joshua's spine slammed into the piling. The death grip on the back of Solomon's neck released. Immediately, he lunged for Joshua's throat and tore away a gaping section just behind the jaw. He backed away from the flowing blood and watched the feebly kicking body sink.

You have extinguished my light.

Go in peace, my brother.

Solomon turned to find Daniel and saw a young gator floating on its back, obviously dead. Another drifted toward the bridge. Neither was Daniel. He could see the remaining adversary fleeing rapidly toward Joshua's encampment.

Daniel?

No answer.

Solomon felt the burning on his belly from Joshua's raking and slowly swam toward shore. As he pulled himself onto the bank, he saw Daniel lying in the grass. Blood flowed freely from the young one's belly staining the ground.

Daniel?

The feeble response was barely detectable.

Solomon?

Why did you join in my contest?

The younger gator's eyes were beginning to glaze.

You are my lord. I could do no other.

Solomon could feel his young friend's spirit ebb.

Oh, Daniel. You were to succeed me. I shall miss you.

Daniel attempted to lift his head, but he didn't have the strength.

There is another more worthy than I.

You mean Lucent?

He is born of the light. I have always known.

Solomon lay his head on the ground with his snout touching Daniel.

He is not ready. We need you.

Daniel again attempted to raise his head then gave up the effort.

You must prepare him, Solomon. And you must live until he is ready. Are you injured?

It is nothing. I will heal.

Daniel heaved a ragged sigh.

I'm so tired.

His eyes closed and his breathing ceased.

Goodbye, my young friend.

Solomon rested his head on Daniel's back and stared into the swamp.

Aaron Trout.

Alone in his quarters, Aaron glanced up from the report he was preparing. He closed his eyes and tried to envision the massive gator lying in the swamp at sunset.

"I am here, Solomon."

Come to the bridge and bring the Chosen One. Jillian.

"Is she in danger?"

No.

"Then it'll have to wait. I have reports to file, and I don't even know where Jillian is."

Jillian is in her quarters. Come now.

Aaron closed the file he'd been editing. "Look, I can't just drop everything and rush out into the swamp every time you beckon. I have work to do. I'll come tomorrow."

Now. Aaron Trout.

Slowly, the pressure began to build between his temples. Aaron recognized the ploy and resisted the relentless force. He succeeded in pushing aside the pain temporarily. Then Solomon cranked up the wattage. He felt his skull would split. A wave of nausea swept up from his gut.

"Okay, I'm coming."

Immediately, the pressure subsided. He rested his head in his hands and waited for his body to cease trembling. "It will take me a few minutes to collect Jillian."

I shall be waiting.

Aaron entered her building and nervously approached the communication panel. He passed his hand through his hair and straightened the collar of his uniform.

"Jillian Rozner's quarters, please."

She answered on the second tone. The panel dissolved into an image of Jillian in a flowing blue gown, standing by a large floral arrangement. "Good evening, Aaron. What a lovely surprise."

"I apologize for interrupting your evening, but I need you."

Her smile lit up the screen. "I'm flattered, Aaron. It's certainly a bold approach."

He felt the blood surge up his neck and color his face. "That isn't exactly what I meant. I.... I...."

She lowered her eyes in a coy gesture. "Perhaps you had better come up and tell me what you have in mind, but pass through the dryer first."

He glanced down at his saturated uniform and realized that he hadn't even noticed the rain. He'd completely forgotten to wear his rain gear. "Yes, yes. I think that would be best."

Her apartment portal irised open as he approached. She stood in the doorway, a faint hint of amusement in her eyes. Aaron felt like a schoolboy on his first date.

"I need to speak with you. Something's happened."

The laughter left her eyes. "Come in."

"Solomon wants to see us immediately. We're to go to the bridge. He's waiting."

She sat down. "Can't it hold until morning?"

"That's what I suggested, but he's insistent."

As she rose from the couch her gown separated revealing a long expanse of bare leg. Aaron tried not to stare. She stood before him. "I have no desire to go into the swamp tonight, Aaron. Go, if you must, but I'm staying here."

She leaned forward and her eyes lost focus. Raising her hands to her temples, she gasped. "Okay, I'll come."

Aaron reached out and touched her cheek. "Solomon?"

"Yes"

"It must be vital. He's never bullied us before."

She stood and leaned against him. "I'm frightened, Aaron."

He put his arms around her and held her tightly. "It'll be okay. I don't believe he'd actually harm us."

She pulled back and studied his face for a long moment. "No, I don't suppose he would. We'd better go. Lewis can supply you with weather protection. We'll roust him on the way out. Just give me a moment to change."

When they'd suited up, they left Jillian's building and stepped out into vast sheets of rain. Gusts rattled their suits and made walking difficult. They leaned into the storm and headed for the trailhead. As they passed the outer marker, the wind began to subside, but the rain intensified.

"Great night for a date, Aaron. Haven't we done this before?"

He laughed. "I only take you to the best places."

"And only to meet the best people."

At the bridge, Aaron led the way. Jillian followed a step behind. He stood leaning against the railing and concentrated.

"Solomon?"

I am here.

Aaron pulled his light stick and focused the bright beam on the water. Solomon lay directly below. "Why have you summoned us?"

The massive gator thrashed his tail. Water sprayed into the air and up onto the bridge deck.

My brother, Joshua gave up his light. I grieve.

Aaron could think of nothing to say.

Solomon continued.

That is not all. You must know. The Dark One is no more.

"Pierce?"

Yes. Jillian, you are free.

Jillian joined Aaron at the railing. "I don't understand."

The Dark One is no longer. I, Solomon, have extinguished his light.

Aaron stood with his arms rigid, his fingers frozen on the railing. "You killed him?"

He no longer is.

Jillian grabbed Aaron's shoulder. "He's killed Pierce."

I know.

Aaron stared at the now-calm gator. "Why? How?"

It was necessary. Dr. Rozner's drives could not remain in the Dark One's control.

Jillian cried out and grabbed the railing. "But they weren't deteriorating."

Aaron stared at her, glanced at Solomon, then back to Jillian. "I don't understand. I thought you said that each successive drive delivered less power. The entire corporation is trying to solve the problem."

She slumped against him. "There is no problem."

Aaron pushed her away and held her at arm's length. "What do you mean, there's no problem? I've seen the numbers. The test results were on the vid. Somehow, that reporter from Intergalactic acquired a tape of the destruction of the lab. Everybody knows about it. The miner's are preparing to strike. Pierce was furious."

Jillian turned and stared into the water. Solomon moved closer to the bridge.

The Constant is secure. The data is false.

Jillian leaned over the railing. "You knew?"

The truth was in me.

"And still you killed Pierce."

His light is extinguished. It was time.

Jillian sank to her knees.

"I knew the stakes, but I didn't want anyone to die because of me. I killed Pierce as surely as if I had done it myself." She pounded a fist on the railing. "And the worst part is, Grandfather left me no choice. I had to do it." Great sobs racked her body.

Aaron dropped beside her. "I don't understand any of this."

Her shoulders heaved. "You... You... couldn't. I couldn't tell you. Too many people were at risk."

He reached out and gently turned her to him.

"Tell me, now."

🐾 🐾 🐾

Aaron watched Jillian as she sat stiffly on her living room couch. After a scalding drink, she was finally ready to talk. Aaron leaned forward with his chin resting on his clenched hands and listened. All the way in from the bridge, he'd been trying to piece it together. It still didn't make any sense.

Jillian sipped her tea, apparently trying to decide where to begin. Finally, she glanced up.

"The drives are normal. That would have become apparent if they were actually installed in ships. I was counting on the weak data to prevent that from happening. No captain would ever accept new drives without reviewing the test results. I arranged to have the numbers successively diminished with each new unit. I don't know what happened to the last one yet."

Aaron watched her closely. "But you weren't even in the assembly plant. How could you alter anything?" Then it hit him. "You had help. Someone on the inside following your instructions, falsifying test results."

She set down her mug on the endtable. "That's why I couldn't tell you. Several lives were at stake. Please try to understand."

Aaron rose from his seat and paced the floor. "You had someone inside the lab. Someone who knew the systems and could sequentially alter the numbers."

Jillian nodded. "A very good friend."

Aaron continued pacing. "It had to be someone Pierce trusted. He would have checked the data. He was a scientist, after all."

Jillian said nothing.

Aaron stopped and faced her. "It had to be driving Pierce nuts. You're right. He would have killed your man if he'd found out. It would not have been difficult to track down the source. How did your inside man do it?"

"The test equipment was recalibrated each night after Pierce left, then reset after each test in case Pierce wanted to examine it, which he did. Once or twice, it was a near thing."

"So, all of those drives in storage, marked defective are actually perfect?"

"Yes."

He looked directly at her. "Someone risked their life for you?"

She smiled. "You did, Aaron, again and again, and so have others."

He felt the warmth of the statement and wanted to hold her again but waited for her to continue.

She hesitated a moment. "I don't suppose it matters now that Pierce is gone. His name is Chester Wiggins. He's the lead lab technician and metallurgist. He's been reporting to me all along. I can never repay him for what he's done."

Aaron sat back down in his chair. "You can try."

"Yes. I can try."

He reached out, took her hand and held it briefly. "What did you hope to accomplish?"

"I never meant to hurt anyone, even Pierce. I thought, if I could discredit the product under his management, he would be forced to resign."

Aaron moved onto the couch beside her. "And then there was Solomon."

"Yes."

"Old Solomon knew that Pierce would never let go no matter how discredited his administration became. Our mentor solved the problem his own way. Where do we go from here?"

Jillian shook her head. "I'll start by rebuilding confidence in the drives. The word is out that we had a problem. But I don't have the strength to start again today."

He stroked her cheek with his thumb. "You don't have to, there's always tomorrow."

She studied his face for a long moment. "Will you be around to help?"

Aaron leaned over and kissed her.

Jillian sat behind the massive desk that had been her grandfather's. She glanced around the office, taking in the citations from governments, corporations and the Federation of United Worlds. She had grave doubts about living up to his reputation even if he wasn't the saint she'd envisioned. Well, she'd just have to create her own.

Solomon's judgement of Adak had certainly been harsh. From Pierce's viewpoint, Grandfather was nothing more than a robber baron. Had Adak been treated unfairly or had he warped history to justify his anger? She would never know.

She had the corporation back but the cost had been enormous. Both the gators and the humans had suffered losses. Her tenure had begun in blood.

A quiet knock interrupted her reverie and her new assistant leaned through the door. "Dr. Wiggins is here to see you."

"Thank you, Lucy. Show him in."

He entered tentatively, as Jillian rose to meet him. "Come in, Chet. I need to speak with you."

Jillian guided her guest to the couch beneath the window and settled in the chair across the low table. She poured the tea she'd had sent in earlier and handed him a cup.

"There's no way to thank you for what you've done. I'm well aware that you laid your life on the line for the corporation and for me."

He glanced up over the rim of his cup. "I did it for Dr. Rozner. I could not let that bastard, Pierce, destroy what we'd worked so hard to build, and he would have destroyed it. He'd have sold it or even allowed war to break out before admitting defeat."

"I agree." Solomon was right. One thing still worried her. "Chet, what happened with the last drive you tested?"

He glanced around, obviously uncomfortable. "I had detuned the test apparatus as far as possible and then tried to adjust the drive itself. It nearly recreated the *Majestic Vagabond* disaster and in that case, we would have had a front row seat. At least we finally know what caused the ship's explosion. You may be assured that all of the other drives are fine. And, I will add a new failsafe before we ship them."

Jillian breathed a sigh of relief.

He looked around her office. His lab coat didn't fit in these formal surroundings. "And what happens now?"

Jillian waited until his gaze resettled on her. "We go on, and I will need the best people I can find. I don't pretend to comprehend the Constant or the process that creates it. Oh, I have all the technical information, and I will share that with you, but there's an enormous leap between knowing and understanding. I will need all your help."

"You can count on me."

Jillian smiled. "I know I can. That's why I'm appointing you Director of Production for the entire corporation."

He froze with his cup halfway to his mouth. "But I need to be in the lab. That's what I know. If we fail to test correctly, people die. I care about that."

"I know you do, and that's precisely why I want you to supervise the entire assembly process. I can't leave it in better hands, and there's nothing to say you can't do that from the lab. I'll get you all the help you require. Just tell me what you need. It takes time to get used to being in charge."

He set down his cup. "I'll do the best I can."

🐟 🐟 🐟

Garrett McPhee stood in the center of an ancillary room of the newly reopened Bore 19 watching his men work. Henshew, frustrated by his morning's lack of success, pounded on the wall with the handle of his digging tool. Garrett had no idea what he was doing.

On the west wall of the room, the Indian surgically excised a beautiful nodule from an apparently large nest of the precious orbs. His uncanny success continued. Lately, Garrett had to work hard to convince himself that it was luck. Something in his brain whispered, "The Indian knows."

Jeremy came running into the room and approached his boss. He spoke between attempts to catch his breath. "She's...she's here."

Garrett stared at him. "Who's here?"

Jeremy straightened up, still breathing hard. "Dr. Rozner. She's at the top of the shaft. Safety just cleared her to descend."

Garrett felt his jaw drop. "Dr. Rozner's coming down here?"

"Apparently."

"Jesus, even the old man never did that. I'd better go greet her. I wonder what she wants."

Jeremy shook his head. "After the events of the last few days nothing would surprise me."

As Garrett entered the main receiving chamber, Jillian, clad in coveralls and a miner's hat, stepped out of the lift. She smiled broadly and extended her hand.

"Hello, Garrett."

He shook her hand, fully conscious of the grimy nature of his grip. She didn't seem to notice. "Good afternoon, Jillian. What brings you to my office?"

She chuckled and glanced around the room. "I wanted to speak with you and I was hoping for an impromptu tour. This is amazing."

Garrett nodded. "They did a wonderful job of restoring 19 after the flood. Would you like to see the rest now?"

"Let's talk first."

He glanced around, looking for something to sit on. "I'm afraid I can't offer you a chair."

She smiled. "That's all right. I've been sitting all day. I planned to leave a message for your men with you, but I see that won't be necessary. She tilted her head toward the tunnel entrance behind him.

Garrett turned to discover his entire crew anxious for a glimpse of their new boss. "Come on in, guys. Dr. Rozner wants a word with us."

They shuffled forward and arrayed themselves in a small semi-circle behind him. Jillian looked at each man, then focused on the foreman. "I know that the last few weeks have been unsettling and that you have many questions. I promise you they will all be answered as quickly as possible. For now, know these things. The new Rozner Corporation will treat you fairly."

They shuffled their feet. Garrett knew they'd heard it all before. Nothing had come of any promises since Rozner's death.

Jillian nodded. She'd apparently read their mood. "Let me begin by declaring an immediate twenty percent increase in the commission you're paid on each nodule."

That brought their heads up. Garrett heard the collective gasp behind him.

Jillian continued. "Secondly, no one should have to worry about basic survival. Henceforth, you will be paid a base wage sufficient to sustain you regardless of how many nodules you locate in any given week. Garrett and I will negotiate that figure over the next few days. And Garrett, you'll need to pick a job title, as you are now my liaison to all the miner's on Rozner's World."

Cries of "Alright," and "It's about time," filled the air.

"Your production commissions will be paid on top of that figure. In other words, the worst you can do is eat well. The upside potential is unlimited."

Silence. Garrett knew it would take a few minutes for the men to absorb the implications. Frankly, he was stunned. The other men's faces reflected similar wonder.

Jillian again looked directly at each man. "Full medical benefits have been restored. I will hold Garrett responsible for seeing that any injury receives immediate attention."

A broad grin spread across her face. "One other thing. On your rest days, beer at Salvation is on the house."

The room exploded with loud shouts and applause. Garrett saw the twinkle in her eyes. She held up her hand.

"Don't get me in trouble with that last one, guys. If it gets too rowdy, I'll have to rescind it."

"We won't." "Way to go, Jillian." "Henshew will drain the place." "Back up the truck." They crowded around her and she shook hands with each of the men.

She turned to Garrett. "Now. How about that tour?"

As she walked through the lateral shaft heading for the current excavation site, Garrett fell in beside her. "I think you just won their hearts, especially with that last bit."

"Well, they deserve it."

He hesitated, afraid to push his luck. "There is one other thing . . . ."

She glanced at him. "Yes."

"These men have all heard about the pleasures of Heaven but none have ever been up there. They simply can't afford it and they won't be able to even with your generous new wage package."

Jillian was silent for a moment. "The problem is capacity. I have plans to build additional towers and other amenities but for now, we're constrained. Maybe we could work out a rotation that would give each man an opportunity to visit."

He felt a great rush of warmth for this bold young woman. "They'll follow you into hell."

She laughed. "Let's hope that won't be necessary."

Alice banked into the sunset over the swamp behind Bore 19 and fell in behind a flock of sea birds.

Jillian watched them scatter. "You'll never grow up, Alice."

"I hope not."

They cruised in silence for a moment. "Jillian."

"Yes, Alice."

"I'm monitoring the *Windflower Vagabond*. She's still in the early phases of acceleration. Her drives are newly tuned and running very smoothly."

"That's nice, Alice?"

"Did Shelly tune them?"

"Shelly and her crew."

Unbidden, Alice turned and headed for home. "I'm not hearing any more rumors about defective drives. There used to be a lot of talk about that, but nobody ever saw one."

"We'll try to keep it that way, Alice."

As they approached their building, Alice decelerated and her garage door opened. "Aaron looks very good in his new uniform, Jillian. You made a wise decision appointing him as Head of Security and Special Projects. Aaron loves the sun. He'll see that the new towers are splendid."

"I'm glad you think he's a good choice."

"Are you and Aaron going to be Life Partners like Laz and Shelly?"

"Alice."

As she settled into her garage, Alice began her post-flight procedure. "I think you're going to see him very soon."

"Why do you say that?"

"I just let him into your apartment."

Acknowledgements

The myth of the lonely author slaving away in isolation to produce his tome is precisely that, a myth. While much of the writing is done in solitary confinement, the final product is the result of the efforts of many talented people.

I want to thank Pamela Goodfellow - teacher, editor, friend. Anything I know about writing, she taught me. Matt Buchman, the best "critiquer" I've ever known, for formatting the novel, and my family and friends who wouldn't let me quit.

A very special debt of gratitude goes to the members of my weekly writing groups who dissected every scene. I look forward to returning the favor.

Solomon, you bastard, I've told your story. Now leave me alone!

Goodfellow Press
16625 Redmond Way, Ste M20
Redmond, WA 98052-4499
(425) 881-7699
Available from Partners Publishers Group

AS YOU LIKE IT - A Goodfellow Imprint

An Unobstructed View by Jenness Clark. Life's unobstructed views, while desirable, depend on where one is standing.   ISBN 1-891761-02-1 $12.99/$13.99 Canada.

SPRING/SUMMER 2000 RELEASE

Howl at the Moon by Polly Blankenship. On a dusty country road in Texas, a woman and a boy come face to face with a nightmare.
ISBN 1-891761-07-2

The Girls from Hanger B by Kristin Campbell Nail. WWII, the union and men are no match for four women when they decide to break all the rules.
ISBN 1-891761-08-0

Between Two Worlds by Suzi Prodan. As the new nation of Yugoslavia rises from the ashes of WWII, rebels learn the price of freedom.
ISBN 1-891761-12-9

FALL/WINTER 2000 RELEASE

Exit from Ecstacy by Jim Flint. Smut, squalor, male sexual angst and a healthy dose of Buddhism.   ISBN 1-891761-05-6

An Unfamiliar Hymn by Doug O'Connor. A man, bound by his principles, tests his family's strength as they cross the country in a mule train.
ISBN 1-891761-06-4

Diamond Life by Johann Sorenson. If you have found your one true love, what do you do when the past shows up?   ISBN 1-891761-09-9

2001 RELEASE

The Altar Stone by Robert Hackman. Possessed by two ancient Amazon gods, a young scientist and a tribal queen are forced to confront their own inner darkness.
ISBN 1-891761-14-5

Goodfellow Professional Services
16625 Redmond Way, Ste M20
Redmond, WA 98052-4499
(425) 881-7699

Goodfellow Professional Services is dedicated to the education of writers and the promotion of the written word, not only as a vehicle for pleasure, but as a work of art. To this end the following services are available:

♦ Editing Services

Editing is performed by Pamela R. Goodfellow, Editor-in-Chief of Goodfellow Press, or by one of her dedicated staff of Associate Editors. All editing is done with two goals in mind: supporting authors to reach their highest potential and aiding them in creating a work of fiction viable in the commercial market.

♦ Weekend Writing Workshops

These two to five-day workshops offer students complete immersion in the writing process. Sessions are led by Pamela R. Goodfellow, Goodfellow Press authors, and a variety of guest speakers. We have found that this forum provides authors, both burgeoning and experienced, with a motivational boost out of all proportion to the time spent.

♦ Ongoing and Private classes

Educational opportunities are available in several other formats including: evening classes for groups of six or more, on-going weekly critique sessions mentored by a Goodfellow Press editor, and weekend seminars by request for groups of fifteen or more.

♦ Speakers Bureau

Authors, designers, and editors are available as speakers for classes, seminars, luncheons, professional societies and conferences. Topics include all aspects of book creation, from writing to publishing.

Goodfellow Press/**Rozner's Constant**

Please check all that apply

1. Approximately how many novels do you buy each month? ____
   How many do you read each month? ____

2. What types of fiction do you usually buy?
   __ Historical   __ Western
   __ Science Fiction   __ Action/Adventure
   __ Romantic Suspense   __ General Fiction
   __ Mystery   __ Time Travel/Paranormal
   __ Horror   __ Other _____

3. Why did you buy this book?
   __ Front Cover   __ Know the author
   __ Liked the characters   __ Back Cover
   __ Like the ending   __ Heard of publisher
   __ Like the setting   __ Purchased at an autographing event

4. For what reasons would you recommend this book to others?
   __ Character Development   __ Setting/Location
   __ Plot/Story Line   __ Writing Style
   __ Overall balance of book

4. For what reasons might you NOT recommend this book to others?
   __ Character Development   __ Setting/Location
   __ Plot/Story Line   __ Writing Style
   __ Overall balance of book

5. What is your education?
   __ High School or less   __ College Graduate
   __ Some College   __ Post Graduate

6. What is your age group?
   __ Under 25   __ 36-45   __ Over 55
   __ 26-35   __ 46-55

7. Have you ever: __ written fiction __ wanted to write fiction?

We would like to hear from you. Please write us with your comments.
Thank you, Pamela R. Goodfellow, Editor-in-chief

Goodfellow Press
Suite M20
16625 Redmond Way
Redmond, WA 98052

Place
Stamp
Here

----

fold here and tape, do not staple

Please include your return address if you wish
to be added to our mailing list.

_____

_____

_____

_____